To

Hannah,

# *FOREVER LOVED*

## *A sequel to Forever Lost*

*LAURA MORGAN*

Lovely to meet you!

Laura Morgan x

*FOREVER LOVED*

Limitless Publishing, LLC
Kailua, HI 96734
www.limitlesspublishing.com

Formatting: Limitless Publishing

ISBN-13: 978-1-68058-688-6
ISBN-10: 1-68058-688-2

# Dedication

For Ells. Sweetie, you rock, and don't ever forget it! You're an amazing friend, mother, and all-round human being. Thank you for just being you. xxx

# Chapter One

"Do you have any chardonnay? I'm not really one for champagne," said a voice from over Cassie's shoulder, and she trembled at the sound. She knew that voice oh-so-well, and dared to hope that it wasn't a fantasy. Those deep, raspy tones had haunted her hopes, dreams, regrets, and fantasies for years, and her heart fluttered wildly in her chest. Everything about her mind and body was drawn to that voice, but at the same time, she was terrified of what it meant for him to be standing behind Cassie in her theater. She turned to stare up at him, and felt her knees grow weak when his shadow fell over her. He was evidently no apparition at all.

"Leo. Are you really here?" she asked, and lifted her hands to touch him, still checking he was real. The pair of them stared at one another for a few seconds, mesmerized by the faces neither of them had seen in well over a year, and yet it seemed as if their souls reconnected with one another's right away. She then heard as Leo's breath caught in his throat, and he took her in for a few seconds while the world around them seemed to fall completely away. Standing there in front of Leo's statuesque frame, she felt as though they'd never been apart.

Cassie's breath hitched, and her body ached for him in a primal, desirous way. Leonardo Solomon looked older, wiser, and more broken than she'd ever seen him before, but the determination in his stare stirred her senses in a bittersweet array of both the terrific and the terrible. In that moment, Cassie wanted desperately to forget all about their shared traumatic past. The cause of that hurt, Victor Sanchez, and his memory loomed over them both like the proverbial elephant in the room, but they were free from her oppressive ex and knew he could never hurt either of them again.

She forgave Leo for everything he'd done. It no longer mattered how the past had gone, only how Cassie's present had turned out. It didn't matter that the Mexican gangster, whom she later married, had taken her away from Leo's grasp. Her marriage to Victor was a relationship borne out of manipulation and forced submission, rather than love, and none of that had been Leo's doing. Victor had stolen her away from the man stood before her, and then made her his obsession. In the end, she'd had no choice but to kill him to obtain the freedom she now cherished.

Cassie knew that underneath it all, she was still that timid young woman who had been forced to set out on her own after her disastrously failed life in the States. Perhaps she always had been. After not one, but two failed marriages, she'd sworn off men in the hope she could hide from her past, but was quickly realizing there was nowhere it couldn't reach her. Where *he* wouldn't find her…

She thought back to how she'd been a lonely recluse when Leo had come along and everything had changed. There'd been no refusing the advances of the gorgeous, yet intimidating gangster who had wooed her from atop his New York empire of women and drugs. Despite those sides of him, she knew she'd been done for the moment he'd laid eyes on her, and yet had adored every minute of their time together.

Cassie had loved Leo once, albeit so very long ago. She knew she still did, and excitement welled in her chest as she remembered their initial game of cat and mouse from their days across the pond years before.

"How could I be anywhere but here? I had to come and find you, Cassie. There's no going back to anything I thought I knew before. All of that means nothing to me without you in my life—safe and free," he answered after a few minutes. "You take my breath away, you're so beautiful."

Tears pricked at her eyes as his words washed over her. Cassie shook her head, feeling utterly dumfounded at his presence in both the UK and in her theater. She had no idea what to say or do; all she could do was stare.

"Is there a problem here, Ms. Philips?" a deep voice then asked. Cassie and Leo turned to look at the voice's owner in shock, their bubble having burst. Her personal security guard, Roger Haynes, stood just a couple of feet away, and with a look on his face that meant serious trouble for Leo if she gave him the go-ahead. He didn't make it obvious, but Cassie knew Roger was well armed, and she appreciated the close attention he always gave her when they were out and she was vulnerable. She paid him well to do it of course, but he'd been a necessary addition to her staff since leaving the States, as had the change of surname. Cassie hadn't stopped looking over her shoulder since that first day back on English soil, but having Roger on hand had helped to ease her fears, and even put a stop to the nightmares that had plagued her for months following Victor's demise.

After having a constant bodyguard with her at all times of the day and night in Mexico, she'd actually gotten used to being watched over while under lock and key. Grayson, her Gentle Giant, had even become a friend of sorts during their time together, and she still wanted the security that having a consistent protective presence gave her. In some ways, freedom scared her—not that Cassie would ever tell anyone that. She'd had to force herself to stop from going back to being a recluse at first. It'd become evident she was just a stone's throw away from becoming an agoraphobic for a while back then, but Roger had swiftly become her rock. They'd not grown as close as she and Grayson had, but they definitely had a tight bond that'd been deeply forged during the past year, and she wouldn't be without him. Cassie was also quite sure he'd recently moved into an apartment near hers purposely so he could be close by if she needed him. He continually went above and beyond the job description, and she'd been grateful for every single step he took to keep her safe.

"It's all good, Rog. Thanks," she told him with a smile. "Leo here's an old friend." Upon hearing the name, he immediately nodded and backed off. Roger knew all about her history—it was one of the things he'd insisted on knowing when he'd taken the job—and so he knew that Leo wasn't the man or his cronies she'd run from. He returned to his spot across the room, but his eyes never left his mark, and she turned her head back up to meet Leo's gaze.

"Good girl," he told her with a smirk, and Cassie shrugged. She knew she didn't need to explain Roger's presence to him, or the change she'd made to her identity. He seemed impressed that she'd taken extra methods to ensure her safety, but Cassie figured he had to have expected it. Either way, she said nothing more about Roger or his place at her side. Leo would just have to understand that they'd be under his constant scrutiny while out in public.

Without hesitation, Leo offered her his hand and together they followed the swarm of people that were attending the opening show at the *New Beginnings Theater*. She'd almost forgotten all about her commitments and responsibilities to the playwright, Alex, and his performance. In many ways, she felt out of sorts, like she had no idea what was going on around her. Cassie was still very much in shock at having bumped into Leo, and while she put her thoughts back in some semblance of a reasonable order, she let him lead the way. He grinned and held on to her hand tightly the entire time, and she knew he was enjoying having her at his mercy again after so long.

"Where are you sitting?" she eventually asked, joining the sea of guests heading toward the stands. As owner, Cassie had one of the front row seats reserved for her, and she followed him down the long pathway that led toward the stage. She felt emotionally disheveled, and lost in a sea of wondrous inner reactions to Leo's almighty presence in her new world. The old and the new were uniting around her, and Cassie didn't fight it for a second. She'd wanted him to come and find her for so long, but had never dared to dream it might actually happen. And yet, here he was, and it was a beautiful feeling having him close again. Regardless of where things went for her and Leo in the future, she knew she would cherish tonight's reunion forever.

She felt herself holding on to him tightly, just to be sure it was real, and Cassie looked up at Leo as he walked her to her seat. He was still the same handsome, powerful man she'd known a lifetime ago, but now he seemed softer, gentler. Leo had the weight of the world on those broad shoulders of his, there was no doubt about it, but he'd chosen to come back to her, and she would never forget that he'd decided to seek out her company when it'd come time for him to move on with his life like she'd done eighteen months before.

"I'm right here." He pointed to the second seat in, which just so happened to be next to hers, and Cassie chuckled.

"Of course you are."

Together, they watched the amazing performance hand-in-hand. She barely said a word,

6

but smiled to herself many times over the course of the show, regardless of the storyline being played out before her eyes. Cassie was thoughtful yet relaxed, and her body ached for Leo in a way she'd forced herself to try and forget since being dragged away from his side. It was the first time in years she'd even felt the rush of adrenaline that spiked from her heart and fluttered down into her belly, but it was a more than welcome return.

A huge part of her wanted to sit him down and talk over everything from the past. They needed to put it all behind them, and yet right now, she didn't want to take turns dredging up their history. Cassie only wanted to move forward. She wanted to be with Leo, to have him hold her close and wordlessly let her know he still cared. She'd never stopped loving him, and knew by his presence here that he'd felt the same.

"You're my soulmate, Cassie. I love you," he whispered in her ear during one of the quieter moments of the play, and she peered back at him through the darkness. He'd never told her that before, but she trusted that he meant it, even after having spent such a long time apart.

"I love you too," she whispered in return, laying a soft kiss on his cheek before turning back to the stage with happy tears in her eyes.

*\*\*\**

"Whoa, who's that?" Cassie's new personal assistant, and now close friend, Siobhan, asked once the play had finished. The pair of them were going over the last couple of items on the itinerary while working the crowd, and Siobhan told her how she had noticed their attractive guest right away.

Leo had left her to do her job, seemingly understanding how important the night was for Cassie, but he still watched her as intently as Roger did on the other side of the large hall. He'd walked off to chat with some of the other attendees while she and Siobhan finished their networking, but she felt his presence and hoped his mind was on her the entire time.

"That's Leo." Cassie grinned as she answered. She knew she was glowing, and figured her eyes were undoubtedly more alight than they'd been since moving back to England the year before. Siobhan smirked and wriggled her eyebrows, making Cassie smile wider. She thought back to when she and Siobhan had met during the stringent interview process to find her an assistant shortly after her return to the UK. Cassie had wanted only the best, needing someone she could truly trust at her side, both professionally and personally, and together she and Siobhan had made a fantastic team.

She'd been both a colleague and a substitute best friend to Cassie since taking on the role, and was as invaluable as Roger. Siobhan had become the person who'd seen her at her highs and her lows, and who hadn't judged her at all when Cassie had finally opened up about her past. Her weekly sessions with her counselor also couldn't be hidden from her assistant, and despite her best efforts, there'd still been rumors that followed Cassie over from the States regarding her past. Many of the new people in her life had questions that'd never been spoken aloud, and Cassie had never opened up, but her silence hadn't helped dispel Siobhan's intrigue about her past.

After she had a meltdown the night of the anniversary of Victor's death, Cassie had finally revealed all. She'd needed to offload and had been rewarded with a deeper understanding from someone who had not only accepted her story as truth, but who never treated her like a victim afterward.

"Leo? As in, *your* Leo?" Siobhan asked, snapping her boss out of her reverie. Cassie watched her take a good look at the impressive man who stood a few yards away. He was talking politely with a few of the actors, but his attention still seemed solely on his once-lost lover, and even Siobhan flushed crimson.

"Yes, *my* Leo."

# *Chapter Two*

After the theater was emptied and left for the cleaners to finish up, Leo offered Cassie a ride home. He then listened in polite silence as Roger gave her the "talk" before he'd let his boss go, reminding her to use her panic button at any time during the night and he'd be there in just a few minutes. She thanked him and nodded, smiling sweetly up at the burly man with an affection that made Leo's blood boil, but he made sure to keep his emotions in check. He didn't want to ruin things quite so soon by pitching a fit and knocking out Cassie's new bodyguard simply because he was being overprotective, when in fact it was the one thing he respected the guy for.

"Call me when you're home safe," Roger insisted, and she agreed. Leo said nothing, but gave Roger a courteous, respectful nod as he passed on his way out. He couldn't deny, he really was pleased that she'd found someone trustworthy to take care of her, but the pang of jealousy he felt at watching their closeness and familiarity was hard to quash. However, so many people in her past had let Cassie down, him included, and she deserved to have good friends around her. He would simply have to tolerate this new bodyguard if it made her feel safe and confident. Cassie's security and happiness was all that mattered.

They drove in relative silence, each seemingly mulling over the past that still hovered over their heads, but Leo didn't care about any of that. Having her back was all he'd been dreaming about ever since the day she'd left for Mexico with Victor. It'd been the worst day of his life, but it felt good that he'd eventually made things right. She'd been saved, not all thanks to him, but Leo knew he'd played a big part in her release from the cartel's clutches, and seeing her happy and strong again helped to ease some of his many burdens. The knowledge that she'd gone back to England and made something of her life while he'd served out his prison sentence was enough to dull that awful, screaming guilt he'd had to live with. Over that year while she'd been forced into submission by his cunning nemesis, Leo had died inside, only to reborn through his need for vengeance and his desire to save her. He just hoped that now she might be able to save him in return.

"What was it like?" she whispered, staring out the windshield thoughtfully. "Prison, I mean," she clarified, and Leo tensed. He hadn't wanted to lie to her quite so soon, but knew it would be better for her if he skimmed over the details of his incarceration rather than be honest. Better to save Cassie from taking on some of the demons from his deep well of guilt and regret.

"Money talks, love. Yes, I've spent the last eighteen months locked in that cell, but it was just a light sentence thanks to my cooperation with the FBI." Leo shrugged for added measure. "I paid my way through the entire thing. I bought myself protection and benefited from the dirty wardens who happily lined their pockets with my money to keep me safe, fed, and watered."

He watched Cassie's reaction to his dismissiveness to his time away. She seemed to accept that he'd bought himself a relatively carefree sentence, and part of him wished he hadn't been so blasé. In truth, he'd had to fall upon both his mental and physical strength and his superior survival instincts on a fair few occasions inside. He'd only barely made it through some of the brawls in one piece, and had made sure he'd ended up one of the most feared inmates. Despite his wealth, Leo hadn't wanted to pay for protection. He'd wanted to earn it in blood, and thanks to the anger he'd kept bubbling beneath the surface, he'd managed it.

"I'm glad it wasn't so bad," she said, and turned to look at him. Leo saw the pain and fear creeping into her eyes, as if she was going to ask those dreaded words, *honestly, Leo?* Or, *you can tell me...*He was far from ready to divulge his deepest and darkest secrets, so he reached out and took her hand in his.

"Piece of cake," he joked, making her smile again, and he was happy to see the sparkle return to her eyes. He knew he'd done the right thing in not telling her the truth, and honestly didn't want to add to her worries. It was better for everybody if she saw him as the same guy she knew and fell for years before, not a brute who'd willingly embodied the persona of the common criminal while behind bars. Leo knew it was time to move the conversation on. "As soon as I was free, next came the extradition to the UK. I've been informed that I'll be watched, but I don't care. My life of drugs and whores is behind me. I'll happily walk away from that world, trust me on that."

"I do, Leo. I believe you. Hanna told me Jamie's taken over?" she asked, talking about her New York best friend and her former drug-dealer husband. Cassie was right. Leo had left his entire empire for Jamie to look after in his absence, and knew he'd made the right choice. Jamie had not only turned the call-girl agencies and strip joints Leo owned into more profitable establishments, but he'd also helped take them in a more legitimate direction. Without his cartel connections, the drug business had run dry long before Leo's fateful birthday party, during which he'd lured Victor Sanchez away from his Mexican fortress to have him arrested. He'd made a deal to turn both himself and Cassie's husband over to the FBI, and although he hated being a rat, it had been a necessary step to ensuring her freedom. But, as plans do, they'd failed—and for the better. Victor was gone for good, not just for a stint in Chino. Either way, the end result had been the same for Leo because of his deal with the Feds, and Cassie had walked, which was all that mattered.

"Yep, I've left everything in his very capable hands," Leo told her. "In preparation for my incarceration, I'd already been mentoring Jay to become my new man at the top for a while, probably permanently now that I'm back over here. He's maintaining the string of businesses that are legit—on the outside. They're still fueled by the cash I made from selling drugs and girls, but he has a tight grasp on the boundaries, and drugs are no longer part of our deal. I trust him," he added, being honest, and she seemed to appreciate it.

Leo really had stepped away. His vast wealth and regular income would be more than enough to set him up for life, thanks to his stateside assistant, Tina. She'd arranged numerous offshore accounts for him and regularly deposited his cut into them, so much so that his move back to London hadn't been an issue financially.

He'd known Cassie was still living in the capital city thanks to Jamie keeping him up to speed with how she was doing and what she was up to. Leo hadn't been able to stop watching over her despite Cassie being thousands of miles away, and he doubted that would ever change.

"I'd trust Jamie and Hanna with my life, and agree you made the right choice with him," she replied, pulling him out of his thoughts, and Leo nodded.

Rather than talk any more, he then focused on the feeling of her hand in his, and the caressing movement she was doing with her fingers as he drove. He was already aching to feel her skin against more of his body, and thought of the few times she'd touched him, loved him, and gave his body the releases he'd craved. He hadn't been with another woman in that way since long before his incarceration, and the feel of her hand against his brought back that welcome yearning inside.

"Here we are." Leo rested the car at the entrance outside Cassie's new apartment and waited.

"You know where I live?" she asked with one eyebrow raised suggestively. He detected a teasing edge to her tone, rather than annoyance, so he shrugged.

"Of course, love," he admitted without a care. The moment he'd stepped off that plane, Leo had tracked her down. He'd used his intel to check out the safety of her new place, as well as secure himself a ticket to the opening night of Cassie's recently refurbished, *New Beginnings Theater*. He hadn't wanted to wait or play any games.

He'd watched her from a dark corner of the theater for a while before approaching, taking in her confident strides and charismatic nature with a swell of pride. Cassie was no longer that lost young woman he'd seen at the trial. She was strong and seemed to have her shit together at last, and what was most impressive was that she'd gotten there all on her own. Yes, she'd had to be saved from the violent and oppressive grasp of her now dead husband, but the timid girl she'd become under his control was very different to the woman he had seen commanding the room and keeping cool under the pressure of her opening night, and that was all her own doing.

"So, Mr. Solomon. Are you coming up for a drink?" Her soft voice interrupted his reverie again.

"Only if you've cheap wine on the menu, and if

there are jellybeans involved," he teased, smirking across at her, and Cassie giggled. He loved how they could still laugh and joke together, and that they could still have their private joke after all the chaos. He remembered that laugh so fondly, and shuddered as the sound cascaded over him. He wanted to hear more of it.

"I'm sure I can rustle something up," she told him with a wide smile before climbing out and ushering for him to follow her.

Leo tailed Cassie up to her apartment, feeling nervous for some reason. There was still so much love and passion between them he could almost feel the tension in the air all around, but it also scared him. The old Leo would've acted on those urges without a care in the world, but not when it came to Cassie, not anymore. With her, it was all about being patient and gaining her trust again. There would be no rushing any of this. She needed to know he had her heart in his sights, not just her body.

\*\*\*

Once inside, Cassie deactivated the security system and quickly set about pouring them two glasses of wine. She then grabbed a half-eaten box of chocolates from the fridge.

"These will have to do, I'm all out of jellybeans," she informed him with a smile, and he plucked out a small chocolate with a matching grin as if not caring at all that she was out of her promised candy.

They watched one another for a while. One hundred unspoken questions hung in the air between them, but Cassie wanted to push them all away and start again. She didn't want to have any of the dark and depressing talk. Tonight had been a huge success for her theater and Cassie wanted to celebrate, not relive the awful past. She certainly didn't want to deal with the doubts that niggled in her gut about whether or not being back in Leo's arms would be a good idea. They'd been through so very much, both while together and apart, and now it was their chance to start over. She wanted it so badly it hurt.

"Milk chocolate, my favorite," Leo murmured as he leaned over and nabbed another small cube from one of the plastic trays. Cassie followed suit, grabbing a caramel one.

"So, where are you staying?" she asked, unable to help quizzing him a little.

"In a rented apartment not too far from here, just for now. I plan on buying something big and lavish soon, but first I'm focusing on looking for a business startup."

"Girls?" she asked, peering at him over the rim of her wine glass.

"No, never again," he answered, and Cassie breathed a sigh of relief. Part of her wanted to ask if he'd been seeing anyone since her, or if any of his old employees might've been around to keep him company during his visitation time while in prison. She couldn't bring herself to utter the words, knowing she'd despise the answer if he admitted her assumptions were true. "Just nightclubs. Maybe

17

casinos if I see a good investment opportunity. I've got contacts over here who've already agreed to partnerships, it's just a matter of getting set up."

"You make it sound so simple," she replied, thinking how hard it'd been running her own business this past year, and she envied his nonchalance.

"Nothing's ever simple, you just have to be ready and willing to make it work. I approach everything that means something to me in the same way. If you want something bad enough, you'll get it. Even if it takes forever to get there."

Cassie's heart fluttered in her chest. Leo's dark brown eyes were staring so intently into hers that she couldn't pull her gaze away. She didn't want to.

"Do you want *me* badly enough?" The words left her mouth before she could stop them. Her cheeks burned, and Cassie knew she must be blushing.

"Good, bad—any way I can, love. You're all I want, and everything I need. I can never apologize enough for what I did to you. But, if you can find a way to forgive me, I'll make it my life's work to make sure you never regret it," he told her, and the sincerity in his gaze made her breath hitch.

Despite his height and huge frame, Leo looked small somehow. He seemed frail, broken, and in need of as much comfort as he evidently assumed she was. Cassie saw through his front and wanted to comfort and care for who she found there. Beneath that mask was a ruined man. He'd been battered and bruised in ways far different than she'd been, but he needed saving all the same, and she knew she had to be the one to do it.

Cassie stepped forward and slid straight into Leo's embrace. She wrapped her arms around his back, resting her palms on his shoulder blades, and squeezed tight.

"Of course I forgive you. None of this was ever what you wanted, Leo. I chose to be with you back then knowing there were risks, and I still want you now."

They stood like that for a long time. Each held on so tightly to the other that there was no denying their pain, or the openness of their feelings. Cassie was glad he'd stopped faking it and just let her hold him. Leo was a proud, defiant, and dominant man. She knew he hated being seen as vulnerable, but wondered if perhaps he simply wasn't strong enough to hide it anymore.

They eventually moved into the living room, where Cassie showed him the photographs of the renovations she'd done to the theater, and of Hanna's recent visit with her daughter, Sandi. He seemed to enjoy seeing the happily captured moments for himself, and stopped her when Cassie went to put the albums away.

"I want to see more," he said, looking at the shelf, which had three more volumes on it.

"There aren't any more. Those albums are empty. I bought them because I know I'm going to make lots of new memories, and those are the ones I want to capture forever."

"We can make them together." He smiled, looking up at her tenderly in the dim light. Cassie leaned down and placed a gentle kiss against Leo's lips, and adored it that he didn't press her into him to deepen it, he just let the softness be. They let the delicate kiss go on for a while, and Cassie liked how tender he was being with her. He'd been a true gentleman when she'd needed him to be after they'd first met, and seemed to be doing it again without her even needing to ask. It was marvelous how in control he was of his once so domineering sexual prowess, and she appreciated the chance to take things slower.

After she pulled back and relaxed into her seat, Leo excused himself and headed to the bathroom, leaving Cassie alone with her thoughts. She wanted to push away every doubt and fear and enjoy this reunion in the most wonderful way she could imagine, naked and between her sheets with this man—her man.

The last person she'd had sex with had been Victor. He'd forced her down and fucked her, while Leo had watched from the shadows. At the time, she'd had no idea he was there simply biding time until the police arrived. She'd thought he was there to watch Victor force himself on her for some sick thrill, but had gotten it all so profoundly wrong. He'd watched to save her, to protect her. Leo had taken charge of her fate that night, and ensured her freedom come the end.

Raw, unadulterated heat swept over her body, and Cassie pulled off her jacket. Regardless of how demoralizing that experience had been, just minutes after Victor had finished taking her, she'd murdered him in cold blood. Strangely, that memory didn't bring with it fear. Instead, it brought her an animalistic desire to feel that power again.

As her blazer hit the floor, Cassie quickly set about sending the rest of her clothes cascading to the ground around her feet. When she was standing buck naked, she grabbed Leo's jacket and slid it over her skin. She loved how it was so big it hung off her, and how it smelled of him.

Doubt flared inside. Was this right? Was she rushing things? Both sides of the argument were buzzing through her mind so loudly that it took her a moment to realize she was no longer alone.

"What are you doing?" Leo asked from right beside Cassie's ear and she sucked in a breath. His voice was so low, deep, and gruff. Full of desire and passion. "I asked you a question," he growled, and Cassie was immediately reminded of their one and only night together so very long ago. She'd given herself to him at last, but only after he'd taken the lead, and Cassie knew she needed that from him again. She needed for Leo to push her over that cliff she knew she would teeter on forever if he left her there.

"I wanted to feel something of yours against my skin," she replied, her voice breathy and ragged.

"Take it off," he demanded, and grabbed at the collar from behind before sliding the jacket down her arms and to the ground. Leo took a sharp intake of breath at the sight of her nakedness and then gripped her bare shoulders in his hands, pulling her into him, and Cassie could feel his need pressing against her ass from inside his pants. "Tell me what you want, Cassie. Tell me everything you want me to do to you."

"I want you, Leo. I want you to own me." Cassie

was shocked at her words. After forcing herself to submit to Victor, here she now was, asking for exactly the same thing from Leo. She'd promised herself she'd never let a man possess her in that way ever again, but now she wanted nothing more than for him to take every inch of her body and claim it for his own.

Cassie reached back and gripped Leo's waist with her tiny hands, pulling him even closer. "I want you to take away the pain of the past and leave me with only you, Leo. Will you do that for me?"

"Abso-fucking-lutely," he replied, and nibbled her earlobe as his hands slid down to her voluptuous breasts. He traced circles around her already hardened nipples before gripping each tightly and massaging them into soft peaks of heightened sensitivity. Leo then answered her unspoken pleas for more as he turned Cassie to face him and captured one of the tender buds in his mouth. He fell to his knees, trailing his kisses over her belly and down to her bare mound. "This is mine, Cassie. Do you understand?" She nodded profusely.

"I'll die before I let another man touch me ever again," she promised, and cried out when Leo's tongue lapped at the already throbbing bead atop her thighs. She didn't care about her scars, or her old hang-ups. She didn't care that he might still be one of the bad guys. All Cassie cared about was her violent need to become Leo's one and only— forever. It'd kill her if he let her go again, she just knew it. She wouldn't survive having her heart broken again, but she let all of that fear go. Trust was the only thing she could cling to. Cassie knew she had to learn to trust Leo before they could even begin to find their way, and she would start right now.

Her hands fisted in his hair, pulling him closer to her aching core, and he groaned in response. He nibbled at her clit and then thrust two fingers inside her soaking body. Years of pent-up emotion came flooding out of her when she came, and Cassie's knees gave out. Luckily, Leo was ready to catch her, and he lifted her straight into his powerful arms.

"I've got you, Cassie. I'll always be here to catch you," he promised, kissing her neck as he laid her down on the sofa. He climbed over her, still fully dressed, and continued his kisses while his hands roved over every inch of her body.

Cassie made quick work of the buttons on Leo's shirt, and her hands were at his belt before he could even finish pulling it off. She was desperate to feel him inside of her, and craved the stretching resistance she knew she'd feel to his presence within. It was a welcome end to her chaste life since leaving the States, and the anticipation was driving her wild.

With his pants around his ankles, Cassie lifted her hips and guided his rock-hard cock inside. She didn't care about anything other than getting her fix of him, and Leo immediately began thrusting hard. He was like a man possessed, seemingly on a mission to claim her as well, and it wasn't long before he pulled himself free and came on her belly.

"I'm sorry, love. I couldn't hold on. It's been so long," he groaned, kicking off his boxer shorts, which he used to clean her up with. Cassie laughed, grinning up at him. She didn't care in the slightest, and knew they'd be going again within minutes. She guessed they both should've known their first time back together would be frantic and over too quickly. The suppressed sexual tension that had built up for years wouldn't take its time to release, and she loved that they'd had to have one another in such an animalistic way.

"All I care about is having you with me again," she whispered, kissing him deeply and pulling him back into her embrace. His body melted into hers. Their lips collided, and as soon as he was ready again, Leo slid inside her wet opening without any need for her to ask. He thrust into her slowly this time, watching her as he moved, and Cassie surrendered to the sweet passion with a greed for him she couldn't hide. She felt whole at last.

Cassie burned for him, hotter and hotter, until a climax exploded out of her and she saw stars. When she opened her eyes again, she saw how Leo had climbed up into a push-up position so he could watch her as she surrendered to her ecstasy. He grinned, but shook his head when she grabbed his forearms and tried to pull him back down against her.

Leo then reached down and lifted her hips up off the sofa, his eyes roving over her body as he made love to her, and he pressed himself deeper into Cassie's still throbbing core, taking his time while she continued to unravel beneath him. He watched every slow, sensuous thrust, and bit his lip.

"You're so beautiful," he sighed, stroking her clit

with his fingertip, and she bucked in response to his touch against her sensitive bead. "I want to watch you take me all night, love. I need to see this perfection," he said, before finally leaning back down to give Cassie a deep, longing kiss.

"I'm far from perfect, Leo," she mumbled, finding it hard that he could love what she still considered to be a mutilated body.

"Perfect. Even if you don't see it, you're absolutely fucking flawless, Cassie. I love you," he whispered in her ear, nibbling his way down to her throat and back up to her swollen lips. "I'm never leaving you again, baby. Never, ever." He thrust deep and emptied into her, shuddering and panting for breath when he was finally spent.

Cassie let a tear escape her eye and fall down her temple into her hair, but it wasn't a sad tear, it was the happiest one she'd ever shed in all her life.

# *Chapter Three*

Leo didn't leave Cassie's apartment until three days later. They simply couldn't give each other up, and blocked out the world while they reconnected again, both physically and emotionally. Leo pushed every one of his meetings back, and she ignored her calls for as long as she could, but they knew the time was coming when they'd have to be apart again. The bittersweet knowledge that he'd always come back made it easier for her to let him go, though, and Cassie couldn't hide her constant smile.

Cassie flushed, thinking back to all their hot and steamy antics, and she felt bad for having ignored the world outside. They'd had no choice other than to let their hearts and bodies become one in the only way they could, through pure and endless love. Letting him see her naked after so long took some getting used to, especially seeing as they'd only actually spent one night together after months of dating and tiptoeing around her hang-ups when they were together before. Even with everything that'd happened between them, the scars from her first husband's frenzied and addiction-fueled attack made her hate her body. Her dominative second husband had helped cure her of her insecurities regarding those scars, but by sheer force more than compassion. Through Victor, she'd lost her modesty, but not her fear, and it was hard letting go, even for Leo.

She hadn't had much luck when it came to men, but she hoped her luck might just be about to change. She had Leo back and their whole setup was far different to how it'd once been. Neither of them had the upper hand, except where the other let them, and she saw it as the fresh start they both desperately needed.

She also had a new man, and friend, in her life—Roger. Despite Cassie's regular text messages informing him that she was okay, he'd turned up halfway through the second day to check on her, and she felt her cheeks burn at the memory of him finding them the way he had. He was furious at her for not having kept him properly up to date, but after seeing her happy face, it was clear he couldn't stay mad. He'd simply reminded her to answer her calls in future, and went on his way again. It'd seemed as if he didn't want to be the one to burst their happy bubble and she'd been grateful for his discretion.

"What's next for us?" Cassie asked as she watched Leo pulling on the only clothes he had at her apartment—his suit from the night of the play. She knew he had to go. He had his empire to get set up, and had already kept his associates waiting long enough, but it didn't make it any easier contemplating spending the rest of the day alone. Cassie had already decided to touch base with Siobhan and Roger, though. They'd overseen the aftermath of the theater's opening night for her, and she owed them both an explanation as well as a huge thank you.

"Everything," Leo replied with a wide smile. He leaned down onto the bed and kissed Cassie with everything he had, driving her wild. She was tender, satiated, and exhausted, but her body still responded to his kiss like it was the first time, and she had to force herself to rein it in. "The world's our oyster, Cassie. I'm gonna do everything in my power to make you the happiest woman alive, I promise. I'll die before I let anyone hurt you or take you away again."

"You and me against the world?"

"Absolutely," Leo agreed, sliding away and blowing her a kiss before he shut the door behind him. Cassie flopped back with a sigh, and could tell without even checking in the mirror that she had the cheesiest grin on her face.

\*\*\*

"Let's call it fifty grand and you've got a deal," Leo offered the man sat opposite him, who, although he clearly hated accepting the low offer, accepted. Dennis Sampson, current owner of *Sampson's Billiards Hall*, shuffled forward in his seat and stretched out his hand. Leo took it and grinned across at his aging companion. Not only had he finalized his first purchase of a casino that

28

morning, but he'd also gotten wind of a certain pool-hall owner with some serious gambling debts owed to his newest establishment. Leo had then made a point of visiting Mr. Sampson in person to discuss the full repayment. He didn't want to inherit bad debtors after all, so focused on cleaning up their balance sheets from the get-go.

As it happened, Dennis was so far under that his only option had been to sell Leo his business. The pool hall was worth a few hundred thousand pounds, minus his debt of course, so he was lucky to even have the opportunity to walk away with money in his pocket at all. "Don't screw me over on this, Dennis, otherwise I'll be visiting your home next time. What is it, two sons you've got?" he said, and Dennis paled as he gave a slight nod of his head. "Seeing as I'm in a good mood, you've got until the end of the week. Get your shit together, the paperwork signed, and leave my lawyer the keys. Got it?"

"Of course, Mr. Solomon. Thank you," he replied, and squirmed in his seat. Leo had made it quite clear he wasn't against sending in the heavies, and how he would be happy to teach Dennis a lesson with his fists if necessary. Although his days of whores and drugs were behind him, Leo figured there were only so many new tricks an old dog could learn.

In just one morning's work, Leo knew he was already establishing himself in the city as someone not to be messed with, and he liked it. He'd had associates in London for years, as well as his extended family, so walking into his role as business mogul had been relatively easy, but he wasn't going to waste a moment not enjoying his spoils. People all across the city had apparently heard of him and his US empire, and foolish nobodies like Dennis Sampson were already cowering before him, which Leo loved. According to his new right hand man and cousin, Brian, stories of his time spent as gangster-turned-crime-lord in prison had preceded him. Leo was the notorious drug-lord who'd taken on the Mexican cartel and won, and he knew he could use his notoriety to his advantage.

He left the pool-hall and climbed into his new ride. His wheels were a flashy black sports car with every added extra, and more than a fair share of horses under the bonnet. Leo's days of being driven around by his men might be behind him for now, but he was going to enjoy the in-between time with another of his new toys.

"Brian, have the manager in my office waiting for me, will you?" Leo barked into his cell phone as he parked in the lot behind his new casino. He was eager to show his new employees he meant business, but that he was also approachable. Brian had been there all morning, and had made sure everything was already set up for his sit-down with the manager, Stuart Smith.

"Sure thing, boss. I'll grab him now," his steady voice replied via his hands-free speakers, and Leo ended the call without another word.

Although he was family, Brian was still a relative stranger after all Leo's years spent in the States, and it'd still be a while until he was more comfortable with the guy. For now, though, his cousin was the closest thing he had to a trustworthy ally, so he'd have to do.

Leo locked up and headed inside, keeping a watchful eye on everything going on around the lobby area of what would soon be renamed *Solomon's Casino and Bar.* He nodded to the reception staff, and had to laugh when one of the women went to stop him as he pressed the button to call the elevator reserved only for management. Her colleague shushed her and whispered in her ear, clearly informing the young woman that he was the new boss. The poor girl went a deep shade of crimson, and Leo found himself amused by it all the way up to his new office.

"Mr. Smith, it's a pleasure to meet you in person at last," Leo said as he came inside, and Stuart started, but quickly stood to greet him. "I get that there will have to be a transitional period, but know this—I'm no fool. I understand this business better than anyone. Do not teach me to suck eggs and never lie to me," he added, taking his seat.

"Absolutely not, Mr. Solomon," Stuart replied shakily. "I would never," he began, but halted when Leo raised a hand for him to stop. He wasn't interested in Stuart's ass-kissing routine. In fact, he'd only said it because he wanted to deliver a warning to his new employee right from the start. *Let it be known, you do not fuck with Leonardo Solomon,* he thought with a smile.

"Tell me about this place. Do you have any issues with the staff? What repairs or updates are required? I need specifics." Leo went straight into figuring out his new establishment from the inside out, and Stuart seemed shocked that he was even interested.

"Most other owners haven't bothered learning my name, let alone cared about the rest of the employees," he said, his eyes widening. "Since before I took over, the owner's office has only ever been used once a month for financial meetings, nothing more." Leo couldn't tell if Stuart appreciated his promise of a more regular presence or not, but he didn't care. This office was going to be his daily base of operations from now on, regardless of whether his manager and the others were used to things working that way.

"Well, that's not how I like to run my business. I'll be using this office every day, so get used to seeing me around. You're welcome to come in and speak with me about anything, anytime," Leo said, dangling the proverbial carrot after his initial threat. "But I want to know everything about everything first, understand? No cutting corners. If someone fucks up, including you, they need to come clean right away or they're out. I've no time for weakness."

Stuart paled at Leo's harsh words, but then sat taller in his seat, clearly appreciating his chance to be heard by the new boss. He proceeded to tell Leo all the ins and outs of his new venture, the positive and negative, as well as outlining the members of staff who he'd had his eye on for one reason or another. Leo wrote notes the entire time, staying quiet while Stuart spoke.

"And lastly, there's Suzie, the barmaid and

receptionist," he said, his expression turning darker. "She's a fucking tease. All short skirts and smiles, and she isn't a team player. I've had to keep her late numerous times for not doing her share of the work."

Leo stared at his employee, reading between the lines, and he didn't like what he found. He considered himself quite an expert at reading people. In fact, it was one of the ways he'd survived so long in a profession most ordinary guys would only last five-minutes in. If a predatory manager was exploiting his employees, he wasn't against using every tool in his box of tricks to nip it in the bud. Having spent years taking care of his girls back in New York, he knew exactly how to handle situations where men thought it was acceptable to take advantage. The location and type business he was in had changed, but Leo could still bring out the big guns if necessary.

"Now then, Stu. You wouldn't be trying to get this girl into trouble would you? I wonder if perhaps she wasn't interested in showing you personally just how much she wanted to keep her job, am I close?" he asked coolly, his dark brown eyes boring into his employees. "I don't want to walk in here and find a sexual harassment case on my hands."

"No, of course not!" Stuart's voice was a little too high-pitched to be the whole truth. "She won't be any trouble, I'm sure. I was just making you aware."

Leo slammed his hand down on his desk and stood, making Stuart jump.

"Very well then, let's go and you can introduce

me to everyone," he told him, walking out into the hall, and his eager new helper quickly followed. *Here boy, be good and you'll get a treat,* Leo joked to himself, but also had to admit he enjoyed having his new lackey hot on his heels.

Leo spent the next few hours meeting the staff and memorizing their faces and names. He chatted with them all in relaxed and calm tones, ensuring they felt comfortable with him as a first impression, but he also ensured he let them know he wasn't going to put up with any nonsense. It went well, and by the end of his first afternoon, Leo already knew he was going to enjoy having a busy new project to focus on. He began making plans for gala events and other revenue enhancers, and his mind wandered over which other businesses might be worth his money and effort now that he was finally back in the swing of things. London was his now, and Leo was planning on taking her for everything she had to offer him.

\*\*\*

Cassie spent her entire day catching up with the reviews and follow-ups from their opening night, and was overwhelmed by the positive response to both the play and her theater. The playwright, Alex, had left her a basket filled with gifts as a thank you for helping his dream become such a success, and she beamed as she opened them. He'd been incredibly observant and had given Cassie a bottle of the perfume she wore every day, some posh wine, a stunning silver necklace from her favorite jeweler, and a gift card for a massage at an amazing Thai place around the corner from the theater. They were each the sorts of things she'd treat herself to here and there, but he'd chosen them all with such care and attention to detail that she simply had to ring him up and thank him profusely. They'd both been in tears by the end of the call, and she loved how she had only cried happy tears in such a long time.

Siobhan skipped in and out of her office with messages, coffee, and even a fresh baguette at lunch when she'd lost all track of time. Cassie had to admit, she enjoyed being busy. It stopped her thinking of Leo too much, and helped calm her overwrought thoughts about how scarily wonderful it was to have him back in her life. She'd worked hard to stop the nightmares from creeping back in the past year, and the worry from invading her everyday thoughts and emotions, but now that Leo was back she had a whole new set of fears to add to her already huge load. She wasn't scared of him, but was frightened to lose him. Cassie was terrified that he might change his mind or find someone new, and a huge part of her wanted to turn full-blown stalker and find out everything about his new life in London in order to try and settle those worries.

She was already fighting imaginary scenarios in which the "big, bad Mr. Solomon" was bending a new voluptuous stunner of an assistant over his desk and having his fun, all the while laughing at his foolish girlfriend for naively believing his promises. Cassie had somehow managed to convince herself that she wasn't enough for him, and knew it would take a lot to change her low opinion of herself. When she'd kept him waiting so long to be intimate before, he'd gone elsewhere for the release she wasn't giving him, and it made her want to vomit even contemplating that he might ever feel that way now that they were back together. Leo had promised her that he hadn't slept with anyone since before the night of his fateful birthday party, and she believed him. His imprisonment helped her trust that story, but there would always be a teensy bit of doubt. She knew he wouldn't have been using the other men around him to relieve that pressure in prison, but struggled to believe she could be everything he needed going forward.

Cassie pushed the despair away. She had Leo in her life again and knew that it was a time for celebrating, not for dwelling on her fears. The pair of them had barely left her bed those few days after getting back to her place following the play's opening night, and it'd been wonderful. Cassie knew she had to get over her hang-ups and trust Leo to keep his word. They had a lot of making up to do, both in and out of the bedroom, and she couldn't expect it to happen overnight.

"Who pissed on your chips?" Roger said with a cocky grin as he came into her office and took a seat without bothering to ask permission. Cassie giggled, but screwed up her nose in disgust at his rough British tone. He was clearly letting his Cockney accent out more than usual for comic effect, and it worked.

"Nice." Cassie shook her head, but continued to laugh. "And, you don't make any sense, by the way!" she added with a smile.

"I don't know. You live away for a few years, come back with a weird accent, and now you seem to have forgotten all the Great British slang!" She really did like Roger, and loved the playful side he only showed once he'd done all of his security checks and had let his guard down a little. He was right though, and she hadn't realized it while still across the pond, but her accent was now a mixture of British with the odd inflection in tone or American word. She was still struggling to drop her New York lilt even after having been away for so long, and being with Leo again didn't help matters either, as his accent was even more of a mixture.

"You're a good man, Rog. But you're talking to a lady, and I would never say such vile things before or after my time spent living away," she said, sticking her nose high up in the air with a cheeky smile.

"Yeah, yeah. Come on, Lady Cassandra, the theater's about to open and you said you wanted to be there to greet the guests," he reminded her, standing and ushering her outside.

The day really had flown by, but Cassie was glad for the busy time spent doing what she wanted to do with her life at long last. No one was telling her what to do, well, aside from the obvious with Roger, but he was doing it for her benefit. Despite their budding friendship, she was his employer, and knew all she had to do was say the word and he'd back down in a heartbeat.

\*\*\*

It was well after midnight when Cassie left the theater, and Roger insisted in driving her the mile or so to Leo's casino. She'd had a few texts off him over the day, mostly confirming her suspicions that he was incredibly busy as well, but she knew that he too was thinking of her and their amazing few days spent entwined on her sofa, floor, bed, and bath. When she arrived, the busy casino was still alive and bustling with clients, and it took her a few minutes to locate the private elevator Leo had told her about. Roger stayed on the periphery, having promised to wait patiently until Cassie found her man before he would clock off for the night, and she was glad. The bustling lobby and loud chimes from the casino were off-putting, and it was good to have him close by. She stared at the keypad, wracking her brains to remember the code Leo had told her, when a voice stopped her.

"Excuse me, Miss. But that lift is for staff only," a scantily clad woman who was caked in thick makeup and teetering on six-inch heels told her with a scowl. Cassie smiled falsely, remembering back to when she was the penniless waitress and clueless escort, and rather than reply angrily, she gave the young woman the benefit of the doubt. Cassie looked at her nametag and addressed her politely.

"Good evening, Suzie. I'm here to see Mr. Solomon, is he free?" she asked, and the girl's eyes lit up. Jealousy flared in Cassie's gut and she wanted to slap that smitten grin off Suzie's face, but forced her fake smile to stay put.

"You need to check in with us here first," Suzie replied matter-of-factly, sauntering over to the reception desk and ushering for Cassie to follow. She did, and was sure to give Roger a wave to indicate for him to stay outside rather than come in to check on the hold-up. She didn't need him stepping in while she was asserting her right to be given access to Leo's private domain.

"It's okay, really. Leo gave me the code, I just can't remember it right now," Cassie replied, but followed her over to the desk. She leaned against the counter and stared into the forced smiles of Suzie and the other two young women, and none of them said a single word of welcome to her. It appeared they didn't believe her story either, and Cassie couldn't wait to see their faces when they finally figured it out. One of the girls picked up a handset and pressed a couple of buttons.

"Mr. Solomon, there's a woman in reception who says she knows you?" she said into the handset, before slamming it down and turning to Cassie. "He's on his way, wait here," she barked, earning herself a scowl, but she didn't seem to care.

Before Cassie could reply, the *ding* of the elevator had her turning her head, and her gaze fell on the huge, gorgeous man who stepped out into the lobby. She sucked her bottom lip as she watched him stroll toward them, clearly the alpha of all that he surveyed. Leo's business mask was firmly in place, and his eyes were ablaze, but he was so hot he took her breath away.

Cassie knew she wasn't looking at Leo. She was looking at Mr. Solomon, and she loved seeing how he commanded the room without even trying. He looked amazing in his perfectly tailored suit and designer shoes, and Cassie adored the way he'd styled his dark hair in a short sweep over to one side. She spotted his diamond cufflinks and expensive watch as they glistened in the bright lights of the lobby, and had to smile. He looked every inch the rock-star chief executive, and she was pleased to discover him atop his throne again. She also knew that no matter what worries or doubts she might still have, that man was all hers, and his dominative stare as it washed over her told everyone so.

"Ladies, when Ms. Philips comes to see me, you absolutely do not detain her, and you most certainly don't ever keep her waiting. You escort her immediately to wherever I am on the premises without delay. Is that understood?" he bellowed, and the three women all jumped in surprise, as did a few nearby patrons. They clearly hadn't taken him for the "steady relationship" type, but Leo didn't seem to care. He fixed each of the women with a hard stare, earning himself mumbled apologies while they blushed scarlet and looked down at the floor.

"Oh, Leo. Don't upset the poor girls, they were only doing their job," Cassie said, stepping closer and then gasping when Leo wrapped an arm around her back and pulled her into him with such force it made her head spin. He kissed her deeply, seemingly wanting to make it known that she was his girlfriend, as if they hadn't guessed that already.

Cassie also appreciated the opportunity to show Suzie and the other girls that he was well and truly taken, so she kissed him back just as hard. Staking her claim over a man had never felt so satisfying. "Can I see your new office now?" she whispered in his ear when he finally leaned away, and Leo hummed softly in response before pulling her off and into the private elevator with a sly grin.

Roger was still waiting patiently outside the huge revolving doors. He gave her a nod from the doorway before he went on his way, and Cassie could do nothing but smile.

As soon as the elevator door was closed, Leo pinned Cassie to the wall and lifted her thighs up around his waist. He pressed his already rock-hard need into her and she groaned, pushing off the mirrored wall against him. They kissed with a desperate demand for one another that neither of them seemed able to fight, and Cassie was glad he didn't hide his love for her, no matter where or when.

"I cannot wait to bend you over my desk and fuck this sweet pussy," he whispered in her ear before finally letting Cassie drop to her feet. "It's time to christen the office, love." When they came to a stop, Leo grabbed Cassie by the waist and marched her down the corridor quickstep, clearly eager to have her naked as soon as possible.

\*\*\*

Once inside, Leo turned the key in the lock and watched as Cassie removed her coat and hung it on his stand. He loved seeing her jacket hanging next to his, and guessed it was the little things that made a relationship work, not just the obvious. He stayed silent as she took in his new office, running her hands over the desk and his high-backed chair. She was so tactile, and he found himself envious of the plush leather and heavy wood. It got to enjoy her touch while all he could do was stand back and wait his turn like a good little boy. Her smile was infectious though, and Leo was grinning just watching her.

"No cameras this time?" she asked, catching him unaware, and Leo shook his head.

"There are cameras, but they've been deactivated. I won't record us here, or at home. Not anymore," he promised, and was surprised that it was all she decided to say on the subject. He knew she'd found out just how far his obsession had gone with her in New York. He'd bugged her cell and placed cameras over every inch of her apartment without her knowledge, and although that surveillance had come in handy many times, Leo knew it was wrong to invade her privacy like that. He hadn't ever said sorry, though, and hadn't once bothered to explain his reasons why. Leo honestly didn't think there was any need. Cassie knew what he was and how he'd operated back then, and she'd accepted him for all those flaws when she'd given him her love. However, he was a changed man now, whether he liked it or not, and from now on he promised himself he wouldn't betray her trust in him. He'd still kept tabs on her, but no way near what he used to do, and as far as Leo was concerned, that was progress.

"Good," she replied thoughtfully, and then began unbuttoning her blouse after checking that each of the blinds was securely closed. Leo's cock pressed into his pants and he was desperate to rush over there and take his lover hard and fast, but instead he forced himself to calm down. He watched the show, delighting in every movement she made as each item of clothing was discarded.

"Perfect," he whispered. Leo watched as she perched on the edge of his desk and opened her legs. Cassie untied her hair, and the long dark ringlets fell across her shoulders and back. She was truly stunning, and yet he had the sneaking suspicion she was still unaware just how beautiful she was. Leo adored how confident she'd become, and waited with a patient smile as her hands slid over her glorious body to tease him.

Cassie started with her large breasts, cupping each one before kneading her nipples between her fingertips, and then she carried on down so she could rub gently at the apex of her thighs. Leo ran his thumb over his lip at the memory of having that same sweet spot on his mouth the night before, and finally stepped forward. He couldn't wait any longer, and pulled off his shirt and tie in record speed before kicking off his pants and shorts.

It was then, under the light above the desk, that Leo noticed a small scar on the inside of Cassie's upper arm. He ran his finger over it and frowned. Leo hated to see that her perfect, delicate body had been hurt again.

"It's okay, Leo. It's an implant," she told him, pressing his finger into the flesh right above the scar. He felt something there beneath the skin, evidently a small piece of plastic, and raised an eyebrow at her quizzically. "It's contraception, silly. I had it put in about six months ago after my periods were all over the place." She giggled, and although Leo loved the sound, he couldn't keep from silencing her with a kiss.

"I did wonder why you hadn't asked me to get some condoms when we got back to your apartment the other night," he admitted, kissing the small silver mark. Leo then headed toward her mouth again, but he took the long route via her nipples. Cassie arched her back, inviting him to return to her taught peaks, and he obliged. Leo sucked, licked, and nibbled at her, relishing in her elated sighs and blissful moans. When his hand crept up her thigh and he slid two fingers straight inside her, Cassie gushed and writhed against his hand. "Let me feel you come, baby. Let me see you," he pleaded, and she came for him within seconds. Leo watched as her cheeks flushed and her skin puckered like gooseflesh, while her thighs trembled and she panted in shallow, delicate breaths.

"Leo," Cassie sighed, leaning her head against his chest, and she was limp in his arms. "Make love to me." He placed her back on the desk, one hand on the back of her neck while the other continued to stroke at her core. Leo held her safe, slowly commanding her, and she followed his lead. When she lay open and ready before him, he spread her thighs and guided himself inside. He hissed when she clamped around him, both gripping and stretching for him. Leo then began moving in time with her breaths, while Cassie peered up at him through hooded eyes.

When she came again and screamed his name, Leo couldn't hold back any longer. He pressed himself deep inside her tightly clenching core and let go. His life flashed before his eyes—so many bad things and bad people, but then there was her. Cassie brought him back from the edge of his despair yet again, and he thanked God for sending her to him.

# Chapter Four

Leo stood staring down into the broken and bloody face of Hank, the mole. With another crack of his fist, Hank fell to the ground and stopped his foolish begging. The only sounds that came from him were the gurgles of his blood-filled lungs, and the only movements were the spasmodic twitches that signaled his impending death. Leo planted two more punches to his face, just to be sure, before climbing off and pounding on the closed door.

"I'm done," he called, stepping back so his fellow inmate and newest minion, Chris, could come inside.

"Nice. Go get cleaned up and get outta here. I'll sort this out," Chris told him, and Leo nodded. He said nothing to explain what'd happened or thank Chris for his help. Leo simply wiped his hands clean of Hank's blood and changed into a fresh set of clothes.

In prison, Leo had become a man of few words, but many actions. He played his own game, and did whatever he had to in order to ensure the longevity *of his enterprise and the safety of his criminal comrades. He'd earned the other inmates' fear from his first day, when he'd beaten the reigning prison king black and blue and subsequently put him in a coma. On the back of that fear, he now had the proverbial throne and the respect of his fellow convicts. It didn't matter that he wasn't staying long, Leo had a lot of anger to offload, and prison was the best place in which to do it.*

*When he reached the yard, Leo nodded to his informant and headed over to his table, only to be intercepted by a piece of shit named Lenny. He'd been trying to get in with Leo for weeks, but had apparently decided he was done sucking up to him, because he stuck a shiv between Leo's ribs. He growled and dived for Lenny. He grabbed his throat and held on to it tightly, squeezing and pressing down on his windpipe until he felt the bone break. Lenny immediately went limp. He dropped the stupid kid to the ground and looked up to find his cronies staring at him in shock, but not because of what he'd done—because of how much he was bleeding. Leo went to speak, but only managed a mumbled gurgle before coughing up a mouthful of blood and falling to his knees.*

*He stared up at the sky and prayed, not for his own life, but for Cassie's. He did what he'd done every day since losing her, and wished to all that was good and right in the world that she was safe and happy. Her face was at the forefront of his mind when he blacked out, and Leo knew that if death was coming for him, at least he could still see it one last time, even if it wasn't real.*

"Leo!" Cassie's screaming voice pulled him out of his dream, and he shot up from the bed in shock. He looked around, getting his bearings, and was grateful for the darkness to hide his confusion and fear. He'd been trying so hard not to show her how broken he still was, but his nightmares had seemingly given him away.

"I'm sorry, love. Did I hurt you?" he had to ask, terrified that he might've lashed out at her in his sleep.

"No," her soft voice chimed. "You were..." She hesitated, and he felt her slide her tiny hand into his. "You were crying and calling out my name."

"Oh," was all he could manage. He didn't want to tell her why. He wanted to keep it all locked away. Leo knew it was killing her not knowing what he'd dealt with, but there was a huge part of his recent past he simply couldn't bear to share with her. He pulled on his sweats and headed to the bathroom, where he splashed his face with cold water and sat on the closed lid of the toilet. Leo kept the lights off, not wanting to see the state his dream had left him in, and he just sat there staring at the floor for what felt like hours.

***

Cassie stood in the doorway, watching him despite the dead of night. If he had noticed she'd followed him out of bed, he hadn't said a word. There was no telling what horrors he might still be seeing in his mind's eye, and Cassie was shocked at seeing him so broken and fragile. She did the only thing she could think to comfort him, and climbed into his lap and held him tightly. It was like hugging a stone cold statue though, like he wasn't even there anymore and had left his empty shell behind. Cassie held on anyway. She hated that he wouldn't tell her the truth about his past. She knew he was just trying to protect her, but it was hard watching him fall apart internally while not letting her even attempt to help him fight those demons.

Cassie didn't care whether or not Leo wanted her in his arms; she had to be there for him. He had to know that she cared and loved him, no matter what'd gone on in the past. It had been a couple of weeks since he'd waltzed back into her life with a sexy smile and a desire for her he hadn't hidden, and Cassie was thankful for every day since then. Whatever he needed from her she'd give him, and she knew he'd do the same for her.

They sat like that for so long Cassie drifted back to sleep in his arms, and roused when she felt him lift her and carry her back to the bed.

"We're both fucked up, Leo. Let's just be crazy together, okay?" she whispered, draping herself over him in an attempt to warm his ice-cold body, and was glad when Leo continued to hold her close.

"Okay, love. I can do that, just please don't ever stop holding me in your arms and telling me it's okay to be screwed up," he said, stroking her hair affectionately, and Cassie nodded. "One day all of this will go away, and I hope it's soon, but as long as I know I have you, I'll make it through."

"Me too, baby. Me and you against the world," she replied, nuzzling deeper into his hold, and she soon began drifting back off to sleep.

The next morning, Leo was his bright and cheery self again, and Cassie knew not to bring up his nightmare or his reaction to it. Part of her wanted to demand he tell her so that they could clear his conscience and move on, but he wasn't that type of guy, and figured she'd have to let him deal in his own way. She knew all too well that her past had messed her up pretty badly, but had no idea just how tormented Leo had also become since they'd been together years ago. He hadn't cared about anyone or anything before, and had never apologized for any of his brutish or chauvinistic behavior. But now, he truly had changed, and it stunned her to see just how much.

"So, I was thinking when your lease is up maybe you should just move in here with me?" she slipped into the conversation while making tea and toast for them both.

After a second's silence, Cassie went to turn to her suddenly quiet lover, but was stopped in her tracks when his huge arms grabbed her. Leo swung her around and grabbed her chin, pulling so she had to look up into his eyes. He kissed every inch of her face and neck while grabbing her ass and lifting her up to sit on the counter. Cassie hooked her legs behind his thighs and pulled him closer, earning herself a deep growl. "Well?" she insisted, peering up at him in the morning light, and she loved the infectious smile on his handsome face.

"Yeah, go on then," he replied, his tone relaxed and full of tease. Leo's eyes were alight with what she could only assume was happiness, and she lapped up his adoring gaze. He then carried Cassie back to the bedroom, where he picked up where they'd left off the night before.

\*\*\*

The next evening, Leo held a party to officially open Solomon's Billiards. Cassie stood by his side the entire time. She smiled sweetly and chatted warmly to the guests, her natural allure shining through, as well her varied experience of such things. Her days as an escort might've been long behind her, but the instincts and natural charm she'd relied on back then were quickly and effortlessly remembered without her even having to try.

She'd brought Siobhan and Roger along for the night as well, and watched from afar as he whooped her assistant's ass game after game. When Leo was finally more relaxed and she felt they'd worked the crowd long enough, she headed over to their table with a smile.

"Okay, okay. Best of nine!" Siobhan was begging, giggling across at Roger when he rolled his eyes.

"Shiv, let me handle this," Cassie interjected, snatching the cue. Her opponent grinned, clearly guessing she would be just as easy to beat as her assistant, but Cassie smiled sweetly and bounced around the table to break the triangle of pool balls at the other end. With her first shot, she potted four balls, and laughed at Roger's reaction to her prowess with the pool cue.

"We got a hustler on our hands or what?" he

said, eventually taking his shot too. Cassie had to admit, he was a good player, but she still beat him and took an overdramatic bow when she potted the black.

"Can I play the winner?" a sultry, heavily accented voice asked from behind her. Cassie turned to find a dark-skinned man watching them from the nearby bar. She went to say no, but stopped herself when Siobhan gave a squeal of delight from beside her and ran to the man.

"José, you came!" she exclaimed, and threw her arms around him. He smiled and kissed Siobhan's cheek.

"*Sí*, baby. Of course," he replied, stepping forward to greet Cassie and Roger. Siobhan made the introductions, explaining that José was an old flame that she'd recently rekindled. She told them how he worked as an accountant in the city center, and they'd happened upon one another when Siobhan had been out buying groceries one night after work. "I moved back to Spain for a while, so lost touch with this *Inglés aumentó,* but then we found each other again, as if by fate," he added, grinning down at her with a smile.

"English Rose," Cassie automatically translated the language she'd hoped to have forgotten by now, but knew was probably engrained in her mind forever.

"*Sí*, you speak Spanish?" he asked, seemingly impressed. Cassie shook her head, not wanting to get into the details with this stranger.

"Just a little," she replied with a shrug, and Roger immediately took notice. He stepped closer to his boss-lady, and Cassie was glad he'd picked up on her unease

"So, José. You playing then or what?" he asked, handing him the cue. José took it and set up the balls, while Cassie leaned in close to Siobhan.

"Can I trust him?" she whispered. Siobhan nodded profusely.

"I promise, Cass. I've known him since we were kids, you can trust him."

"Good to hear it," Leo's voice chimed in from behind them, and both girls jumped. He grinned down at them, but Cassie watched him take in José with a dark expression. He too seemed uneasy about their new arrival, but not overly concerned. Cassie took a deep breath and reminded herself that she couldn't be scared of all Latinos she came across. She thought back to the personal vow she'd made that there would be no more running from her past, just the chance to show strength and independence in the face of whatever life threw at her next.

Cassie shook off her unease, stepped closer, and took her shot with a kind smile at José. Her unease slowly dissipated, and she was glad when their fun and carefree moods returned. He won the game, but only marginally, and was gentleman enough not to gloat. They were about to call it quits when Leo took the cue from her and indicated for José to set the balls up again.

"Loser buys the next round," he said with a wink at the girls. Cassie knew their new friend was being hustled. She watched Leo stalk and prowl around the table, stopping only to give her the odd kiss before taking his shot. With that kiss, he was staking his claim on not only his woman, but on the entire place, and it was good to watch his confident prowess come out again.

José was quickly relieved of his title of reigning champion, and his drinking money, when Leo beat him effortlessly. He wasn't a sore loser, though, and came back to their table with a bottle of posh champagne for the girls to share.

"*Cerveza?*" he asked, handing Leo and Roger two bottles of beer, and they each took them with a smile. Something struck her as strange. None of the others seemed to notice the change in his accent, but Cassie picked it out straight away. He'd pronounced the word slightly differently to any other Spaniard she'd met.

She hoped she was just being paranoid, but couldn't stop watching him carefully, listening to every inflection in his accent, and wondering if he might not quite be who he said he was.

\*\*\*

Leo cleared the place out around midnight. He'd had enough playing nice Mr. Host, and was ready to play a game in private with his girl. He locked up and walked back into the hall, finding Cassie stood leaning against the only table still lit. When he reached her, she immediately turned and bent down to take the first shot on their new game. The move was perfectly timed, and Leo couldn't stop the deep growl that emanated from his chest as she pressed her ass back into his groin.

He loved watching Cassie play. It reminded him

of the night they'd first met at his New York mansion—the night their game of cat and mouse had begun. She'd been bent over at the pool table before him that night too. He had to admit, the view had only gotten better over the years. Leo pressed himself into her, delighting in her soft cry as she gasped and splayed her hands on the green felt beneath her.

"Good girl. Now, you keep those hands exactly where they are," he told her through gritted teeth. Cassie nodded and he could hear her soft, shallow breaths as he kneeled behind her and slid down her panties. He devoured her. Every inch of her gushing core was right before his eyes, and Leo took no time at all in delivering his lover a scream-inducing orgasm using only his mouth. When he was finished, Leo stood and unbuttoned his pants. He took a moment to enjoy the sight of Cassie still clinging to the table in front of her, doing just as she'd been told.

Sliding inside her wet opening was effortless, and as soon as she clenched around him, all of Leo's worries and fears simply melted away. No matter what'd happened in the past, they were together now, and he would die a happy man if things could stay the way they were. Leo gripped her hips, pulling Cassie back to meet his thrusts, and when she came again he was right there with her.

\*\*\*

*Pain. Gut-wrenching, agonizing pain shot*

*through Leo's body as though he was on fire. He tried to move, but stopped when the agony in his thighs rendered him useless. Leo opened only his right eye, namely because the other one was swollen shut, and took in the horrendous scene before him. His assistant, Tina, was whimpering on the floor, and her body was covered by a scrawny man who was grunting and thrusting on top of her. Leo didn't need to ask what he was doing.*

*"Oh good, you're awake," Victor Sanchez's disturbingly upbeat voice chimed from beside him, and Leo groaned in disgust.*

*"Leave her alone," he said, knowing that his attempt at chivalry toward his oldest friend was fruitless, but he had to try.*

*"Oh, her? She already told me everything I wanted to know. This is just for fun," Victor teased. "She spilled her guts about your precious Cassandra as soon as I put a bullet in her leg. After all, I wanted the two of you to have matching scars," he added, pressing down on one of Leo's bloody thighs until he cried out in pain.*

*"Fuck you!" he hissed, spouting as much venom as he could, but Victor simply continued to grin down at him.*

*"Oh no, I'm saving myself for that sweet piece of British pie you've been hiding from me." Regardless of the pain, Leo saw red at Victor's words. Closing his eyes, he sent a demand to his bone and muscle to move and release him from the restraints. He wanted to wrap his hands around Victor's throat and keep hold of it until the last beat of his heart. He wanted to crush him, beat him, and*

*kill him. Every animal instinct inside of Leo screamed for bloody vengeance, but his broken body refused him.*

*"Where is she?" he finally mumbled through gritted teeth. "If you hurt her, so help me God."*

*"Now, now. There's no need for that." Victor paced slowly up and down in front of the chair Leo was tied to, and checked his watch. "I guess you've not realized it's nearly dawn? You've been out cold for half a day, my friend. A whole evening in which I not only tracked down your darling Cassie, but also delivered her with an offer I know she won't refuse."*

*"You leave her alone, Victor. Please," Leo begged, feeling desperate and so incredibly foolish for having let her down so profoundly. Victor didn't answer. Instead, he nodded to someone behind Leo, and walked away while his men beat their prisoner some more and then gagged him.*

*"Leo!" Cassie's voice woke him from his black stupor, and his body sang as he drank in the sight of her and the sound of that wonderful voice. Then, reality kicked back in. He begged her to leave, not to choose his life over hers, but he was powerless. She'd already decided.*

*He could do nothing but watch as Victor put his hands all over her with a disgusting grin on his arrogant face. When she uttered the devastating words that she was leaving with him, Leo fell to pieces. He could only blame himself for all of this. He, who thought he was untouchable, was dying from the inside out thanks to the decision she'd made to save him. When Victor's gun slammed into his temple, Leo welcomed the sweet release from reality. He wouldn't have to deal with the fact that Cassie was gone if he was out cold, and as the blackness enveloped him, he knew it was selfish, but he even prayed for death.*

Leo jumped awake and clutched at his aching chest. The dreams were coming more and more frequently. They were reminders of a past he'd refused to deal with and knew wouldn't release him until he did. But he simply couldn't get past his male bravado and reveal how broken he truly felt inside. Leo peered down at the scars on his thighs. They were his everyday reminders of that terrible time in his mansion, and of that morning he'd let Cassie slip into the clutches of a dangerous predator. They marked not only the loss he felt that day, but also the failure he'd become after losing her. Leo pinched the scar tissue with his fingertips. The sensitive welts offered him a sharp shot of pain, but it wasn't near what he knew he deserved.

After shaking off his sleepy haze, Leo realized Cassie wasn't lying beside him, but he heard her voice from elsewhere in the apartment, so instantly calmed down. He was glad she hadn't been there to see him wake, and hoped she'd never have to witness him in the throes of one of his nightmares ever again.

He pulled on his sweats and padded down the hall toward the kitchen, where it sounded as though Cassie was on the phone. He stopped before going inside, a lump rising in his throat as he overheard her conversation.

"He's messed up, Rog. More than me, and that's saying something." Her voice sounded pained and fretful. "He has terrible nightmares, but he won't talk to me. There are scars all over his body, and not just the old ones from Victor. Some are relatively fresh, but he won't tell me how he got them. What can I do?" There was a short pause, and Cassie sighed. "Time, patience, and trust—I know all about the need for that."

# *Chapter Five*

Cassie set down her cell and peered out the window at the bustling city street below. She'd turned to Roger for advice on what she might possibly do to help Leo overcome his demons, and was grateful, as always, for his guidance. Cassie hated how Leo was internalizing everything. She wanted nothing more than to ease his pain, but he wouldn't let her in, and it was driving her insane. Cassie guessed she had to remember that she'd had almost two years of time and therapy to help her move on from the ordeal with Victor, while Leo had only just left prison before returning to England a few weeks before. He had to be exactly where she'd been when she landed back on home soil, and only her patience might help him recover fully.

After a deep breath, Cassie decided to follow Roger's advice and offer Leo more space. She'd asked the same of him once upon a time ago, and he'd given her exactly that. It was the least she could do after everything he'd sacrificed to free her.

"Morning, love. Did I hear you talking on the

phone just now?" Leo asked as he walked into the kitchen, rubbing his bleary eyes. Cassie's heart lurched, and she hoped to God that he hadn't overheard her conversation, but her lover was giving nothing away.

"Yeah, just checking in with Roger. Are we still heading out tonight?" she replied with a smile, and Leo nodded. He stepped closer and gathered her up in his huge arms, kissing her lips gently at first, then deeper and more passionately.

"I can't wait to show you what's gonna be my new nightclub," he told her, his eyes ablaze with what seemed like excitement, and Cassie loved how enthused he was about his next venture. "I'm gonna rename it as well," he added with a sheepish grin.

"Oh really, what to?" she asked, tracing the lines of his collarbones with her fingertips before travelling down the contours of his pecs and abs. She loved him, there was absolutely no doubt about it, and every inch of her body screamed for him to take her back to bed and have what was his.

"Casanova," Leo answered, peering down at her. Cassie's smile dominated her face within seconds, and she could tell he was pleased by her response.

"You're really gonna do that?"

"Of course, love. It's perfect, just like you," he replied, and sealed his mouth over hers before she could respond to his compliment. He then picked Cassie up and carried her back to the bedroom, where he undressed her slowly. Leo kissed and nibbled at her curves, stroked and caressed her skin with gentle touches. He was languid and sensuous, taking his time to show her how much he cared.

When she was finally naked, Leo pressed Cassie's thighs apart and smiled down at the sight of her.

"What?" she asked, her hands going down to instinctively cover her exposed core. With one shake of his head, Leo stopped their progression.

"Look at you," he whispered. "There was a time when me touching you would make you tremble and cry. Now?" His fingers caressed her swollen nub and then delicately traced the tiny scars she'd once hidden away from him in fear. "Now, you own these. They're your flawless imperfections, Cassie. I love that you've stopped letting your past rule you." After a soft kiss to her nether lips, Leo kissed his way up toward her mouth.

It was all a little too much for Cassie. Despite what he thought, she felt like a fraud. There were so many times it was as if she was barely holding it together. Cassie wanted to be strong and independent. She wanted to be free and happy, but wasn't sure if it was actually possible with all the baggage she had dragging behind her.

Jonah had given her those scars—and he'd died because of her foolish attempt at retaliation for them. Victor had taught her not to fear the scars—and he'd died proving just how much he thought he owned the rest of her. Leo wanted her to own them, and yet Cassie wasn't sure she could.

If anyone had conquered her trauma that'd once been so debilitating, it certainly didn't feel like her. Cassie had asked Leo to own her, and he'd accepted. Perhaps he'd taken ownership of her flaws too? She felt like hers was acceptance out of necessity more than progression. So many worse things had happened since Jonah had gone crazy and hurt her, and sometimes staying numb to all of it was the only option she had left.

"I don't own them, they're simply no longer the worst of my scars. The ugliest ones are on the inside. I don't want them to hurt, but they do. I want to be over it, and I want to be beautiful and strong for you. But sometimes I can't do it." Cassie took a deep, faltering breath. "Hold me, Leo. Please," she begged, and knew she'd caught him off guard by the look in his eyes.

He immediately pulled her to him and fused their bodies together. Leo nestled himself between her thighs and she hooked her feet around his ankles so that they were truly intertwined.

"I'm sorry. I'm so sorry," he whispered, over and over again. "I love you. You're more than beautiful to me. You're perfect."

*** 

Later that night, Cassie took Leo's arm and let him lead her into the heaving nightclub. They bypassed the queue and were immediately taken to the VIP area, where champagne awaited them. Roger watched from a few feet away, as did Leo's hired help, and Cassie did her best to ignore their goon squad and enjoy herself.

"I like the music," she told Leo with a seductive smile, finding the beat inviting. "Would you care to dance, Mr. Solomon?"

"I would, but you're terrible at it," he replied

with a wink, and then seemed to change his mind when she pouted playfully. "It's a good thing I'm just as bad, if not worse." He grabbed her hand and led the way, but not before stopping to speak with the DJ first.

Cassie raised an eyebrow inquisitively, but her man was giving nothing away. Leo just pulled her close and took charge of her willing body. With his hands on her hips, he guided her to the rhythm and the beat, while his kind smile and heated gaze told her she was doing well. Cassie swung her hips, and knew she'd surprised Leo with her new prowess on the dance floor, but couldn't bring herself to tell him it was thanks to Victor's cousin who'd taught her how to salsa back in Mexico.

She sighed. Not all the memories were awful, and she genuinely hoped Gabriela and the rest of the Sanchez family were doing okay. It couldn't have been easy on them losing another member of the family the way they had, and while she'd never once felt the need to mourn Victor herself, she hated having brought them such loss.

A kiss to her temple brought her back to the present, and as the track started to change, being mixed expertly by the DJ, the lights dimmed. Darkness soon enveloped the crowd, and Cassie gasped when Leo grabbed her and pinned her to him. She was blind, but felt safe in his embrace, and almost squealed when his mouth found the sensitive spot just beneath her ear. Leo's tongue slid the length of her jaw and over her mouth. He then delved inside and claimed her. Cassie melted in his arms and felt her body turn to liquid. She was molten lava ready to be caressed and molded in whatever way he commanded. All thoughts or reminders of anything else left her, and the blissful peace of his hold made her smile.

The beat kicked in again and the lights returned, but Cassie was lost under Leo's spell. Her powerful man, who had remained masterful in all things, was the only person in the entire club. Leo had become her haven, and she basked in the warmth of his body and the unspoken promises behind his eyes.

"I love you," she whispered, leaning up onto her tiptoes to give him another kiss.

"You're everything to me, Cassie. Everything," he replied, gripping her waist and pulling her closer. "I'd die if I lost you again."

"Then let's make sure you don't." They kissed and clung to one another while the song burst to life around them. Cassie could hear the lyrics now, and grinned up at him when he finally pulled away.

*"I'll be your Casanova, your Romeo. You'll be my Juliet, don't tell me no."* Base throbbed in her chest, along with her heart. "Mr. Smooth," she teased, but loved his choice of song.

When they'd had enough of the crowded dance floor, the pair slid effortlessly through the crowd back toward the VIP area. Leo's commanding presence alone seemed to be enough to part the sea of writhing bodies, and Cassie was proud to be on the magnificent man's arm. Their night out wasn't anything like when Victor had taken her to his club back in Mexico. She'd been nothing but a trophy he was showing off to his minions that night, and she felt more like a whore than he'd ever treated her before or after. Cassie had worn what he'd instructed and acted as he'd demanded, but still Victor had belittled and humiliated her in front of his men.

She shook off the memory by force, and grinned when they reached their table and found Siobhan and José waiting for them.

"Hey, you made it," she cried, hugging her new friend before accepting a kiss on the cheek from the man she still found hard to trust. There was something about José that simply didn't add up. She'd heard him talking in Spanish, and it was the right dialect for the European language rather than the South American variation, but every now and again she was sure she heard it slip. Cassie told herself countless times she must be imagining it. That she was probably distrustful of all strange men—not just those with accents that sent her mind reeling with past trauma. For Siobhan's sake, she had to force the mistrust away, or at least hide it to stop from hurting her feelings. Cassie couldn't bear it if she alienated her dear friend over such a senseless reason as her having a Spanish boyfriend.

They chatted for a while and Cassie settled her thoughts, enjoying herself as the drinks flowed and she relished the company of her friends. She was safe here, not only under the watchful eye of her protective lover but with Roger and the others close by too. Trust had to be earned, but she chose to give José the benefit of the doubt until he'd earned her trust fully. Siobhan had already earned it, and she'd vouched for him, so that had to mean something.

"Well, we have some news," Siobhan said,

squirming excitedly in her seat. "José proposed!" She thrust her hand in Cassie's face, showing off a glittering diamond that Cassie was surprised she hadn't already noticed. She leapt out of her seat and hugged her friend tightly, while Leo congratulated José on their engagement.

"I'm so happy for you," she told them as she accepted a fresh glass of champagne from Leo. "Cheers." They all clinked glasses with wide smiles. "So, any plans on dates or venues?"

"I said I'd quite like to elope," Siobhan replied, leaning into José as he wrapped a loving arm around her. "Maybe with just a couple of good friends there to be our witnesses…that's you two, in case you were wondering."

"What?" Cassie was taken aback, yet honored. "It'd be wonderful to be there with you guys, of course!"

"Phew, she was hoping you'd agree," José chimed in with a gentle smile. "I said what about the Bahamas, or Mexico?"

"No!" both Leo and Cassie shouted at the same time, shocking the groom-to-be with their outburst. Leo recovered quickly, laughing off their reaction.

"It's just, everyone does that. It's too obvious," he said. "What about Mauritius or Thailand? I know some great places."

"Yeah, I told you the US wasn't a great idea. Visas and stuff can be a nightmare," Siobhan agreed, covering for them. Cassie was pleased to discover she hadn't told her fiancé about her and Leo's past or that they weren't allowed back into the States, but could tell he was still suspicious.

"Anyway, there's plenty of time for all that. Tonight, we're celebrating!" Cassie told them with a grin, glad to have the chance to change the subject.

Leo pressed his lips to her temple and slipped an arm around her waist. He then pulled her further into the seclusion of the booth while their lovesick companions headed to the dance floor.

"Would you ever do it again, with me, obviously?" he whispered in her ear.

"Wow, what a romantic proposal," Cassie teased, but her smile let him know she wasn't being serious. "No, I don't want to get married again. As much as I'd love to be your wife, I don't want to jinx what we've got." This time she absolutely meant it. Leo was clearly disheartened, but Cassie knew he understood her reasons why, and was glad when he didn't push her on it.

"Okay, just let me know if you change your mind. The ball's in your court, love."

"It always is," she answered him playfully, before jumping up and heading back to the dance floor. Leo finished his drink, and then followed behind her with a sly smile. Feeling his eyes on her, Cassie swayed her hips as she walked. Before she even reached their friends, his hands were on her, pulling her into him.

"I can't wait to get you home," his voice growled in her ear. "You won't be able to sit down for a week when I'm done with you."

Cassie grinned and arched back into him. She knew he wasn't joking, but couldn't wait either.

# Chapter Six

"You're doing so well in our sessions. Why aren't you making more progress at home, Leo?" Mrs. Jones, the psychiatrist, watched intently from behind her square glasses. Her hand was poised, as always, to write down his answer, and he despised her for asking. It might be her job to determine his state of mind, but Leo hated that it gave her permission to pry into his personal life.

"I can't offload my shit onto Cassie, I just can't. She doesn't even know I come here." Leo rolled his eyes. "I'm a monster, plain and simple. I've hurt people, used and abused them, and then thrown them away when I'd had enough. I already dragged her into my crazy once before, and I can't do it again."

"Then why not just tell her that? Explain to Cassie how you feel about yourself and the past? It'll help you accept the changes you're going through as well as make her understand your transition better."

"I've killed people, and I'm not talking about a

long time ago. I don't want her knowing what a cold, heartless murderer I became after she tore my world apart. I don't care about anyone anymore, and it scares me. There's only one. It's a single purpose I have in this entire world, and that's Cassie. I live and breathe because she needs me to. I function and survive, because *she* needs me to. I love with all my heart, because she loves me." Leo knew he was ranting, but it was all scarily true.

"There's no need to try and convince me you're an obsessive sociopath, Mr. Solomon. I already know that," Mrs. Jones said. "You cannot fool me, and I don't believe for a second that you're fooling her. Open up, what's the worst that can happen?"

"She'll leave me again."

"That might happen anyway, it's only a matter of time." The pity in her smile made Leo want to trash her perfectly laid out office. "Our hour's up. See you next week, Mr. Solomon."

Leo left the psychiatrist's office with a scowl. He tried hard to lock down those emotions again, and cursed again how as part of his parole he'd agreed to attend regular sessions with the shrink. He was happier just letting it all go, but Mrs. Jones had to drag it all up again week after week. Cassie didn't need to know how fucked up he was. That is, if she hadn't already figured it out, of course.

The mixed emotions stayed with him as he stalked through the crowded street back to his casino, and he let the flow of people guide him. Leo had learned soon after beginning the sessions to walk there and back. He wasn't much company until he'd calmed down, and didn't want anyone from his office to see beneath his cool, hard shell. Leo was pretty certain that the time spent walking by himself was actually as necessary as the session itself.

His mind was racing. Might Mrs. Jones be right? All that he said and did was meticulously planned and orchestrated, but lots of people were like that. He was a control-freak. Could it really be a matter of time before he ruined everything and broke Cassie's heart again? He couldn't be that guy who opened up to his girl about each and every emotion he had. He certainly wasn't the type to sit up all night talking about his past and crying on her shoulder about it. Every time an emotion welled inside, he quashed it. That'd always been his nature, and what did it matter if it made him an obsessive sociopath, as Mrs. Jones had delightfully put it? He'd cared about others when it truly mattered.

She was wrong anyway. As far as Leo was concerned he couldn't be a sociopath. He had empathy and remorse for the things he'd done—but only when it came to Cassie. Everyone else meant nothing to him, it was only her. *That's something else entirely, an obsessive sociopath with only the one catalyst. What a lucky girl she is to have you fixating over her day and night.*

Leo shook off his antagonizing thoughts, not caring that he was a mess. He could still love with every fiber of his being. He could still put another person before himself at every turn. Everything Leo had done since getting off the plane from New York had been for Cassie, and he didn't intend on ever stopping.

Romance and affection he could do easily. Picnics in the park, movies and date nights were effortless. He'd made it his mission to fill Cassie's world with laughter and love, and watching her smile was the only reward he needed. Well, then there was the sex. Leo's heart beat fast even thinking about their lovemaking, and he had to adjust himself in his pants just envisioning how different she was now.

Cassie had truly been awakened since they'd last been together, and he loved how they'd not only rekindled their physical love for one another, but started a fire so strong it was now unstoppable. He still couldn't believe she'd made the moves on him that very first night he'd come back. She was so confident, beautiful, and incredibly sexy. He'd gone weak at the knees just catching sight of her wearing nothing but his jacket over her tiny, perfectly curvaceous frame. At the time, he hadn't remotely expected their physical relationship to begin again so quickly, but had adored her eagerness for more, and remembered that night with a smile.

There still was one aspect that'd been a hard realization recently. He'd thought for a long time that she'd learned to own her past and had moved on, but now he knew she was far from it. When he'd first met Cassie years ago, she'd been haunted by the monstrous memory of Jonah, the addiction-addled husband who had mutilated her body while out of his mind. How she'd let him stay in her life was beyond Leo's comprehension, and she'd insisted all along she wasn't a victim—when clearly that's exactly what she was. Cassie had made Leo wait so long to be with her that it'd driven him crazy. He still hated that he'd used a whore to satisfy those needs she couldn't, but that was in the past. There was only one woman for him now, and he knew he'd never so much as look at another one again.

Cassie hadn't really moved on from being that timid girl she once was. Only her monster had changed. The metaphorical dog that bit her and made her scared to pet another one had turned into a wolf, and he'd hunted her and preyed on every one of Cassie's weaknesses. Victor was that wolf. Leo knew he had to have genuinely fallen in love with her, or else he would've never married and protected her the way he did. When he'd taken Cassie away, it was to be a whore, and they'd all known it. However, something had changed, and Leo still didn't truly know exactly how or why Victor had altered his plans for her. But, that obsessive love had been his undoing in the end, and they'd all lost something along the way.

Yes, Cassie no longer trembled and hid her scars from him, but Leo had been forced to see for himself that it wasn't because she'd overcome them. It was because the scars now ran deeper than simply on her skin. She was riddled with them inside and out, just like he was, and he hoped that despite his downfalls, he could be the one to help her overcome the past.

Together they'd move on and be happy. Leo relied on her for that at least. His only chance at redemption was to die knowing he'd done everything he could to make things right by Cassie.

The empire he'd built in New York, and that which he was cultivating in London, meant nothing, whereas they had once meant everything to him. Leo still wanted wealth and power, those needs were in his blood, but only if he got to share them with Cassie.

Coming to a stop, he steadied himself, took a deep breath, and then pushed through the doors to his huge casino. With his icy demeanor back in place, Mr. Solomon headed straight upstairs to get back to business.

\*\*\*

Cassie waited patiently for Leo in his office, having been assured by Brian that he'd be back in no time. It'd been almost an hour. As far as she knew he didn't have anywhere else to be other than the casino, though, and Cassie was growing impatient. Part of her thought about quizzing him when he got back, but she was loathe to turn into that girlfriend who wanted to know where he was and what he was doing all the time.

When he stormed in and almost threw his jacket onto the coat stand, Cassie flinched. He seemed colder and more distant than ever. Leo was hiding under not just his normal layers of closed-off indifference, but an extra few for some reason.

He jumped when he caught sight of her on the sofa, reading through a manuscript she'd been sent—her newest project. Cassie tried her best to stay relaxed, and she smiled over at him. She began gathering up her things, sensing the tension rolling off him, figuring it might not be a good time to visit after all.

"Hey, I thought I'd stop by and see if you wanted to grab a bite to eat, but…"

"Sorry, love. I've been out." She wanted to roll her eyes and point out that he was stating the obvious, but stopped herself. Cassie went over to him and stared up into his hard face. The lines seemed deeper, and his eyes held no warmth. She didn't like the man standing before her, it wasn't her Leo. "I'm too distracted tonight. How about we do it another time?" he offered.

"Okay." She smiled, despite her hatred for the big, bad gangster persona he was wearing. Cassie never had been a fan of Mr. Solomon, and wasn't too disgruntled at being dismissed from his presence. "I'll go and meet Shiv for drinks instead."

He agreed and let her go with nothing more than a chaste kiss on her cheek. Normally, she'd wrap her arms around him and wait for the calm, gentle Leo to return, but this time she was more than ready to get away from the closed-off man she knew wouldn't answer her questions. She had no idea what was eating him, and guessed he wasn't about to enlighten her.

Cassie left the casino, and was glad to be out of there. She had to shake off the memory of his soulless stare. He still hid so much away, and she hated the unpredictability of him.

She called Siobhan and arranged to meet her at a bar just around the corner from her apartment, then hailed a cab. She rang Roger as well, informing him of the change in her plans. He wasn't impressed to hear she'd left the casino without a chaperone.

"Leo let you leave without checking you were covered?" he barked down the line. She could hear the rustling of him presumably dressing while maintaining their call. "Go back to the lobby and wait for me."

"Too late, I'm already in the cab," she informed him, and heard him curse. "Meet me at the bar, okay?" Cassie added before ending the call. She spent the cab journey checking her emails and messages, keen for a distraction from the memory of the pain in Leo's eyes, or his eagerness to get rid of her. She had to wonder where he'd been or with who. It had to be someone who had the power to chill him so effectively. It hadn't been his cousin; Brian was at the casino with her. God, she wanted Leo to dig deeper, and hated knowing she probably wouldn't get him to even if she begged him.

When she reached their chosen venue, McGill's Irish Bar, she hovered outside, looking for her friends. Cassie suddenly felt an icy chill sweep over her, and she peered up and down the street. It was busy enough that she felt safe, but something still made her feel uneasy. It was as though she was being watched.

"Hey," José's kind voice called from across the street. He crossed over to join her when the traffic slowed. "Are we the first ones here?" Cassie guessed Siobhan must've invited him along. She didn't mind, but in all honesty she'd wanted some girl time to discuss her closed-off man with her friend in confidence. Cassie nodded and accepted a kiss on the cheek from Siobhan's fiancé in greeting, once again pushing her doubts about him aside. He'd sensed them, though, and evidently decided it was time to address her unease. "There's something I've been meaning to tell you, so it's good we've got a minute," José said, and her heart lurched.

"Let me guess, you're not quite who you say you are?" she jumped in, unable to bite her tongue. José looked shocked, but his smile stayed on.

"Yeah, I suppose so," he answered. "Listen, I do work in the city center, but I travel a lot more than I can talk about. My job has taken me to many, ah…obscure places."

"Like Mexico?"

"*Sí*, like Mexico." He softened the "x" as he pronounced it properly, whereas she'd refused to use her knowledge of the language when she'd spoken. It was a silly act of defiance, and yet she could never resist doing it.

"Are you here to hurt me or my friends, José? I'd appreciate a heads up if I'm in trouble." Cassie wasn't afraid; in fact her cold numbness had returned and she felt ready for anything he might try and throw at her. It was a handy reaction to being under pressure. Utterly calm and collected, she regarded the man standing before her.

"No, nothing like that!" José held up his hands to signal he meant no harm. "I just know who you are, that's all, and I wanted to be honest. I think you're incredibly courageous."

"I'm no one, José. I survived something terrible—end of story. Please remember that." Cassie could hear the ice in her tone. She wasn't ready to discuss her past with someone she barely knew, yet who appeared to know who she was beneath the new name and persona, and had all along.

Roger appeared at that moment, stepping out of a cab in black pants and a shirt that actually made him look rather handsome. She was used to his bodyguard combo of white shirt and chinos, and had to admit he scrubbed up well.

"Hey, you two okay?" he asked with a concerned look on his face, and Cassie guessed she must be scowling. She let go of the anger that'd been building inside of her and forced a smile.

"Sure, just waiting on Shiv and we can head inside," she answered, pointedly ignoring José. "You boys wanna go grab the drinks and a table while I give her a call to see where she's got to?"

They did as she suggested, but Roger didn't look happy. He stayed near the door and kept watch over her, even when Cassie could see José attempting to make conversation.

Just as she pulled out her cell, Siobhan arrived, walking fast around the corner that led to the tube station. Cassie hugged her.

"Hey, what's up? I thought you were heading over to see Leo?"

"He's snowed under," Cassie lied. "I thought I'd leave him to it. Gives me some time with you guys," she added with a wide grin. She still couldn't figure out what was up with him, and his dismissiveness of her company weighed heavily on Cassie's mind. He'd never let her leave without either him or Roger before, and her imagination immediately went haywire with thoughts of trouble back in the States, or perhaps run-ins with the police here in the UK.

She hadn't heard from Hanna for a few days, and made a mental note to text her as soon as she had a free minute. She and Jamie were due to visit soon, and Cassie wondered if Leo might try to keep Cassie at arm's length because of something to do with them. Were they still coming? Had Jamie gotten in some kind of trouble? Cassie hoped it was all her frenzied mind playing tricks on her, fooling her into thinking the worst. She jumped when Siobhan laid her hand on her shoulder.

Cassie forced another smile, then followed her friend inside. They joined the guys in the bustling bar, where two large glasses of chardonnay awaited their attention.

"Come to momma," Siobhan whispered, grabbing her glass and then taking a long sip. Cassie giggled and snatched her own from the bar.

"We eating or just having a liquid dinner tonight?" she asked, and Roger's raised eyebrow informed her that she'd better prepare for an interrogation very soon. For a man whose job it was to remain stoic and mysterious, he didn't hide his emotions well at all. He could blend in with any crowd, yet was never able to mask his concern for her wellbeing. She guessed he could read her like a book too, and he seemed to know that things weren't quite right.

José didn't ask any questions. He simply ushered them to a table, where he handed each of them a menu in answer to Cassie's question regarding whether they were having a "liquid dinner." After rolling their eyes playfully, the two women admitted defeat and made their decisions.

They enjoyed plates piled high with burgers and fries, followed by chocolate sundaes with cream and hot fudge sauce. Cassie ate so much she felt like she might fall asleep right there at the table, but the flowing wine kept her with a nice buzz, and she found herself relaxing thanks to the wonderful company.

After a long session of what Cassie could only describe as "eye-fucking" Siobhan and José made their excuses and left. Roger then leaned forward, watching her intently from across the table. She envied Siobhan in that moment, and wondered what Leo was up to. Cassie missed him. When she grabbed her purse to leave, Roger shook his head.

"Tell me what's bugging you. Why did you leave Leo's, and what was going on between you and José outside?" he demanded without showing even a flicker of guilt over his intrusiveness.

"Leo was being cold, emotionless and distant— so nothing new there," she snapped, and regretted it instantly. Whatever Leo had going on behind those walls of his, she knew he wasn't doing any of this hiding because he preferred it that way. Cassie understood that he stayed guarded out of necessity, and just hoped he'd open up when the time was right. She took a deep breath and sighed. "I didn't mean that. It's just sometimes it feels like he's so very far away. Like…"

"Like maybe he simply moved from one prison into another?" Roger finished her train of thought.

"Yeah, and it's one that only he can break out of.

No matter what I do—or don't do—he's trapped until he decides it's time to open up." Roger reached across the table and gave her hand a little squeeze, and Cassie was reminded once again just how great the man sitting opposite her was. She felt a tear slide down her cheek and quickly wiped it away with her free hand, but she knew Roger wouldn't draw attention to it anyway. He certainly wasn't the type to cause a scene or encourage her to "let it all out," but he was there for her when she needed it, and that was what mattered. Cassie was grateful for the lack of fuss he caused whenever she had a girly moment in his company, and his calm demeanor helped to keep her grounded.

"And what's the deal with José? You looked upset when I got here." Roger moved the conversation on effortlessly, but kept his hand over hers on the table.

"There's something about that guy I don't trust," she replied. "The way his accent sometimes changes, and he's aloof when it comes to talking about his job. He told me right before you got here that he 'knows who I really am.' What the hell is that about? I couldn't figure out if it was a threat or a warning…"

"He asked me about your history a few weeks ago," Roger interjected, putting a stop to Cassie's rambling. "I did some digging, and that guy does have a past that seems a little too clean. There wasn't much I could find on him, but his financial career seems legit, and he has travelled the world at the behest of his company's wealthiest clients. It's quite probable he's worked with Victor's cartel, or

81

perhaps his colleagues did back in the day. You've got to remember, despite you changing your name and moving across the world, you were big news a couple of years ago to anyone watching the money scene."

"I was big news?" Cassie was surprised by Roger's comment. "There was hardly any press coverage of my trial, and the only thing that really made the headlines was Leo's arrest. It was mentioned that he took down Victor in the process, but otherwise my involvement was kept quiet. The US authorities took care of that."

"I know, but it was still newsworthy that one of the largest drug cartels was almost taken down in one night by the leader's wife and her lover. José told me once how he'd seen a photograph of you and Victor during a visit to one of his Brazilian clients, and then he'd heard you'd dropped off the radar—until he met you here in London."

"Will I ever be able to leave it all behind, Rog? Or is Victor going to haunt me forever?" she asked, and her voice was almost a whisper.

"You'll always have him hovering over you, Cassie. But that's why you hired me, and why Leo keeps tabs on you like he does. Safety can only be maintained by being careful and staying strong. The moment you do something foolish is the moment you're potentially in trouble." Roger's whole demeanor had changed. He was in full protective mode, and Cassie knew he was right. No matter what, there would always be a risk of the past catching up with her. All that mattered was that she was prepared and protected as much as possible when, and not if, that time ever came.

"I think I'm ready to go home," she told him, and Roger waved to the waitress to bring them the check. He said nothing else, but stayed close and watched over her as they rode in the back of a cab to her apartment. He saw her inside, gave the place a once over, and made to leave, but she stopped him. "Stay and have a cuppa with me?"

"Sure." He ditched his jacket and took a seat at the dining table while Cassie made them a pot of Earl Grey tea.

They'd switched back to cheerful, chatty mode by the time Leo came home. Roger had Cassie howling with laughter over a story he was telling, and both of them greeted Leo with a smile.

"Hey, love. You two having fun?" Leo asked as he poured himself a shot of vodka from the freezer and joined them. Cassie leaned in and gave him a kiss on the cheek, having decided against pulling him up on his cold behavior from before. There had to be times she let it go, even if everything inside her wanted to shake him and scream at her man to tell her what was going on.

"Just keeping your lady company is all," Roger informed him. "Tonight was supposed to be my night off, but instead I got roped into dinner with her, Shiv, and José. Turned out to be a fun night, you should've come."

"Too much on, but maybe next time," Leo replied as he stood and replenished his glass. He was giving off an icy vibe that both Cassie and Roger picked up on, but she knew he just wanted to be alone with her. After helping her clear up their cups and teapot, Roger waited for her to give him a nod, and then left.

Cassie hovered by the doorway to the kitchen in silence. Leo was hunched over the counter, staring down into his empty glass. "You just gonna stand there and stare?" he growled, but didn't bother turning to look at her, and it shocked Cassie to hear his cruel tone. He'd never held on to his angst for so long before, and she didn't feel equipped to deal with his offhandedness right now.

"No, actually, I'm going to bed," she retorted, and turned on her heel. She headed for the bedroom, where she stripped off, showered, and then slid on a set of pajamas. After tying her damp hair back in a long ponytail, she took a deep breath and set off in search of Leo again. No matter what she'd said, she refused to leave him to wallow, regardless of whether he'd tell her what was eating him.

He was exactly where she'd left him, and however many shots more inebriated. Without saying a word, she pushed her way between him and the counter top and wrapped her arms as tightly around his waist as she could. Leo didn't say anything, but after a few minutes she felt him start to relax and lean into her hold. He buried his face in the crook of her neck, and Cassie held on for as long as he needed.

When he eventually pulled away, she led him to the bedroom. Leo followed her without a fuss, and let her strip him in tense silence. There was nothing sexual about how they both felt. Instead, Cassie was soft and gentle with her touch. He needed it, she could tell. They then climbed beneath the sheets on their huge bed. A hundred questions were rolling around in her head, desperate to be asked aloud and answered at last, but she forced them away.

"I'm sorry," Leo's voice reached her ears, and it was nothing more than a sigh.

"I know," was all she mumbled in reply before sleep claimed them both.

# *Chapter Seven*

*Cassie was gone. She'd left in the clutches of that monster, and there had been nothing Leo could do to stop her. He'd begged, pleaded, and even prayed for his death over her imprisonment, but it hadn't been granted. After months of rehabilitation, his wounds were healed, and he could properly walk again. Pain still shot through his thighs every now and again, but they were his reminder of what a failure he was, and Leo relished the pain he felt he deserved more of. He'd failed everyone, including himself. His life meant nothing without her, but Cassie had gone. She'd left him behind.*

*And now she was married. Mrs. Fucking. Victor. Sanchez. Cassie had become the wife of the man he hated more than anyone else in the world, and she'd said yes—willingly. She'd posed for pictures and screamed his name while he'd fucked her on that live stream Leo had been forced to watch. Hardly a powerless victim like he'd thought. Hate surged through him, giving Leo the shakes. He wanted to punch something, to lay ruin to something beautiful.*

*Leo needed a distraction. He knew he should've called for a tall blonde, but instead the dark-haired, big-breasted girl lay on the bed. She'd been his favorite for months—no guessing why. Spread before him on her belly, her long hair draped over her curvy ass, it could almost be Cassie lying there. And wasn't his gluttony for punishment just the reason why he'd chosen her time and again?*

*"Don't make a sound, and don't look at me," he ordered, climbing behind her. The girl didn't respond. She kept her face buried in the pillow of Leo's guest bed—like the good whore she was. After pulling on a condom, he palmed her ass cheeks and pulled her hips up to meet his. Leo hesitated, wanting to stop what he was about to do. This wasn't helping him move on. If anything, being with her was keeping one foot in the past he was so desperately trying to run from. He felt like curling into a ball and crying, but his stubbornness forced him to see it through. He pushed himself inside, over and over without a care for the act itself—only the gratification his tainted heart demanded. He was hard and fast, but didn't care. The softer, gentler Leo had gone away, probably never to return again.*

*He couldn't finish. The emotionless fucking was doing nothing to curb his needs, and he guessed he should've known the release he was looking for wasn't ever going to happen with the dirty slut bent over before him.*

*Leo wrapped her hair in his hands and pulled her up off the sheets, relishing in her shocked gasp. "You're loving this aren't you? You filthy whore."*

*He tugged harder. His hips still moved, but they felt like they were on autopilot. The only enjoyment he was getting was the sick satisfaction of having this slut completely at his command. She cried out and he rammed her harder with his unsatisfied hard-on. "You're a whore, Cassie. Look what you've done to me! Nothing but a fucking whore," he screamed at her, and the girl just trembled before him, evidently too scared to say a word.*

Leo woke up drenched in sweat and tears. His hands were fisted in the sheets, his body was trembling, and his cock was so hard it was painful. That dream, just like the others, had hit him where it hurt. The memories he'd been trying so desperately to force away returned to him over and over again each night, and he knew he had to do something. He had to learn how to open up.

He looked around, glad Cassie wasn't in bed with him, and wondered if it was morning already, but then movement in the shadows by the end of the bed caught his attention. Cassie was stood there watching him with wide eyes that told Leo she was terrified of what she'd just seen. Her arms were wrapped around her body tightly, as though shielding herself, protecting herself—from him.

"Don't," she whispered when he climbed up off the bed. He wanted to go to her, to wrap her in his arms and make her feel safe again. Leo didn't listen to her plea. He climbed closer but was immediately halted in his tracks when she flinched.

"No, please. I need you, Cassie. I need you to understand, and to love me despite all my shit.

Please," he begged.

"I'm trying, Leo. God knows I'm trying." She sighed, turned on her heel, and stomped toward the doorway, where she stopped for just a second and peered over her shoulder at him. "So, I'm nothing but a whore, am I?" Cassie added, and just like that, she broke through his barriers.

His heart sank. Leo knew then that he must've been shouting out in his sleep, and he wanted to make her understand that he hadn't said it to her per se. He hadn't been thinking those things while lying asleep next to her in bed. Maybe a long time ago when he was hurting and lost, but not now. The dream flooded his senses again, as did the memories of that time in his life. He'd started using all sorts of drugs and bingeing on alcohol back then, and his mind had been a wreck, just like his heart. Cassie was lost to him, and he'd had no idea if or how he might ever get her back. He'd been ready to burn his entire empire to the ground because of his failings, but hurting or name-calling her had never been what he'd wanted, only what his pain had demanded in fucked-up retribution.

"No, Cassie. It's not what it sounded like, I wasn't saying it to you. I was saying it to…" The agony in his voice surprised him. He wanted so desperately to tell her the truth, but didn't know where to begin, and his hesitation only seemed to make her angrier. It was Cassie's turn to be cold now, and Leo knew he deserved it.

"I need a minute," she replied, and her voice was just as pained. "Don't follow me." This time, Leo did as she asked.

He climbed back under the sheets and stared at the ceiling for hours, waiting for her to come back to bed, but she didn't. Mrs. Jones had been right; he would lose her anyway if he kept on hiding the truths from both past and present. Things had to change, before it was too late.

\*\*\*

Cassie lay on the sofa, staring up at the ceiling. Had the man she loved so much, and thought loved her in return, really just woken her up grabbing at their bed sheets while screaming that she was a whore? His nightmares had been plaguing them both ever since he'd come back, but never had she seen or heard that side of him come out from his subconscious. The venom in his voice when he'd said the words still haunted her. *"You're a whore, Cassie. Look what you've done to me! Nothing but a fucking whore."*

Tears rolled down her face, landing in puddles by her ears. She'd stopped wiping at them now. There was just too much pouring out of her to bother cleaning them up, so she simply lay there and sobbed as quietly as she could. Pain was always hard to bear, but she was starting to realize just how many forms of pain there were for her to endure. Love really could do a number on you if it wanted to, and it seemed despite their incredible attraction, she and Leo still had more hard times ahead. They weren't out from beneath their dark shadows yet, and Cassie could only hope that he might eventually let her in—before his iciness ruined them both.

The next morning, she woke with a stiff back and dry, sore eyes. At some point she must've stopped crying, but she knew she'd wept for hours before finally falling into an exhausted sleep. After a quick search of the apartment, Cassie realized Leo had gone out. There was no note and no text message telling her where he was or when he'd be back. He'd just gone.

"Here we go with the cold-shoulder routine," she mumbled as she climbed into the shower. "Well, two can play at that game."

Within the hour, she'd gone to her theater and buried her head in the proverbial sand. Siobhan plied her with coffee and seemed to know not to ask questions, while Roger watched with concern etched all over his face. By late afternoon, Cassie decided enough was enough, and swapped the coffee for something far stronger. "You two coming for a proper drink or what?" she demanded.

"Sure thing, boss," Roger replied, and Siobhan grabbed her purse. Neither seemed interested in questioning her motives, and Cassie was glad they'd taken her not-so-subtle hints to keep the hell out of it.

"Where're we headed?" Siobhan asked as she climbed into the back seat of a minicab with Cassie and Roger. Cassie answered her with nothing but a sly grin and a wink before quietly instructing the driver where to go.

They started with cocktails, quickly followed by wine, and then took a pit stop for junk food from an old-fashioned fish and chip shop. Roger tucked into a huge plate of battered cod and vinegar-soaked fries, but he drank nothing more than soda while Cassie and Siobhan ate their meals with another bottle of wine to share as an accompaniment. He played protector while the girls had more than his share of booze, and soon Cassie and Siobhan were swaying and hugging each other tightly while they stumbled along to the next bar.

"You've been the best friend I could've wanted here, Shiv. The best!" Cassie proclaimed. "You're gonna be married soon, and leave me to go and have Spanish babies. But I don't care, because if you're happy—I'm happy."

"No way, I'm not going anywhere." Siobhan shook her head and the fast movement made her wobble. "José knows I'm not leaving my career behind, nope. Nor you. You're my best friend too, I love you!" They squeezed one another tightly and shrieked, but didn't care who was watching. Cassie adored having such a great friend by her side, and wouldn't ever apologize for expressing how happy it made her having Siobhan in her life.

"Girls, how about we take a break and grab some coffee?" Roger tried, but his attempt to cut their conversation short only brought him into it.

"Roger!" Cassie screamed. She'd almost forgotten he was there, and grabbed him, flinging her arms around his shoulders. "You are my best boy friend. Not as in *boyfriend*, but—you know?" He nodded and tried to pry her arms from around his neck, but without success. "You're so cute, you know? I wanted you and Shiv to get it on, but she's got her Spanish heartthrob now, so we need to find you a lady friend. What do you like? Blonde?

Brunette?"

"Boys?" Siobhan asked, and they both creased up laughing.

"None of the above," he replied with a smile. "Redheads every time." He then took one of each of their hands in his and led them toward an all-night coffee shop, but Cassie had other ideas. With a twist, she had her hand free, and she stormed straight inside an entryway she'd spotted a few doors down marked *Club Alpha*.

She paid the entrance fee and dived right in, and the others could do nothing but follow her inside. Cassie grinned at the sight that welcomed her. Male dancers were everywhere. Some were dressed up in costumes or ripped jeans, while others had on tiny thongs or what looked like socks covering their manhood. A select few were on a stage, and were completely naked. Their epic rods stood to attention while they gyrated and danced, and their adoring public screamed for more. Cassie blushed at the sight, but refused to walk away.

"Table for three, please," she instructed the waitress, who spotted Siobhan and a very red-faced Roger trailing in behind her, and the young woman beckoned for them to follow her. They sat around a tall circular table, and Cassie immediately ordered cocktails. "Keep them coming," she instructed, handing a wad of cash to the girl, who nodded. Within minutes, two of the strippers came over, each carrying a tray adorned with colorful drinks and bowls of seductive looking canapés. They soon began offering the women a taste, while Roger stared the men down, letting them know he wasn't there for the show, or to be waited on.

A tall, blond Adonis gave Cassie his undivided attention for the entire duration of their drinking session. He was stunning, but she wasn't interested in anything he had to offer except the fun and flirtation. The man was oiled and waxed to perfection, and while she appreciated the view, it wasn't why she was there. She was teaching her own Adonis a lesson. Eyes were on her, and not just from the still disgruntled Roger sitting opposite, but from others who had been tailing them all afternoon. Cassie had known for a while that she'd been watched at all times, and in her anger had decided to give Leo's cronies something to report about.

When Mario, or so he said his name was, offered to feed her a cherry on a cocktail stick, she accepted. When he held a glass to her lips and tipped it for the perfect mouthful, she didn't object. He told her not to lift a finger, and she didn't. "A girl could get used to being waited on hand and foot," she told him after Mario wiped her lip clear of any remnants from her Screaming Orgasm with a napkin.

"I aim to please, madam." His baby blues bore into hers as he leaned in closer. "There are many ways I could wait on you. Many of which are not on the menu. All you need to do is ask."

Cassie gave Mario a coy smile, trying to act as demure as possible while her insides screamed in embarrassment. She had no need to trade sexual exploits with her almost naked bartender, but took the gesture as a compliment.

"I'll just take another one of these for now, but thank you," she replied, pointing to the empty glass.

"I'd like to give you more than just another Screaming Orgasm, but I guess it'll do," Mario teased before he stepped away to fulfill her order.

Cassie took a deep breath and looked across at her friends. Siobhan seemed to be in the same mood as she was—enjoying the attention while not really being all that interested—but Roger looked about ready to explode. Cassie ignored him. Instead, she watched the show going on near the back of the room as a dancer dressed as a cowboy took to the stage. He quickly started teasing the crowd, and she had to laugh at how the women were screaming giddily for him to take it all off. She wondered if, in another life, she too might've become one of those carefree, fun girls. The ones who had nothing to worry about. If she'd never moved to America with Jonah, she might just have been like them. The call of the theater had proven too enticing for them both in the end, though, and she knew there would always be a huge part of her that regretted taking off to the States with her star-bound husband.

When she sensed company standing close behind her, Cassie spun around, ready to welcome back her sexy waiter. Instead of her half-naked new friend, she collided with a tight wall of cotton-covered muscle. She knew exactly who wore the shirt she was staring at, and had to fight the smile curling at her lips. He'd gotten her message loud and clear, it seemed.

Despite his nightmare-driven cries that still rang in her ears, everything inside Cassie treacherously

95

reacted to Leo's presence. Even though she tried to maintain her nonchalance at finding him standing there, she couldn't resist teasing him.

"I hope you're here to deliver my cocktail?" she asked, staring up into his icy gaze.

"I think you've had enough," he said, and he put a stop to her mischievousness without even a flicker of guilt for his harsh demeanor.

"I don't care what you think, Leo. I'll stop when I say so." She knew she sounded like a petulant teenager, but didn't care. "Where's Mario?" She tried to look around the mammoth man blocking her view of the strip club, but it was no use. He overwhelmed her senses, each and every one of them, and they both knew she'd lose if she tried to fight him too hard on this.

"He's been reassigned." Leo didn't grab her or try to make her leave, but he didn't sit down to join them either. He continued to stare at her, as though disgusted that she'd even set foot in a male strip joint, let alone have enjoyed the attention of the men working there. "You don't belong in a place like this," he said, his voice low.

"I thought this is exactly where I belong? I'm nothing but another one of yours and Victor's whores, after all," she replied bitterly.

Cassie twisted her body sideways, grabbed her purse, and stormed out. She didn't want to cause a scene, so was sure to keep her head high and her forced smile firmly plastered on her face as she waved goodbye to Mario and the others that'd served their table.

When the cool air hit her, she wobbled and

slowed her march to a meander. Cassie knew the others weren't far behind, and was glad when she felt Siobhan's arm wrap around her waist in support rather than Leo's.

"Come on. Let's go home," she whispered, and Cassie nodded. She came to a stop and turned to face the guys just in time to catch the standoff happening between Leo and Roger. She'd missed the start of their talk, but it was clear Roger was stepping up in her defense. Cassie was grateful, but it hurt to think she needed her bodyguard to get between her and Leo. Not once had she ever thought they'd need it.

"I think it's pretty clear she doesn't wanna be around you tonight, Leo. Give her some space. I won't ask you again." Roger stepped directly into Leo's path, blocking him from the girls. She had to give Roger some credit, he had balls. Leo looked ready to explode. He clearly wasn't used to people telling him what to do, and struggled to keep his cool.

"Don't you dare tell me what I can or cannot do," Leo spat, and Cassie could see his snarl over her bodyguard's shoulder. He stepped closer and got in his face, but Roger still didn't back down. "Don't get in my way, Rog. You'll regret it, trust me." Leo added with a growl.

"You can threaten me all you like, but I don't respond to intimidation, nor do I play by prison rules." Roger stepped closer still, their noses almost touching, and Cassie could feel herself starting to panic. The last thing she wanted was to have caused a fight between two of her most favorite people, and her stomach lurched as she watched them.

In a flash, Leo had him by the throat and threw Roger to the ground. No matter his training or strength, Roger seemed no match for the powerful man, and went limp to show Leo he wasn't interested in a fight. But he still didn't seem ready to admit defeat. "Go home, Mr. Solomon. *Your* home." Leo let go, but didn't take his eyes off him as he stood and righted himself.

Cassie tried to ignore the sea of onlookers, and fought back her tears. She and Leo locked eyes for just a second, and she could see he was in pain, but she didn't feel ready to comfort him. Her head started to spin thanks to their drinking session, and she felt exhausted. Most importantly, she was hurting too.

Part of her wanted nothing more than for Leo to take her home and make it up to her, but she knew she had to push him. Her icy man would never learn if she kept letting him get away with keeping his emotions at bay. Only by taking the hardest road now could they possibly hope to move on.

She turned and walked away, and was glad when Roger caught her up and steered the girls toward an awaiting cab. Cassie trembled, fumbling with her purse in a bid to distract herself. She didn't look back as they sped away, and knew she had to stay strong.

They dropped Siobhan off before heading to her apartment, even though she insisted she was sober enough to come back to Cassie's and keep her company. Siobhan was swaying more than her boss, and even Cassie could tell she'd be good for nothing more than falling into bed when she finally crashed.

Roger said nothing as they rode the rest of the way, and he didn't even give Cassie the option of refusing his company when they reached her building. He followed her inside and promptly started the big-brother-style caretaker routine. After helping her out of her heels and jacket, he ran her a hot bath. Their comfortable silence carried on while he worked, and Cassie was grateful for it. She didn't feel much like talking about what'd happened between Roger and Leo on that sidewalk, and she wasn't ready to even consider whether or not they could move on from Leo's behavior.

When she emerged, she discovered that Roger had left a perfectly brewed cup of tea and a small stack of biscuits on her nightstand. Sometimes, those little things he did reminded her so much of Grayson. He'd been the one to keep her safe and bring her food when she was in Mexico, all the while watching over her with a silent affection and brotherly-type love. She still missed him, even after all this time. Not the situation in which they'd met, or how it'd all ended, but she missed her friend and protector. Grayson, her Gentle Giant. She often wondered where on earth he might be now and hoped he'd escaped the cartel too. She prayed he was happy, wherever he was.

After Cassie had dressed and climbed under her sheets, she called to the man she knew would be waiting outside her door.

"You can come in." She smiled when Roger slipped inside her doorway a second later. "Thanks for taking care of me," she added, indicating to her tea and biscuits.

"I thought you might need sobering up, although you're doing far better than I would've thought," he teased gently, but they both knew having fought with Leo was definitely a sobering experience.

"I can handle my booze, Rog. It's not my first night on the town, but I must admit it was my first male strip-joint," she replied with a cheeky grin.

"Mine too." He chuckled to himself as he tucked her in and made to leave, but then turned back. "Whatever he did. I get it that you're hurt, but don't punish him too long. That man's lost without you." It was a relief to hear that he wasn't holding a grudge.

"He called me a whore," she replied on a sigh. "He said I was nothing but another whore. How can I forgive that?" Tears pricked at her eyes as she peered up at him. Cassie then told him exactly what'd happened that morning as Leo had slept beside her, and Roger took a deep breath.

"I hate to be the voice of reason, but I think he deserves the chance to explain. Sounds to me like he's dealing with some serious shit, and not very well. A beaten and broken animal will always lash out at the first sign of a nurturing, kind hand. They don't know any better. Give him the opportunity to learn his lesson and you'll both be better off, I promise."

He left before she could respond, and Cassie sat and drank her tea in stunned silence. Eventually, she turned out the light and fell into an exhausted sleep.

# Chapter Eight

Leo woke up at his desk, feeling stiff and sore after the few hours he'd spent hunched over the hard wooden table. He'd returned to the casino after the altercation with Roger because there was no way he could go to "his home," as Roger had called it. That apartment was nothing but a shell, an empty set of rooms he was just about to give up so he could move in permanently with Cassie. He felt lonely nestled amongst his busy casino with all his employees, and knew he'd be a wreck if he went back to the almost empty place he'd barely set foot in since that night with Cassie after the play. That place wasn't his home, she was. Nothing else mattered, and he missed her so badly that the last day felt like a year. He'd thought after she'd calmed down they would've been able to sort things out like normal, but he'd been wrong.

Yes, he'd had guys following her. He couldn't help himself, but when they'd called to say she and her friends had hit a strip club, he knew she was on to him. Leo had kept his cool when he'd seen the photos of Roger and Cassie holding hands over the dinner table after he'd pushed her away before. Her tears and hopeless expression had consumed him, but rather than be jealous, he was left terrified. Leo swore he'd never be the reason she cried again, yet he'd already broken that self-imposed rule far too frequently.

Roger wasn't a threat; he'd known that since before he'd even met the guy. Leo had learned right from the start that Roger and Cassie's friendship was deep, while not sexual in any way, but last night he'd hated that Roger was the one having fun with his girl and not him. After being informed of their escapades, Leo had seen red. He'd gone straight down there and warned the stripper who'd been flirting with Cassie to back off, or else he'd put an end to his livelihood with a brick to that chiseled face of his. Part of him felt like going back there and doing as he'd warned. Just knowing Mario, or whatever his real name was, had been pawing over Cassie was enough to make his blood still boil. He forced his anger away. They were at a turning point, and there was no going back this time. Mario wasn't to blame, and neither was Roger.

Leo pushed back his chair and headed to his bathroom to get cleaned up. There was nothing else for it; he had to tell Cassie the truth about his dreams. He'd hit a wall, and knew it was make or break time with the woman he loved.

On his way out of the building thirty minutes later, he bumped into Suzie, the receptionist the casino manager had warned him about when he'd first taken over. So far she'd seemed harmless, a little bit over the top with the makeup and blonde dye-job, but not a tease like Stuart had said. Now though, Leo barely recognized her. Suzie had dyed her hair dark brown and was wearing half as much makeup as usual. She looked natural, and prettier than Leo had even seen her.

"Morning, Mr. Solomon. You're here early, or did you pull an all-nighter?" she asked, smiling up at him sweetly.

"Just heading home now. Are you on an early shift?" Leo replied in an attempt to remain courteous, while all he wanted was to get to Cassie. He wanted to make a start on rebuilding their relationship, even if it meant unearthing some of the things he'd tried so hard to keep buried.

"Yep," she said, and Leo thought she seemed awfully bubbly for so close to dawn. "I'm going out tonight so switched shifts. My new boyfriend is taking me to see a play, it's all very exciting." Leo really didn't care. He forced a smile and carried on his way, heading out into the cool morning air to retrieve his car from his private spot by the staff entrance.

Leo cursed under his breath when he went into Cassie's apartment and found the alarm turned off. Even when she was inside, she had been told she should activate it so Roger would be alerted if anyone broke in. His exasperation was soon forced aside when he spotted Roger's jacket hanging over the back of the sofa. He wasn't asleep on it, in fact he was nowhere to be seen, and Leo's stomach immediately lurched.

*No way. She wouldn't. They wouldn't.* His heart was in his mouth, and Leo tried to prepare himself for the worst. If he found the man he'd trusted not to extort his closeness with her in bed with Cassie, there would be no holding back. He knew he'd kill him.

When he found Roger fast asleep, curled into a ball on the hallway floor, Leo was beyond relieved. He knew he never wanted to feel like that ever again—like she might want to cheat on him, or like he'd given her a reason to.

"Rog." He shook him awake gently. "Are you down there acting as a protective friend or a guard dog? I need to know if you're here to keep my girl company or if you're gonna try and stop me getting in there and sorting my shit out." There was no need or time for small talk or pleasantries. He was ready to throw down if necessary, but it wasn't what he wanted.

"Just here to keep an eye on her, mate. Not to fight you," Roger groaned in response, rubbing the sleep from his eyes.

"Good, then let me see you out." Leo helped him up, thanked him, and then did just that.

\*\*\*

Cassie stirred and groaned. Her stomach was rumbling—the first signal that her hangover was already creeping in—and she peeled open her eyes. *Only eight o'clock?* Not bad considering how late she'd gone to sleep. After she stretched and was rubbing her eyes roughly to clear the sleep away, a small cough alerted her to the presence of another person in her bedroom. Cassie sprang upright and looked down at the man watching her from the armchair across the room. Leo looked utterly exhausted. If he'd slept at all it couldn't have been much. Two nights of unbearable distance between them had taken an incredible toll, and Cassie immediately softened, rather than still being angry with him.

"Hey," was all she managed.

"I wasn't calling you a whore." His words caught her completely off guard, but she was glad he was there and seemingly ready to open up at long last. Cassie nodded, wanting him to know she'd heard him, but that she needed to hear more. "I keep having awful, vivid dreams. Like I'm being forced to relive the past. I know you've seen and heard me, and I'm sorry for what I said, but it wasn't to you." Leo let out a sigh and leaned forward, his elbows resting on his knees while his head hung low on his shoulders.

Cassie forced herself to stay put. She wanted to go to him, to soothe his pain, but knew he needed to keep going. They were getting somewhere at last, so she wasn't about to interrupt him now that he was finally offloading about his past. "There was a whore who looked like you. I convinced myself it was okay that I used her as practice because you were so fragile, and because I was such a sexual predator. Even after you were taken, I'm ashamed to say that I still booked her from time to time. With her, I somehow felt close to you, like you were still there instead of gone—snatched away and held prisoner while I festered behind like some kind of zombie."

Her heart was pounding in her chest. Victor had mentioned a whore that looked like Cassie once, in his usual taunting way, but she'd never known if he'd been telling her the truth—until now. She wasn't sure whether she wanted to cry, cuddle him, or throw something.

Leo started talking again before she could react, cutting off her inner turmoil, and Cassie stared at her hands as his words washed over her. "After you'd gone, I was a mess, and whenever I fucked her I was far from gentle. That's what you heard. I was screaming those words at her, hating her for being with me when you weren't, and I hated myself for touching her. I hated myself for needing her. I still do."

"You're a douchebag, Leonardo Solomon," she told him as she looked back up. Cassie's words were said with half-hearted seriousness. Overall, she was genuinely glad to hear the truth at long last. He didn't object. In fact, Leo simply peered over at her, and he looked old all of a sudden, as though just that tiny snippet of honesty had taken a lot out of him. "I'm not the damsel in distress anymore, so stop treating me like I'm gonna fall apart with just a small bit of your truth. This closed-off attitude needs to stop, otherwise it'll break us. Just talk to me, tell me how you feel and what's eating you, okay?"

"Okay," Leo conceded, and he climbed up out of the chair with slow movements that confirmed to her how tired he must be. Leo lay down on the bed next to her, and Cassie slid into his strong arms. She couldn't bring herself to be mad at him any longer. It just wasn't in her to punish his behavior when she knew he was struggling to control all of those emotions bubbling under his cool, hard exterior.

"When are you going to learn that I'm right *all* the time? Just do as you're told and all of this will be so much easier," she teased, and she loved the gruff laugh he afforded her.

"Oh dear, love. You really are with the wrong man," he mumbled. It seemed to take every last bit of energy he had to peel off his clothes and slide under the covers, but he did it, and then pulled her back into his arms. Cassie let herself melt into his embrace and breathed Leo in. She'd missed him the night before. The distance had still been torturous, and she never wanted to go through that with him ever again.

When she felt Leo thrashing beside her a few hours later, Cassie forced herself awake and tried to leave his strong embrace. This was usually her cue to dive out of bed and watch as whatever nightmare plaguing him completed its torment before eventually releasing him. This time though, Leo somehow sensed her retreat and stopped her, grabbing Cassie and pulling her into him. They'd been spooning, her being the little one, and now his thickly muscled arms were wrapped around her along with his legs. She was cocooned in him. Her immediate instinct was to panic, but that was short-lived when soft words filtered through from his subconscious mind and filled the silence.

"How can she still be so goddam beautiful? Look

at her, so broken and scared, yet radiant and gorgeous. She's submissive to him, and he's owning her, but she wants him to." A sob escaped him and he held Cassie tighter. "She hates you, Leo. Keep it together. Don't let Victor see how much you care," he was murmuring in her ear. "Don't let him know it's affecting you. Don't show him how much you miss her, how much you love her. Hold on, Cassie. I'll save you, but you just have to hold on."

"Leo, I'm here. I'm safe now," she whispered through ragged breaths while he pinned her to the bed. Strangely, he wasn't hurting her. If anything, his hold was strangely delicate and protective. Leo was so strong that his grip was utterly unyielding, but she liked it.

Cassie had known for a long time that she was attracted to danger. She'd felt it right from the moment she'd first met Leo in his mansion. He'd been intimidating and scary, but she'd been drawn to that fire inside of him. She'd also known just how easily he could crush her and ruin her if he chose to. According to her best friend, Hanna, he'd done exactly that time and time again to his previous conquests, but she'd still wanted him regardless. Cassie had enjoyed the chase. When she'd finally caved, she also loved the feeling of dominating herself in order to be submissive to him. It was the ultimate empowering feeling to submit to Leo, rather than feeling weak and possessed out of self-preservation like she'd had to with Victor.

With those memories flaring in her gut, she realized she'd always been that way. Cassie had let her world be ruled by the men in it for all of her adult life, and even now she was still the same. There was no fighting it, if anything she knew she wanted more. Being taken care of and led was freeing, and at least this time she'd given herself to her dominator willingly. In fact, she'd outright begged Leo to own her the night he'd come back into her life and to her apartment after the theater's opening performance.

A wave of pleasure swept through Cassie, and she felt the last bit of shielding numbness she'd carried for so long subside. It was replaced by sheer euphoria, and when she felt the tip of his rock-hard cock press into her from behind, she wanted it to find its home. Cassie arched back into him, but he wasn't at the right angle to accept the invitation. "Leo," she sighed, desperately wanting him to wake up and take her.

Still pressing into her from behind, he grabbed her arms at the elbow and pulled them behind her back, pushing her shoulder blades together. Cassie's face and chest were pressed harder into the mattress, while her lower half was still to the side, but she didn't fight.

"Do you want to be free? Do it, Cassie," he mumbled, and his voice caught in his throat. She suddenly knew exactly what he was dreaming of. It had to be the moment when she'd killed Victor right in front of him. Leo had held her oppressor in the same way he was holding her now, and she'd taken the chance she needed to be free of him at last. Cassie knew it was wrong to find satisfaction in that moment of sheer instinct and self-defense, but there was no denying it.

The memory was overwhelming her waking thought, just like it was haunting Leo's dream. But instead of feeling frightened, Cassie felt as though she might burst into flames if he didn't help her reach the explosive climax already building in her core.

She needed Leo to take her and give her some pleasure to associate with that memory forcing itself back to life between them. The transition had already begun, and she was no longer ashamed to admit that deep within lay a truth she'd never spoken aloud before—she'd enjoyed killing Victor.

Cassie summoned her strength and twisted in Leo's grasp. She turned fully onto her belly, her hips moving in line with the rest of her body, and she felt him move with her. This time his hardness found its home, and like two pieces of a delicious puzzle, they slotted together. Her mind was alive with the memory of the moment she'd murdered her husband with his own knife, and she was well aware how soaked she was between her thighs. Cassie cried out when Leo slammed into her from behind and delivered her an almost instantaneous orgasm.

"Leo!" she screamed, and that was when his lips pressed against her shoulder tenderly. He kissed and nipped at her, having let go of her arms, but he kept his fingers entwined with hers at her sides. Leo was awake, Cassie could tell, but he didn't seem interested in fighting this strange urge either. He pushed her thighs closed and continued thrusting inside of her, not needing to ask if she wanted more.

After Cassie came again, he pulled out and

flipped her onto her back. He tore open her thighs and was back inside in an instant. Leo then he covered every inch of her body with his own. Their lips were fused, and their chests and stomachs felt glued together, while Cassie hooked her legs around his waist. Their lovemaking was frantic, chaotic, and hurried, but also bursting with passion and adoration.

When Leo finished claiming her, she peered up into his eyes, and enjoyed the surprised look in them.

"I'm sorry, I..." He stopped when she grinned up at him knowingly. "My dream, it felt so real, but totally fucked up."

"I know what you were dreaming about, Leo," she teased, grinding up against the still hard cock between her legs. "Did you enjoy watching Victor fuck me that night? You were sat so still, and at the time I believed you hated me for having left you. I thought you were there to watch out of some sick satisfaction. Like you wanted to see him own me."

A low growl started from somewhere deep within Leo's chest, and Cassie placed her hand over his heart. It was pounding hard. "But now I know it wasn't that. You loved me even then, and you gave up everything to save me."

Cassie began moving against him from below; gyrating to help push him in and out of her soaking cleft while Leo remained pressed against her, holding himself over Cassie using his powerful arms. He stayed silent, but she felt his eyes on her, watching her grind on him. She arched up even higher on the bed. Cassie rolled her hips, so fluid and sensuous against his hard muscles, building her climax while he did nothing but let her. "Does it make you hard thinking of me murdering him? Because it makes me wet, Leo. It makes me so desperate to be fucked hard…"

Her words were cut short when Leo silenced her with a forceful kiss. In a flash, her ankles were in his hands, being pressed up into the air by her head. With her body curled up and open to him, her voracious lover stopped her writhing by pounding her hard.

Leo took himself almost all the way out, before plummeting back inside and locking onto her g-spot with the head of his hard-on. She was utterly at his command, and didn't fight the loud groans and cries her body emitted in response to his epic thrusts.

He was relentless. "Stop, baby. Stop," she pleaded when her next explosive orgasm ripped through her, but Leo refused. He released her ankles and drew her legs back down to his hips, where he slowed his pursuit to a gentle stroke.

"You always told me not to stop, even when you asked me to." His sultry voice filled her ears. "But I can't ever stop, don't you understand, Cassie? I'll never stop loving you." Leo showed her by making love to her. Slow and deep, he commanded each of her senses before he eventually stilled and groaned as he came. He then wrapped her in his arms and continued to hold on tight for as long as she let him.

They dozed together for a while, but Cassie's hangover came back with a vengeance and she had to give into the hunger growling in her belly. She climbed up and pulled on a shirt, and could feel herself bouncing on the balls of her feet as she headed through the apartment. Finally, they were getting somewhere. Yes, they might both be messed up victims that were potential ticking time bombs of explosive and destructive behavior, but Cassie also felt like they were healing each other with every day that passed. Bit by bit they were recovering, and that was good enough for her.

She was making crumpets and coffee when she felt him behind her. Leo had sneaked in so silently that she nearly jumped, but her body still yearned for his touch, and instead Cassie trembled in sweet remembrance of their day spent in bed. He planted gentle kisses on her shoulders and brought his hands down her arms before he settled them around her slim waist.

"If anyone knew the fucked up things we said and did earlier, I doubt they'd speak to us again," he teased, and she had to laugh. Leo continued kissing her neck and back, but she wasn't hungry for him again, not yet. Cassie still needed answers.

"It's a good thing we can be fucked up together in private then, isn't it?" she replied, turning to face him, a large bite of buttered crumpet still in her mouth. "Tell me about your nightmares, Leo. I need you to be honest with me about what haunts you, not bottle it up."

He closed the gap and pulled her to him. "It wasn't a nightmare this time, love. Usually it's memories replaying in my mind, mostly the bad, but this time it was a good one."

"Hmm, I remember you like to watch." Her eyebrow shot up, and Cassie let him see she was grinning. "Even that night?"

"Yep." Leo took a bite out of her makeshift meal. "It took everything I had to ignore you at my party, and when you guys disappeared I was worried you'd left. I needed Victor to stick around long enough for the Feds to get what they needed, so I went in search of you both."

"And you found us in the bedroom," Cassie murmured, finishing his sentence, and Leo nodded.

"I had to play it cool, when all I wanted to do was kill him. But then, you were such a treat to watch. Seeing him fuck you turned me inside out, but I had to make him believe I didn't care. You helped keep my cover without even realizing it."

"I believed it," she murmured, remembering how miserable she'd been made to feel after Leo had pointedly ignored her presence at his party after everything that'd happened.

"Exactly, and you made him believe. He was unarmed and so arrogant, totally convinced that he'd won." Leo ground his renewed hard-on into her thigh. "Until you took that knife of his and killed him, of course." He was driving her crazy, and she knew if they weren't careful they'd end up back in bed before she could finish her food, let alone her questioning.

Cassie stepped away, shaking her head. "You aren't gonna distract me that easily, Solomon," she informed him with a smile. "I want more, tell me about your dream the other night. I need to know more about that whore." She wasn't going to back down this time, and Leo seemed to sense it. He took a deep breath and made himself a cup of coffee while staring out the window, seemingly gathering his thoughts.

"She was just a means for release at first. I used her only when absolutely necessary, and I am truly sorry for it, Cassie." She believed him, and stepped close behind her man. Cassie slid a supportive hand up his back and rubbed between his shoulders, needing Leo to know she was still there for him, and was strong enough to hear his story. "When I'd healed up and was trying to convince myself I was over you, I started using drugs—you know that." Cassie hummed in affirmation, although she hated the thought of him self-medicating. "Our exploits were anywhere from gentle to harsh, and then we progressed to downright dangerous."

"Like how?" she asked, not taking her hand from his shoulder.

"I never cared what she wanted, I just told her where and when. The fact that she kept coming back when I called was enough to convince me she was enjoying herself with me, but we never talked other than for me to issue my orders. Sometimes I'd gag and whip her, other times I'd beat her." Leo turned to face Cassie, and she could see the regret in his stare. "I'd gone back to the old me, and then some. I paid her well, and I guess she must've been a masochist, 'cause she came back day after day. Always wanting more of the monster, the legend that was Leonardo Solomon."

"Many a woman, both weak and strong, has bowed before you, Leo. Even I wanted a piece of that monster I knew was lurking beneath your gentlemanly façade," she told him. It was the truth,

115

and dangerous or not, she could see the attraction. "Did you enjoy beating her while thinking of me?" Cassie couldn't help asking the question, and she bit the inside of her lip in anticipation of his answer.

"No, love. By that point I think I'd stopped associating her with you at all. I'd tried to force you away as much as possible, to mask my feelings, and the cocaine was helping with that." Cassie nodded in understanding. Although it killed her to think of him fucking that whore, she was relieved to hear that she hadn't been on his mind while he was beating her, and felt herself relax again. "We started dabbling in more BDSM, and I liked it, but then one day I discovered something else."

"Please tell me it's nothing to do with golden showers or ball gags?" she teased, and Leo let out a gruff laugh as he turned to face her.

"Well..." He pulled her close and laughed again, and Cassie was glad to hear that he was staying calm and on top of his emotions. "No, it's something often referred to as 'ravishment fantasy.' You'd given me a taste of it the morning we'd woken up at my place. Do you remember?" She sure did. Cassie thought back to that first night together with a smile, and remembered how she'd asked him to force her after her intense dream the following morning. They'd been refused any other chances to be together after that, as just hours after they'd cemented their relationship at last, she'd caught the attention of the monster who made it his mission to tear her away.

"Rape?" Cassie asked wide-eyed.

"Kinda, but consensual of course. We started out

small, and I enjoyed forcing her. Having her completely at my mercy was a thrill. I ended up texting her to meet me behind one of my clubs one night, where I jumped her. She knew it was me, and went along with it. I liked having her at my command, but I liked it too much. One night I beat her badly in the throes of the roleplay. After that, she was never safe, and I even put her in the hospital."

"Jeez." Cassie peered up at him. "I was getting all hot and bothered until you said that." She meant it. Although she hated that he'd been indulging in those darker fantasies without her, especially with "whore Cassie," the sheer thought of him ravishing her that way had her body aching for him to show her exactly what he meant.

"I was a mess back then, but now I can control it—control myself. I'd love nothing more than to show you," Leo replied, kissing her deeply. "But we need to take it slowly, love. Explore your limits."

"I'd like that," she replied, snuggling into his hold. "I know you don't want to hear this, but Victor showed me some of the things I hadn't thought I'd like too." Leo tensed.

"I saw for myself." His tone was bitter and full of venom. "When I came to visit after you'd just gotten married, he linked the camera feed from your room into mine. I was forced to see and hear the two of you going at it."

Cassie gasped in shock. "Leo, I had no idea about that," she told him honestly, and stepped away with a shudder. "You know I only did what I had to so he'd believe I loved him? I had to be the

117

wife he wanted me to be, or else I'd end up another whore to be used and abused by his men and their clients."

"I know, love. I know." His tone was soothing now, and he recaptured her in his embrace. "At the time I believed it. I'd been bested. I don't normally admit defeat, but in that moment, I was done with you. When I got back to New York, I buried myself in work and pussy. The last time I was with *her* I wrapped my hands around her neck and screamed at her until she passed out. I saw your face again, and felt my anger at you come pouring out of me." He winced, and Cassie knew it was a hard memory for him to relive, either awake or asleep. "That's what I was dreaming about the other day. I almost killed her that night, and after that I never saw her again."

"How did you get from there to deciding to save me?" Cassie absolutely had to know, otherwise she suspected she'd grow scared of him. Leo had shocked her with his explanation of how dark things had gotten for him, and she needed to find out how he'd gotten from there to now.

"I became so terrified of what I'd become that I had no choice but to sort my life out at last. It was only when I was clean and sober that I could see the truth. You were just surviving, of course you were. Anyone would do the same in your position. I did in prison." He stopped short, and Cassie detected a hint of deeper agony there that she knew was a conversation for another time. No matter his nonchalance before, prison was a trigger for him, and she could see it.

Leo had done well opening up as much as he

already had, so she wasn't about to push for more. This was a vast improvement on the stubborn silence she'd had from him so far, and Cassie appreciated that he was trying so hard. She wrapped her arms around his waist again and squeezed, offering support and love wordlessly, and she felt him relax around her. Leo kissed the top of her head and leaned into her, and she just continued to hold on to him.

After the longest time, they finally broke apart. Cassie peered up at her man, wanting nothing more than for him to claim her again. "So, tell me more about this ravishment thing," she said, and her request made him grin from ear to ear.

"Sure, but only if you agree to tell me what other things you've discovered you like. I promise not to get jealous." Leo took a step back and reached out his hand for her to shake.

"Deal," she agreed as she shook it. He then grabbed her again and pulled Cassie up into his arms. She shrieked loudly but didn't stop him, planting kisses all over his face and neck as he carried her back to the bedroom.

He laid her down on the soft duvet and peered into her face adoringly, and Cassie stared right back at him. Leo's arched eyebrow told her he was waiting for her to deliver on her part of the bargain, and she cringed. She felt her cheeks burn as she turned sheepish under his intense gaze, but he didn't budge. Leo continued to stare down into her eyes expectantly, and she found him intimidating, but in a sexy way instead of scary. Wanting everything he had to give, Cassie opened her mouth at last. "I liked it when…" She took a deep breath and held it. "When he spanked me." Cassie screwed her eyes shut in anticipation of his response.

He didn't even acknowledge her.

"Okay. So, let's talk ravishment," Leo replied cheerfully, and Cassie peeled open her eyes to find him watching her with a playful smile. "The basis of the idea is consensual force. You'd willingly let me take you in whatever way I wanted, and whenever I want. You'd be free to fight back, and try to escape me, of course. If anything, I'd like that even more." He winked and slid his hands over her scantily clad body on the bed. Cassie moaned and arched her back, thinking she liked the sound of that too.

"I could run? Fight you?" she checked, and Leo nodded. "I'm guessing that when it's on, there's no stopping the game?"

"Quite the opposite, you'll have a safe word. But if you ask me to stop or scream for help, I'll ignore it." Cassie's body heat turned up about three notches. She liked the sound of that more than she'd ever admit to anyone but Leo. "We need to take things one step at a time, slowly at first. We'll start with basic dominance and go from there. If you like the extra element of the ravishment the first few times, we could then intensify things."

"How?" She was panting now, and knew her body was sending off some serious signals because Leo was short of breath too. His hands roamed over her breasts and down to her soaking cleft, and he took a sharp inhale when he discovered her readiness. He slid two fingers inside and slowly stroked his way up and down her more than ready sex.

"Timing can be part of the fun," he answered, leaning down to give her nipple a quick bite before continuing. "For example, I'd tell you in the morning that at some point over the day I'll strike. You won't know when or where, and the anticipation will drive you crazy." His thumb caressed the swollen bead at the apex of her thighs, and Cassie felt her climax building.

"No matter what?" she breathed, desperate to know more.

"You know me, I'll get creative," he replied with a gruff laugh. "Do you want me to give you a taste?" A groan was her response, and Leo pressed his mouth around her nipple hard enough to let her know it wasn't a good enough answer.

"Yes," she bit out through clenched teeth, and Leo pulled his hand from inside her trembling core. He grabbed her thigh and flipped his lover over onto her belly, and then he gripped her hands and pulled them around behind her back. Cassie squirmed when he held on tightly enough to cause a small spark of pain, and was rewarded with a sharp slap to her backside. The sting made her gasp in surprise.

"Don't move," he commanded, and she purposely wriggled again. A second spank brought her desires rushing to the surface, and when a third, harder slap struck her, she came. The times when Victor had spanked her, she'd enjoyed the mixture of pain and pleasure, but when it was Leo doing it, she was driven wild by his hand. The third strike had been directly to her exposed pussy, and the sting had brought with it a satisfaction she'd never thought imaginable.

Leo was inside her in an instant. He still held her hands tightly behind her back, and thrust his long, commanding cock in and out relentlessly. He was rough, hard, and powerful, and his voracious pummeling quickly solicited another orgasm from his exhausted lover.

Cassie turned to jelly in his hold, and by the time he stilled and shot his hot load into her, she could barely speak or move her spent body. He laid her down under the duvet and held on tight, not letting go for even a second as her mind and body calmed and rested in his strong grasp.

# *Chapter Nine*

Cassie woke the next morning to a surprisingly calm Leo lying beside her. The sun was streaming in through the open curtains, landing on his huge chest, and he looked incredibly beautiful. She watched for a few minutes, loving having found him sleeping peacefully for a change. After a while, her stomach growled angrily, reminding her she'd barely eaten the last couple of days, so she slid silently out of bed and pulled on a fresh set of shorts along with one of Leo's t-shirts. She'd made it as far as the door when she was tackled from behind. Cassie squealed, but didn't fight as he pressed her into the wall from behind.

"And just where do you think you're going?" Leo's voice growled in her ear.

"To get some breakfast. I need some food if I'm going to try and keep up with you," she replied, pushing against the wall with her hands to ensure she pressed her body back into his. Cassie was rewarded with soft nibbles and kisses to her neck, while Leo cupped her breasts roughly and ensured she stayed still. His huge erection delved between her thighs, and she gasped.

Leo curled his fingers and pulled the cotton t-shirt taut before ripping it in two at her cleavage. Cassie squealed in surprise as he flung the torn shreds to the ground, and then ravaged her breasts and nipples with those tremendously powerful hands.

"I'll do the same to those shorts in ten seconds if they aren't off," he ordered, running his hands down to her waist and slipping his fingertips under the band. Cassie quickly slipped them off and kicked them aside, all the while panting excitedly at Leo's show of raw dominance. "Good. Today we aren't wearing any clothes, otherwise there'll be trouble. Hear me?"

Leo leaned down slightly behind her and his hands travelled to Cassie's knees, which he grabbed and lifted her off the ground. Her hands found the wall for support just in time for him to open her legs and wrap her ankles behind his ass. He then drove his hard-on straight into her soaking cleft. After a few long strokes, Leo pressed the head of his shaft into her g-spot and kept it there. Cassie clenched around him and trembled, welcoming the fullness, and felt her body opening up even more. "I asked you a question."

"Yes, Leo. Yes!"

"Yes what?" he asked, pulling back just an inch or so before driving himself back against her sweet spot.

"No clothes," she panted, desperate for him to finish what he'd started. Leo seemed to hear her silent plea, and began pummeling her, hard. He then stopped his pounding and, her hands gripping the wall and her ankles digging into his ass for support, he started moving her on top of him. Cassie was soaring up and down, and it felt amazing. It was like floating, and only Leo's hands on her waist kept her from flying away. Her body roared with heat and toe-curling pleasure, and he didn't stop. Only after she'd climaxed multiple times did he go still and join her in her ecstasy.

Cassie whimpered when he eventually pulled out, feeling empty. Leo untangled her legs from around him and carried her into the bathroom, where he ran her a hot shower. Cassie's knees were weak to the point of wobbling, but Leo held her steady. He seemed to take great pleasure in cleaning her up under the cascading heat, and then toweled her dry with gentle hands and a delicate touch.

"Stay here, Jellybean. I'll bring you something to eat," he told her, settling her beneath the duvet before padding out to the hallway wearing nothing but a smile. Cassie laughed, for no reason other than that Leo and his domineering ways amused her. He was confusing as hell, but she loved his unpredictability and his extreme passion. She knew without words or gestures how much he loved her. He'd shown her in so many ways, and Cassie adored how they'd not only made it through their first argument, but that they'd come out the other side even stronger.

She smiled to herself at his new term of endearment for her, *Jellybean*. The nickname was silly, but she liked it. She'd always told him she was the "cheap wine and jellybeans kinda girl," and he'd never forced her to be anything else since. She was reminded of when he'd delivered her with those exact gifts after saving her from a potentially monstrous lover in the musician, Otis, and then held her tight as she fell apart in his arms afterwards. He wasn't a monster, not then, and not now. Neither of them were; they both simply needed to remember that.

"It's true what they say about makeup sex being epic," she told him when Leo came back in with two plates piled high with pancakes and bacon. He set them down and grinned at her before heading back to the kitchen to grab the coffee.

"I'm sure I'll be a douchebag again soon, then we'll have the chance for more makeup sex," he finally replied with a small laugh.

"Or I'll overreact about something and kick off. Either way, I'm sure we'll be fine," Cassie said with a wink. She wanted him to know that she wasn't a fool. He wasn't always going to be the one causing the fights; it was inevitable that she would cause her fair share of rows too, but that was normal.

"It's strange how I came here to take care of you, thinking you still needed me to save you, but instead it seems you're the one saving me. You're putting me back together piece by piece, Cassandra Taylor," he told her, holding up a forkful of pancake and bacon for her to eat.

Her heart ached for him. Leo was finally learning to open up, and she was starting to see the truth he'd been hiding from her all this time. He really was broken and in need of someone willing to put him back together again. It was Cassie's turn to do the saving, and that was absolutely fine.

"It's my job to build you back up, Leo. Always and forever, I'll be your rock, just like you're mine." She ate the forkful and watched in surprise as he cut her another piece, leaving the other plate untouched. Before she could object, he placed the fresh mouthful to her lips and she took it. The food was delicious, and Cassie was impressed that he'd managed to whip up an American style breakfast so quickly. She missed lots of things about her life in New York, one of which was undoubtedly the food, and she loved how he'd taken the initiative and cooked her something both filling and nostalgic. After another bite, he caught her looking over to his rapidly cooling plate of food and shrugged.

"I need to make sure you're good first. It's my job to take care of you as well, and trust me— there's nowhere in the world I'd rather be than here with you." Leo scooped up the final mouthful and offered it to Cassie, and she basked in the shy smile he afforded her when she took it. His cheeks were flushed, and she could see the pride in his eyes. She'd never seen this side of him before, and wondered if his dominant alter-ego sometimes needed to control her in ways other than just sexual.

He was rewarding her submissiveness by caring for her completely now that he'd had his fun. She'd followed his orders, and was sure that this was how things ought to be. With Victor, he'd rewarded her by allowing her the things she should've had all along, like security, food, and affection. Her submissive behavior had earned her things like the pencils and paper to draw, or the cell phone when he'd let her call Hanna. It was all a game to him, whereas Leo was going about earning her trust in a completely opposite way. He was loving, caring, and providing for her in so many different ways. With every single thing he did, big or small, Leo always seemed to be putting her first and taking care of her needs before his own.

There was no fighting any of it now. Cassie knew she'd loved him from the moment she'd first laid eyes on him at that party, and always would.

"You're a good man, Leonardo Solomon. I feel safe with you," she told him, and he seemed shocked. She realized that she'd never said those words to him before, probably because back when they'd first met he was intimidating and powerful, and he had scared her. Now, though, they were both incredibly different people to who they'd been before, and she thanked God for bringing him back into her life. "Can I feed you now?" she then asked, and Leo nodded. He handed her the second plate, but he left the single knife and fork set on the empty one.

Cassie knew without asking what he wanted. She used her fingertips to pull apart the fluffy pancake, sticky with syrup, and offered him a piece. He opened up and then licked her fingers clean with every mouthful, working his soft tongue over her fingertips in such a seductive way that it made her blush every time. She carried on in silence, and watched enthralled as he devoured each delicious morsel. Cassie couldn't deny she enjoyed the feeling it gave her to serve him, and was sad when the meal was finished.

She had to admit, she got it now. No matter how independent she'd become, Cassie still wanted to be owned, but this time she'd made the right choice in which man she'd given herself to.

\*\*\*

After lying wrapped in each other's arms for hours, chatting, and whiling away the afternoon in sleepy bliss, Cassie finally gave in to her bladder's request to be emptied. On her way back to bed, the buzzer rang on the intercom and she grabbed her robe before padding through the apartment to the door. She picked up the receiver and heard Roger's deep, cockney voice on the other end, so let him up. Cassie deactivated the alarm and opened the door only when she saw him reach the top of the stairs through the peephole.

"I have taught you well, my student," he joked when she'd let him inside and reactivated the system. "Everything okay?" he asked, clearly aiming for nonchalance, and failing miserably. It was obvious he was there to check that she and Leo had made up and were both okay, and she guessed one look at her smitten face must've said it all. "I was just swinging by to check in, I won't keep you," he added with a wink before letting himself out again. Cassie fiddled with the alarm, and was stood contemplating what to do with the rest of their day when Leo's deep voice boomed from the bedroom.

"Cassandra, get in here this instant!" She didn't

hesitate to follow his order and almost ran to him, but stopped dead when his hard scowl greeted her from the bed. He was propped up against the pillows, seemingly lying in wait for her return. Cassie opened her mouth to ask what was wrong when he patted the duvet covering his knees to summon her closer. "Did I, or did I not, give you an order this morning?" She stepped closer, nodding timidly. "What was that order?"

"No clothes." Her voice came out in a timid squeal.

"And yet, look at you now." Cassie looked down at the robe she'd tied around herself.

"I couldn't answer the door naked!" she cried, her insides screaming. While she hated the idea that she'd disobeyed him, the realization that punishment was coming was strangely welcome too.

"I don't want problems, I want solutions, Ms. Taylor." He patted the duvet again and she stepped closer. "The only way you'll be prepared for the next time is for you to be taught a serious lesson on this occasion. Don't you agree?"

Cassie untied her robe and dropped it to the floor. Another step closer had her standing right beside the bed, and she could feel her core tensing in anticipation already.

"Yes, Mr. Solomon." She watched the satisfaction cross his face at her words, and when he smoothed the covers in front of him she knew exactly what to do. Cassie leaned over his lap, trying her hardest to keep her feet on the floor while her arms reached across him, and her torso ended up over his knees. Leo ran his hand from the nape of her neck to the curve of her ass, sending a shiver down her spine, and then struck. She hissed in reaction to the sting, but didn't cry out.

"Good girl." He spanked her again and rubbed the sting for a few seconds while she could only lay there breathless and full of desire. She'd never admit it to anyone except him, but she wanted nothing more than for Leo to strike again, and the sweet anticipation of it was driving her insane.

Her master obliged her wordless plea. He struck that same cheek three more times before moving on to the neglected one. Between each slap, he rubbed the sore spot for a second before spanking her again, and by the time her right cheek was as burning hot as her left, Cassie knew she was soaking. Her thighs were drenched, and she rubbed them together in search of the release she knew wasn't far away. He figured her out in an instant, and pushed her up on the bed over his knees so that her head fell off the other end and she found herself staring at the floor. Cassie went to laugh, but was silenced when she felt his mouth on her.

Leo licked his way up the back of one thigh and lifted her hips, opening her up to him unashamedly before he thrust his tongue straight inside her. Cassie was clenching around him in seconds, but he didn't stop. Leo grabbed her hips and pulled her up even more, arching her back almost painfully, but she didn't care. She was gone, transcending high above the clouds as her pleasure took over and the blood rushed to her head. Cassie saw stars and dug her hands into the carpet beneath her as her lover tongue-fucked her into further submission.

When she came back down, Cassie expected Leo to turn her over and claim her properly, but instead his tongue worked its way upward. When she felt the tip swirl around the back entrance no one but Victor had been inside before, she froze. Cassie expected to hate it, but instead the sensation of his tongue back there was thrilling. Without any penetration, Leo simply caressed her in a way she'd never known before, and it sent a wave of pleasure over her that she hadn't counted on. He thrust two fingers inside her cleft and continued licking in circles around her tight opening, and she soon bucked and began groaning in pleasure.

Before she could even think about what he was doing next, Leo lifted his head, pulled out his fingers, and climbed up over her. He replaced them with his hard cock. While thrusting into her from behind, he continued to caress her burning ass cheeks with his hands—reminding her of the gratifying ache there.

When he came, they both fell onto the bed in an exhausted heap, and he pulled her into his arms. "Jeez, love. You really are full of surprises," he told her, and she could hear the smile in his voice.

"You have no idea," Cassie replied, nuzzling into his neck and soaking up the scent of him. She loved this, loved him, and knew there was nothing she wouldn't try if he asked her.

\*\*\*

Leo lay in bed and watched Cassie doze with a

smile. He was still in shock at what she'd been so up for letting him do to her, but also because of how she'd opened up about her sexual awakenings. She now knew what she wanted, and what she could handle when it came to their exploits, and he trusted her to tell him when she was reaching her limits. Cassie hadn't even hesitated when he'd pushed her and dominated her, in fact she'd almost begged for more. Leo had told himself right from the beginning of their fresh start that he'd take that stuff slowly, and yet she was the one pushing the boundaries he'd set at every turn.

He realized that after Victor had dominated her so incredibly she could've been affected either way, and Leo was glad to see she hadn't gone the direction of the timid girl who wanted slow lovemaking and to give the occasional blowjob. He would've been that guy if she'd needed it, but he much preferred being allowed the chance to have his powerful side take charge.

Leo had issued her with orders and commands without hesitating, and he could tell she'd been shocked, but also eager to serve him. Everything in him wanted her to stay this way. She had asked for his dominance and to have him own her, not because he wanted it, but because she needed it. Their dynamic was perfect, and Leo knew this could really be the start of the rest of their lives together, unafraid to let their sexual fantasies flourish and come to life via their roleplay and experimentation.

He'd thought she was asleep, but soon Cassie pulled herself out of his embrace with a groan. She plodded sleepily to the bathroom, and Leo watched her ass as she walked. Her round cheeks bounced with just the perfect amount of fullness, but what made them the most impeccable sight was the beautifully pink hue of each cheek. She didn't wince or moan as she moved, and she'd been far from upset when he'd struck her. Cassie had wanted his hands on her, wanted him to spank and deliver her a flash of hot pain. When he'd discovered how wet she was after he'd issued with her supposed "punishment," Leo hadn't been able to control himself. He'd had to taste her, and took great pleasure in every delectable lick and plunge inside her amazing pussy. He barely even noticed those scars that were once so debilitating, and she'd certainly not let them bother her when he'd caressed every inch of both openings with his mouth.

That part had certainly been a surprise. Leo had always been an ass man, but had never even broached the subject with Cassie before. Pure lust and the fact that he'd devoured her from behind had led his tongue back and over that tight bud, and he loved that she hadn't pulled away. She'd given in to her own pleasure, and Leo was sure he'd be asking for more of that again soon.

Cassie came back into the bedroom and grabbed her robe off the floor, and Leo lifted himself up onto his elbows to stare down his body at her.

"If you dare put that on, your ass is going to go from a delightful dusty pink color to a hot shade of crimson," he told her with a smirk. She stared at the white cotton, seemingly considering it for a second, and Leo's cock swelled. Did she really want more?

The sly smile curling at her lips told him she might be contemplating it, but her hesitation showed how deep down she knew she might be overdoing it if she pushed herself too far in one day.

"Yes, sir," she eventually replied, lifting the robe and hanging it up on its hook.

"Stay right there, let me look at you," Leo said as he climbed up onto his knees and stared intently at the amazing view. Cassie was up on her tiptoes, casually placing the robe up on the peg, and her body was utterly perfect. He could see just the curve of her breast by her rib, and her long dark hair that trailed down her back almost to her behind. She was lovelier than any model or actress he'd ever seen, and Leo locked the mental image away for him to keep forever.

Cassie peered over her shoulder at him with a shy smile.

"You can stop drooling now," she teased, trying to be playful, but her flushed cheeks gave away her embarrassment. Cassie wasn't used to being adored, and Leo vowed he would change that.

# *Chapter Ten*

Screams erupted uncontrollably from deep within Cassie, and people stared in shock at the outburst, but she didn't care one little bit. She ran toward the bouncing woman standing a few feet away, who was clearly just as excited to see her, and flung her arms around her. Hanna was shouting something about having missed her so much, and Cassie returned the excited greeting while rubbing her best friend's tiny baby bump with her hands.

"Sandi, you're going to be a big sister. Awesome!" she exclaimed as she pulled away and scooped the toddler into her arms. Cassie proceeded to hug her just as tightly as she had her mother, if not more.

"Will you be his god-mom too? Just like you're mine Number Two Mommy?" Sandi's accent was adorable, and Cassie couldn't get enough of hearing her talk. She'd grown so much the past few months that even her speech had come on dramatically even since their last phone call, and Cassie's heart sang with love for the little angel her two dear friends had been blessed with.

"Way to ruin the surprise," Jamie told his daughter as he rolled his eyes and leaned in to give Cassie a kiss on the cheek. He looked older as well. His wrinkles were far deeper than they'd been before, and his hair was speckled with silver flecks that gave him away. "Yes, it's a boy, and we'd love for you two to be his godparents." Cassie's face must've said it all, and Jamie shot her a smile that lit up his eyes. There was the young man she'd once known, and she beamed.

"It'd be our honor," Leo answered for them both, clearly having already understood that Cassie would say yes. She loved Sandi like she was her own, and knew she'd love their new baby when he came along as well. An urge within her had always been drawn to kids, but especially the ones she held so dear. Cassie would give anything to make sure Sandi was happy and safe, and would do the exact same for Hanna and Jamie's new baby boy when he arrived. She pulled her favorite little lady behind her so she could give her a piggyback.

"The more the better, so keep on popping them out, sweetie!" Cassie chimed with a wink, but Hanna shook her head no. As much as they'd wanted their family, Cassie knew having a cheeky toddler on their hands was taking its toll on them both, and she had to admire their readiness to go through it all over again.

Deep down, Cassie wasn't sure if she could even have kids. She and Jonah hadn't ever officially been trying, but for over a year they'd gone without any contraception in the hopes of "accidentally on purpose" conceiving, and the only reason they hadn't gone to get tested was because they'd split up before it'd really dawned on her that things might not be working in one of their downstairs departments. There were even times when Victor had seemed lax about giving Cassie her pill, and she often wondered if the small purple capsule Grayson delivered her each morning was actually her contraceptive or not. Technically, it could've been anything. She'd never been offered the packet to check.

"Are you sure? We kinda wanted to ask you guys tomorrow over dinner or something, but Sandi jumped the gun," Hanna said with a kind smile at her miniature double that was still riding on Cassie's back.

"Of course I'll be his godmother," Cassie told her with another wide smile. "So, how can you possibly know at sixteen weeks that it's a boy?"

Hanna couldn't contain her laughter. "Oh, he had it all hanging out at the scan last week, there was no need to even ask the nurse."

"Rocking out with his you-know-what out, just like his dad," Cassie teased, and she earned herself a laugh from their guests. Jamie simply rolled his eyes and shrugged off her jibe, evidently having come readily prepared for some cracks from their happy hostess.

Greetings over, the group chatted non-stop as they headed through the busy London terminal to the awaiting car. Sandi told Cassie how exciting the takeoff was, but how the rest of the flight was super boring, or *bwoaring* as she'd pronounced it. Cassie loved hearing her explain the trip, and she carried Sandi all the way to the parking lot. All the while, they laughed and played like the kindred spirits they were.

Roger was there to greet them, and he said nothing as he hauled the luggage into the back of the huge minivan they'd rented for the couple weeks' of their stay. Hanna and Jamie both looked exhausted, and Cassie knew they'd hardly slept during the long flight. As with their previous visits, a late night and plenty of alcohol would soon cure Jamie's jetlag, but this time around, Hanna would have to suffer the sleeplessness alongside Sandi. They all napped on the journey back into the city, but roused when they reached Cassie's apartment, and although it was almost midnight in London, Sandi and her parents were ready for their evening meal rather than for bed.

Cassie quickly rustled them up some supper while Leo and Jamie talked business for their allowed quota and not a moment longer. He seemed happy with the goings-on Stateside, and Cassie didn't even bother asking. That world was so far behind her now she wasn't even the slightest bit interested in being dragged back in. She simply delivered the group their bowls of warming and filling pasta bake with garlic bread and hand-grated Parmesan cheese, with the help of her beautiful young apprentice who stood at the ready with a black pepper grinder.

After devouring their late-night meal, their guests all seemed sleepy, and Cassie settled them in for their first night. She then joined Leo in the kitchen, where he handed her a glass of wine and raised his own.

"Here's to us, godparents and all that," he made a toast to their offered roles as responsible stand-ins for their friends. Cassie clinked her glass with his and took a long sip. She watched him curiously, wondering if he truly was as at ease as he seemed. Accepting their offer would mean accepting some moral responsibility for Hanna and Jamie's children, being part of their lives forever, and loving them as their own. Perhaps it was because Sandi loved Leo without ever seeing the monster he thought still lingered within, but it seemed as though he really might be ready for more in his life.

"Do you want children, Leo?" she couldn't stop from asking, and her heart lurched when he gave her a broad smile and an insistent nod in answer. "Me too, but I'm scared. What if we want it too much? Will you still love me if I can't give you a child?" Leo set his glass aside and grabbed the stem of hers to gently pry it from her hand. He then placed the wine beside his on the countertop and closed the gap, forcing Cassie into his embrace without a word of warning. He hugged her tightly to his chest.

"No matter what life gives us or not, it's you and me against the world, remember?" he told her, and she breathed a sigh of relief. "I've been careful all these years because when it happened it had to be with the right woman. If it doesn't happen at all, then so be it. We'll still be together, and you'll still be the only one I ever want. I'm nothing without you. Never forget that, love."

"I won't, I promise." Her shoulders certainly felt lighter, and deep down Cassie just hoped he'd meant what he'd said. Nothing was right back when she and Jonah had contemplated trying, and she knew things would be vastly different when the time came that she and Leo decided to try to start a family.

\*\*\*

The next few days were spent overcoming Hanna and Jamie's jetlag, while also keeping Sandi occupied. Cassie baked cakes and cookies with her, and took her to the nearby park so that her parents could have a nap whenever they were flagging. Leo took as much time away from work as he could, but still had to head in where necessary. He made sure not to miss out on any of the fun stuff, though.

They soon started their whistle-stop tour of the city, and even roped Siobhan in with a bit of babysitting every now and again so Cassie could take Hanna and Jamie on late nights out to the theater or to Leo's nightclub. They'd return home drunk and full of laughter, while their pregnant comrade would simply roll her eyes and thank Siobhan for helping out before seeing her on her way again.

One evening after Sandi had gone to bed, Hanna offered to give Cassie a backrub. She'd noticed her wince when she took her seat, and Cassie didn't have the guts to tell her it wasn't her back aching, but far lower after having spent another evening with Leo's huge hands delivering her with another so-called punishment. Hanna would never let her live it down if she told her why her ass was sore.

Despite her hesitation, Cassie accepted, and pulled off her shirt before lying face-down on the thick rug on the floor of her lounge. It'd been a long time since she'd had one of Hanna's world famous backrubs, and she simply couldn't pass up the opportunity.

The guys were in the kitchen fixing them their promised cocktails and snacks, so when Hanna undid the clasp of her bra and slid the straps aside, Cassie didn't shy away at being half-naked before her best friend. She relaxed into her flattened pose and pressed her breasts into the soft rug beneath her while scooting around until she felt comfortable, all the while grinning with her secret.

After grabbing some lotion from her travel bag and pouring some into her palms, Hanna warmed it. She then began swirling her hands over Cassie's shoulder blades and spine, kneading and pressing into muscles Cassie had no idea were even stiff until Hanna began working her magic. She was soon lost in the euphoria of her massage, groaning in appreciation of the relaxing treat. Time and all thought was gone, and only the sweeping hands of her best friend kept her grounded.

She giggled uncontrollably when Hanna's fingertips glided over her ribs, and it only served to make her do it again. Before long, Cassie was squirming beneath her, laughing loudly until Hanna finally let go of her ticklish spot.

"Still beautiful as ever," Hanna's sultry voice whispered so close to her ear that Cassie jumped in surprise. She turned to look up at her and caught the sexy smile on Hanna's face that told her she was enjoying having her hands on Cassie's body again. She had to smile back, knowing exactly what Hanna was thinking of.

Way back at the mansion when they'd had their threesome of sorts with Jamie under the watchful eyes of Leo's cameras, Hanna had come clean about her bisexual tendencies—especially where Cassie was concerned. They'd been more intimate that night than she'd been with anyone in a long time, and even after her and Leo's recent exploits it ranked as one of Cassie's hottest nights ever. She'd never been with a woman before or since, but she'd enjoyed delving into what at the time was a world of frivolous fun and newly released inhibitions. Cassie didn't know if it was thanks to Leo and her new life full of passion and an "anything goes" attitude when it came to sex, but she wasn't be against touching and tasting that forbidden treasure again.

Shaking off their joint flare of indulgent heat, Hanna went back to work. She sat back on her heels and continued the backrub, while Cassie began shuffling around in a bid to get more comfortable. She then let out a sharp hiss when Hanna's elbow pressed down on her ass cheek, and Hanna quickly started questioning her on why she was in pain.

Cassie knew she must've gone an incriminating shade of red when Hanna immediately burst into laughter and demanded to see. She pinned Cassie down with her powerful arms and pushed her into the floor. Cassie didn't fight her hold, mostly because Hanna had the advantage of being in a delicate way so she couldn't risk hurting her, but also because she didn't really want to put an end to their play fight. It was wonderful being able to laugh so easily again, and Cassie knew Hanna loved seeing her so happy at long last.

She and Hanna had been through so much together that all inhibitions had been thrown out the window years before, and Cassie still treasured how she'd always felt so free in her company. The day-to-day, mundane, and monotonous all drifted away, and it felt good to let go.

The deep rumbles of laughter that filled their ears quickly alerted Hanna and Cassie to the return of their lovers, and they looked up in time to watch as the guys headed into the lounge with clearly amused grins on their faces. Drinks in hand, Leo and Jamie immediately stopped their previous conversation.

They stepped closer and Cassie turned her head in time to catch as both sets of eyes widened in shock. They clearly hadn't expected to find the girls rolling around on the floor with Cassie half-naked, but simply shrugged, took their seats and watched as their playful wrestle played out.

"Don't stop on our account..." Jamie told his wife with a wide smile.

"Show me! What have you two been up to?" Hanna demanded, grinning down at Cassie while still pressing into her.

"Get off me, you dirty pervert," she teased, squirming against her hold. "You had a one-time-only deal with this piece of ass, and you had your fun. Now I belong to him, and I'll only show if he tells me to," she slurred with a giggle. Cassie knew she was potentially sharing a little too much, but Hanna didn't seem embarrassed by her admission of Leo's dominance, and neither did their partners.

They both turned to look at where the guys sat side by side on the sofa, sipping on their gin and tonics in silence. They'd stayed there while Hanna had wrestled Cassie into full submission on the floor before them, neither stepping in to stop their playful teasing.

With their eyes on their lovers, Leo and Jamie leaned in close to talk to one another in private. Cassie wasn't sure what Leo's response would be, and she gave up her fight in time to see him grinning and laughing quietly while nodding in agreement over something Jamie had just said.

"Take off your clothes, Jellybean. I want to see the handprint I left on your butt this morning," Leo's voice chimed.

"You too, Hanna. It's only fair you show off that beautiful body you've got under that dress." Jamie's deep tones echoed from beside him, and Hanna grinned as she released Cassie from her grasp. Both girls climbed up onto their knees and Cassie draped her long hair over her breasts, effectively covering them for the time being.

"As if he tells me what to do," Hanna told Cassie, but she still slid out of her dress and started peeling off her underwear. Cassie loved how she was effortlessly following her husband's order while still maintaining her independence, and enjoyed seeing their balanced relationship style.

After leaving her life as a prostitute behind to be with Jamie, there hadn't been anyone for Hanna but him—and vice versa. Cassie felt privileged to have Hanna's attention on her again, and knew they wouldn't do anything more than simply giving their lovers a good show, just like they'd done before. This time, though, there would be no sharing when it came to their men, and both women seemed to know without asking that their tryst wasn't about to turn into a foursome.

Cassie halted her striptease when down to just her panties, and she took a moment to run a finger over her best friend's small bump in awe. Hanna looked so beautiful, and truly glowed in pregnancy. Cassie was all of a sudden envious of her. She had everything she could've dreamed of without the pain or the heartache, and her own life suddenly felt very small in comparison to Hanna, Jamie, and their blossoming brood.

She wanted it too. In a sudden moment of realization, Cassie was suddenly broody. She wanted a baby with Leo, and was no longer scared to admit it. Cassie forced her attention away from Hanna's rounded belly before her broodiness got the better of her. She focused instead on the full lips before her, and found herself staring at them with a need she hadn't fulfilled in so very long.

Cassie hesitated before kissing them. Waiting was such sweet agony, but she didn't move. She waited as long as she could bear, and was overjoyed when she then heard Leo's voice waft over from the sofa.

"Go for it, love." Even Hanna gasped at his

command, and her eyes lit up as she realized just which route their relationship had taken. Cassie closed the small gap and took Hanna's mouth with hers. Their tongues delved and their lips collided in a passionate display Cassie knew would already be arousing their observers. They kissed for so long she was panting and her lips were swollen when she finally pulled away, and she was glad to see that Hanna was in a similar state.

"Oh shit, sweetie. Don't tell me you want this again, 'cause I'll go there for sure." Hanna's voice was ragged and full of need, and the sound went right to Cassie's core. "I'm horny like, all the time, and now you've got me remembering that night in Leo's mansion. I want it again, but so much more. Can we?" Hanna's soft tones drew Cassie in, and she let out a soft laugh. She looked over her shoulder at their two lovers with a smile, focusing on Leo in particular.

"How far?" The sound was quiet and timid, but she had to know Leo was on board with what was about to happen. She guessed she really had given her full submission to him, as the only thing holding her back from going for it with Hanna was Leo's say-so. She craved his approval, and could tell by the salacious smile curling at his lips he was enjoying her need to obey him.

"I watched you two fool around on that recording hundreds of times. Now I get to see it for real." He leaned forward and rested his elbows on his knees. "Show me what you showed Jamie that night," Leo said, and his command gave Cassie all the approval she needed to carry on. She delved back into her kissing session with Hanna without even hesitating.

After a few minutes of heavy petting, she felt Hanna's hands on the hem of her panties, but before she could pull them down, her hand was yanked away. In her surprise, Cassie looked to Hanna, but it was Leo who answered her unspoken question. "I changed my mind." He pulled Cassie to her feet.

She went to apologize to her friend, but saw the impressed look on Hanna's face and thought better of it.

Despite his forceful way of putting a stop to their heavy petting, Hanna was clearly fascinated by his prowess, and Cassie watched as fire burned in her eyes when she regarded him. Jealousy speared in her gut, and she understood now why Leo had put a stop to their fun. Regardless of their history, she knew she wouldn't share him with anyone either.

Cassie followed him out and down the hall to their bedroom without another word to Hanna or Jamie, but saw for herself how Jamie had already taken her place on the rug, ready to carry on in private just as she and Leo were.

Once they were alone, he pinned Cassie to the wall by her throat and kissed her roughly. "No one touches you but me, got it?" he demanded, and sunk his teeth into her bottom lip. She hissed at the pain, but didn't pull away.

"Got it," Cassie replied, and she pushed her hips against his. He was rock-hard beneath his clothes, and she was almost naked, drenched and ready for him to take what was his.

"Tell me you're mine. Tell me I own you," he

groaned as he unbuttoned his pants and ripp
what remained of her clothing.

"All yours, baby. Always," Cassie cried when h
buried himself deep inside. She told him again and
again while he showed her how crazy she'd made
him with her little show with Hanna. Cassie liked
knowing she could drive him so wild with desire for
her, and she locked the feeling away so it could be
called upon again and again. It felt amazing to have
that affect over her powerful lover, and thanks to his
lasciviousness, she soared once again in his arms.

ed off

# *Chapter Eleven*

After saying farewell to their American visitors, life returned to normal, or at least the version of normal Cassie and Leo were beginning to create for themselves. He moved in permanently, and together they were working hard on their careers while enjoying all the downtime they could have together.

One afternoon while between productions, Cassie suddenly felt compelled to draw. The urge had come and gone over the past year or so, and it was always tinged with the memories of old that crept up on her while she offloaded her emotion onto the page. Through her art, she was somehow able to express herself in a way she'd never been able to with words. The good and the bad oozed out of her, and there had been numerous times when Cassie could barely control the subject or the way the drawings ended up.

Faces haunted her, portraits of those who demanded her attention even after they were long since out of her life. They never left her, only waited their turn to be drawn back to being or else torment her day and night. She fought it, but their ghosts frequently won, and she'd often find herself in floods of tears as she sketched the faces of those she'd much rather forget. There were more pictures in her portfolio than she could count, and along the way she'd even asked Siobhan to help her sort through them. The good, happier sketches were allowed to stay in a neatly arranged cabinet in her apartment, but the ones that came with a hundred sorrows and an agonizing heartache were boxed and stored at the far back of her office in the theater. Victor lived there now, as did Jonah. There were also the people she'd failed and the beautiful places she'd laid waste to in her mission to get home.

Cassie sometimes felt like she was keeping the memories of them alive by drawing them, and often feared what she'd created. It was almost as if her tormentors themselves could rise from the pages like a creature from the other side. Her Blue Period, it seemed, was far blacker than even Cassie was able to comprehend.

Leo came home to find her covered in charcoal from her dwindling pencil, with her head buried in the pad. Cassie was sketching Sandi. The little angel was happy, prancing around in a ballerina's outfit, and this time Cassie was more than happy to show him that day's work.

"Do you ever draw me?" he asked, flicking through her current sketchbook thoughtfully. There weren't any of him in there, and there was a good reason. With a smile, she stood and walked over to a large wooden chest nestled in its spot beneath one of her huge windows.

151

"There are too many for one book," she told him, and lifted the lid. Inside were hundreds more of her sketches, all of Leo. They were dated, and some went as far back as their first days together in New York. In a gesture she could never thank Hanna enough for, they'd been kept safe, awaiting her escape from that ivory tower in the desert. Her drawings were some of the few items she'd brought back to the UK with her, and despite all the baggage weighing on her shoulders back then, Cassie had known she had to keep them.

Leo lifted the top few out. He'd undoubtedly like some more than others, and wasn't surprised to see his expression go from relaxed to scowling, and back again. If her drawings were anything, they were honest. In some he was smiling, in others his flirtatious grin was ever present, but in a few his frown remained, or a glower had hardened his stare. He didn't deny that any of them were accurate, and she was glad that he took them for what they truly were—a way for Cassie to offload some of the demons from one shoulder, as well as the cherubs from the other.

"What about Victor? Do you draw him? And Jonah?" he asked, and Cassie shuddered. She'd barely been able to look at old photographs of Jonah, let alone his portraits, and she couldn't even begin to talk about her art based on Victor. Those works were beyond dark, and if she could help it, the images she'd conceived while in the worst of her grief would never see the light of day again. She knew she should burn them, or throw them away. She'd tried, but had never been able to see it through. They were a part of her, whether she liked it or not.

"They've got a box each as well, but not here. I can't see them, Leo. I can't have them around to take me back to those scary places. I have to focus on the good, and those who give me happy memories." Cassie smiled up at him.

"Like me?" he asked incredulously, as though he couldn't believe her.

"Yes, exactly like you," she replied, and then closed the lid on the faces of Leo's past. They weren't important; only the future could do her harm now, and she was sure each of them would do their best to make sure they had far happier than sad days ahead of them.

***

"I think it's time we went to visit my family," Cassie informed Leo over dinner at their new favorite restaurant, Giuseppe's. Her love of Italian food had never ceased, and Leo knew the reason she so often chose this place for dinner was because it reminded her of Mrs. Brown's restaurant in New York. That old dive had meant far more to her than just a place of work. Working there had provided Cassie with a new home, a fresh start, and a surrogate family she could rely on during her separation from Jonah.

Leo pulled his mind away from their Stateside past. He thought instead about her request for a trip to visit her family, and wasn't at all surprised by it. He could understand her need to introduce him to her parents and brother at long last, but part of him was dubious. Leo wasn't interested in winning over the parents who hadn't been all that supportive or caring—at least as far as he'd seen. Her folks had seemed disinterested in her life and career every time he'd heard her on the phone with them. It was only her younger brother, Will, who cared at all. He was always the one to call her, and he'd even arranged a visit to London a couple months previous, but had to cancel when he'd been offered a job in a prestigious law firm after finishing university. Cassie had been pleased to hear his news, but she'd also been devastated that their trip had to be put on hold.

That conversation had been another hard one for Leo, and not because of his own disappointment, but because he hadn't known how to comfort her. Having never had a close relationship with his own family, he'd always had a hard time associating those bonds with a loving connection, so wasn't sure what was the right or wrong way. It wasn't something Leo was used to. When he was ten years old, he'd lost his father in a car accident. He'd been devastated, but his mother had reacted to the news ten times worse. She'd sent Leo to boarding school rather than deal with being both a widow and a single mother, or so it'd seemed to him, and then taken her own life a year later. He never spoke of her, not even to Cassie, but knew her death had been the start of his retreat from emotional connections and meaningful relationships.

His schoolteachers had brought him up from then on, and of course the family nanny when he stayed with his aunt during the holidays. Leo had turned everything off that made him care about anyone other than himself. He'd then gone on to use that icy, emotionally devoid selfishness to drive him toward his personal successes. As soon as he'd been offered a scholarship in the States, Leo had known he was on the right path. He'd been so business-oriented that nothing held him back, not even the remnants of his family back home. His obsessive need to control everything took him far, and Leo knew it had caused him to become the cold-hearted man Cassie would eventually go on to meet.

Back then, he'd seen women as worth nothing but a quick bit of fun and a feast for the eyes, which was why he'd chosen to invest in the escort business as soon as he graduated. Drugs had been his chosen profession for years by that point, so he'd simply continued on and developed his reach further and in deeper pockets. The world had been his for the taking, and he'd taken every single thing he could get.

Leo had heard the rumors about him supposedly having an ex-girlfriend in England who'd broken his heart, but they weren't true in the slightest. Perhaps his mother had broken it for him as a child, but he would never let himself think that much about what she'd done or how it'd affected him. The only other woman to have ever managed to both thaw and break his heart had been Cassie. The day Victor took her from him had been the worst day of his entire existence, and as he watched her sitting across from him over their meal, waiting patiently for his reply, he did what any other doting boyfriend would do. He agreed.

"Sure, Jellybean. When do you want to go?" he replied, and he adored the sweet smile she afforded him in return. He wondered if she'd expected him to say no, but there was no way he'd ever let her down again. His own family might be disjointed and cold, but that didn't mean he had to push hers away. The only member of the Solomon family tree he could stand to have around was his cousin, Brian, and that was only because the burly man was well connected in the city and had helped get him get set up. That, and because he had already proven himself to be one hell of a number-two. Leo wouldn't even go as far to say he considered Brian a friend, perhaps more of an employee he regarded above all others because of blood.

But, Cassie wanted her family in her life again, and that meant he would at least make the effort to try. He would go and be the respectable gentleman—or the fiercely loyal protector. Whichever one she needed, he'd be, and either way he silently vowed to her that he wouldn't make a fuss.

Cassie smiled that stunning, shy, happy smile she only ever saved for him. She was truly radiant. Beautiful. That look was what gave his life meaning. There were many things that made her happy now, and Leo knew it wasn't all his doing, but he took pride in it. The sweet, innocent smile belonged to him—not the theater or her friends. That smile wasn't even thanks to her independence and freedom. It was only for Leo. A gift she didn't even know she was giving him, and that made him love it even more.

***

Cassie realized without a shadow of doubt that she was madly in love with the man sitting opposite her. She'd known right from the moment Leo had come back into her life that they could get this far if they tried hard enough, and she'd gladly proven herself right. They'd fought each other and learned hard lessons along the way, but they'd gotten through so much together that she couldn't ever imagine a world in which Leonardo Solomon no longer lay beside her at night, or kissed her good morning the following day.

The waiter came and deposited a fresh glass of wine and a beer to their table, interrupting her train of thought, and Cassie looked around at the quaint Italian restaurant they'd found just a few weeks before. A middle-aged woman seemed to run the place, accompanied by her family and other employees, and Cassie felt right at home. She hadn't seen or heard from her old boss, Mrs. Brown, in a long time, thanks to her being technologically challenged, and she missed her terribly. Hanna gave her updates during their web-chats, but other than that she felt completely detached from the world she'd once loved so much.

Even Hanna had moved on with her life in a myriad of ways, and Cassie couldn't blame her. She and Jamie had been a huge part of Cassie's world in New York, but now they were about to have baby number two and he was running Leo's American empire. Cassie wasn't allowed entry into the States after being extradited, not even for a holiday, and hated that she couldn't just jump on a flight and see her best friend and her family. Even though they'd visited not long ago, the euphoria was always short-lived once the routine returned.

"Next week is Will's birthday, maybe we can go down for the weekend as a surprise?" she asked, thinking how lovely it would be to see him. After all the chaos, it'd be nice going for a normal family trip, and Cassie couldn't deny it'd been a long time since her last visit.

Her baby brother had been the one person who'd truly stuck by her. He'd even offered her legal advice regarding her strange inheritance from Victor, and the necessary change of persona. All of it was in his limited experience, but he'd tried hard to make her transition easier, and she was eternally grateful. Will had been the one to greet her at the airport when Cassie had returned to the UK, and he'd been the one to hold her tight when the tears and depression had hit night after night in those first days back. He'd been her rock when she hadn't wanted anything to cling to, and had pulled her back from the edge countless times. She owed her brother a debt worth far more than money or power, yet he'd never once asked her to give him a thing in return.

She thought back to their days before Leo, before Victor, before Jonah. Growing up, Cassie had been close with all her family. Her parents had been proud of her for going off to London to follow her dreams. They'd supported her marriage with Jonah and were over the moon when they'd been offered the move to Broadway. In the same small village in rural Cornwall where she'd lived her entire childhood, everybody knew everyone else's business, and of course that was fine when things were going well. Her mother had actually used the word "scandal" to categorize Cassie's ordeal, and she knew she'd never forget how much distance that one word had put between them. There was so much she'd left unsaid, and at the time she hadn't wanted to rock the boat, but Cassie wished they'd supported her better. Now that she was stronger than ever and healing more and more everyday thanks to Leo's presence, she could see things so much clearer, and couldn't deny her pain at having been discarded so easily. Despite their selfishness, though, they were still her parents, and there was no denying the fact they would always have a free pass no matter how hurt or upset she might be.

"Let's do it, love. Let's go." Leo broke her reverie again, and she caught the absolutely defiant look on his face. He seemed to feel the same, and was clued up on all of her issues when it came to her family. She knew Leo was ready and willing to defend her honor if it came to it, and with that solid force at her back, she was sure she could take anything anyone wanted to throw at her.

\*\*\*

By the end of the following day, the plans were made. Cassie booked rooms at the village hotel for them to sleep in rather than stay at her parents' house. As much as she looked forward to seeing them, being under the same roof for three nights wasn't her idea of fun, and she wanted to have the solace a room of their own would give them if a break were required. She'd booked two adjoining rooms, but was quick to offer Roger the choice if he'd rather not go with them.

"You don't have to come, Leo will be with me," she told him, giving Roger the chance to take some vacation time while she and Leo were away. He shook his head and fixed her with a scowl.

"Do you really think I'll be able to relax knowing you're there?" Cassie shrugged and wondered why not. "Your family is the one outside link people can use to find you. I want this whole trip monitored and your presence there kept as quiet as possible," he demanded.

His explanation startled her. Cassie hadn't even considered that before. The Taylors were an obvious way by which somebody might track her down, and her mind began racing. She was quickly second-guessing her decision to go, but Roger seemed to sense her unease and grabbed her hand from across her desk. "Cassie, I've had eyes on that village ever since I started working for you. I would know if anyone had been there asking questions or scoping the place out. The hotel is a good idea, much better than staying with your folks, and you've booked it under a fake name so it's all good. I just want you to bear in mind that maintaining your safety is my number one job, and rest assured that it's exactly what I'm going to be doing the entire stay."

"Thanks, Rog. What would I do without you?" She shook off the wave of nausea that'd come over her along with the worry clenching at her gut.

"I'm saying nothing," he told her with a wink. "But we both know you'd be lost, heartbroken, a wreck…" Roger lay his hand over his heart and swept his non-existent hair back in a display of mock romanticism, making Cassie laugh loudly. She knew what he was doing. Roger often laid on a bit of comedy when he knew she was getting bogged down with her stresses and strains, but she still appreciated the effort, and it worked.

\*\*\*

The following Thursday, the three of them got settled in the car Roger had rented and headed for the motorway, ready for the long drive ahead. Cassie climbed in the back at first, wanting to sit with Leo while Roger drove, but soon had to switch to the front seat when a blast of travel sickness almost had her reaching for a bag. She'd suffered with it as a child, and had forgotten how badly she could be affected on longer journeys. Tube trains and quick cab rides had a lot to do with that forgetfulness. She'd barely driven anywhere in years, well, apart from the few outings while in Mexico, but she guessed the constant dread overtook her unsteadiness during that period of her life.

Her travel sickness subsided, and she sat back in the chair and watched the world go by out the window. While Cassie loved the city, she realized she missed taking a drive in the countryside or going for a day at the beach, and vowed they would take the time to have more days out. Even if it meant her sitting in the front with Roger while Leo sprawled out on the backseat without her. They needed some time away from work and the chaos of the city, and she figured she could always take a tablet to ease the sickness next time.

After a few more hours, they eventually pulled into a tiny village just outside of Newquay on the south coast of England, and then checked straight into the small hotel. Memories flooded Cassie's mind, all of them good, and it felt wonderful being home again after having spent so many years away. She'd left at the age of eighteen to go to college and had never looked back, but she was now full of nostalgia and even regret at having been so keen to rush off and find an adventure.

When they'd unloaded their things, Roger went into his room to do the same, using the adjoining door, which he purposely left open. Leo scooped Cassie into his arms regardless of the clear message from her bodyguard that he was still keeping an eye on them, and kissed her so hard she was sure her lips must be bruised.

"What was that for?" she asked when he eventually pulled away, and she peered up into his dark eyes lovingly.

"Nothing in particular," he answered with a roguish grin, and leaned in close to whisper in her ear. "I was just thinking how much I want to tie you to this bed and make you scream until the management have to come and tell us off." Cassie felt her cheeks burn, but his offer wasn't an unwelcome one. She turned her head to look at the huge bed, with its chunky wooden headboard and four-poster-frame, and lifted her hand up to tug at Leo's necktie.

"Well then, I hope you have some more of these in that bag?" she murmured, turning back to look up at him. Leo pulled her in for another kiss, and only stopped when an insistent cough burst their private bubble.

"I didn't drive all this way to watch you two make out," Roger grumbled. "Are we heading to your folks' house straight away?" Cassie checked the time and nodded. She'd arranged for her parents to invite Will over after he'd finished work, where they'd meet them as a surprise. It was already past closing time at his law firm, so she guessed he'd either already be there or on his way, and she was excited to see her brother after so long. Cassie stepped away from her beau, after placing one last kiss on his delicious lips, and she grabbed her purse.

They were back in the lobby in no time, and Cassie made a point not to make any eye contact with anyone in or around the hotel. She wanted this time away to be all about her family, not the small village in which everyone knew each other, and therefore knew all about her dark and sordid past. Nothing was sacred in this goldfish bowl, and she was eager to focus solely on those she loved rather than the people from her past who were looking for nothing more than the updated gossip to add to the tales they'd heard about her along the way.

After a quick drive, the three of them pulled into

a driveway outside a bungalow bigger than most townhouses in the city. The Taylors hadn't sold up when their children had moved out; in fact they'd simply utilized the extra space as a library and study. Timothy and Penelope Taylor had both retired a few years before, but having always been busy professionals, they had never quite stopped work entirely. They each had projects in the community they focused on and small businesses they turned around for a while before moving on to the next idea, or so they'd told Cassie every time she called to check in. She didn't doubt it for a moment. Her parents were never ones to sit around and do nothing.

The trio of visitors had barely climbed out of the car when the front door flung open and Will came tumbling out. In his hurry to reach his sister's side, he knocked over a large vase full of flowers on the porch, but obviously didn't care. He scooped Cassie up into a hug and lifted her off her feet, twirling her around while the others looked on with wide smiles.

Cassie gave Will a big kiss and stepped back once she'd been put down on her feet again. Her heart was so full, and she took in the sight of her not-so-small brother before her. He'd changed since she'd last seen him, and had bulked up too. She could feel the thick muscles beneath his shirt, and wondered if he'd started working out. His dark hair and eyes were exactly like hers, but she loved how he'd kept his innocent stare despite having grown in her absence. Cassie prayed he'd never experience the pain she had in life, and hoped that glint in his eye would never fade.

"Will, I'd like to introduce you properly," she told him, leading him over to where Leo stood waiting patiently by the car. Roger was out of the driver's seat and scanning their perimeter already, seemingly giving them a minute to reacquaint themselves without his watchful gaze, and she was grateful to have a moment of their own.

"So this is the infamous Leonardo Solomon. It's an absolute pleasure to meet you at last," Will said, taking the lead effortlessly in his usual calm way. He reached forward to shake his hand, and Cassie grinned as Leo reached out to take it, but then pulled him into a tight hug instead. He patted her brother's back loudly and then pulled away after a couple of seconds, grinning from ear to ear.

"The pleasure's all mine. And please, call me Leo," he told him, and Will nodded in silent acceptance. They'd been the same for years. Cassie and Will had always preferred it that way. The change hadn't started out as an act of rebellion, at least not until their parents had shown how much it'd annoyed them, and by that point the shortened names were absolutely going to happen.

Eventually, their mother, Penelope, came down from the doorstep and kissed Cassie on the cheek before shaking Leo's hand in welcome.

"Wonderful to meet you, Leonardo," was all she had to say, clearly dismissing his preference, as always, but Leo remained cool and simply returned the kind greeting. Her father did the same, all prim and proper, and without an ounce of warmth towards her man. Cassie knew they blamed him for what'd happened to her with Victor. Penelope had

165

outright told her so after the trial, and it was one of the main reasons she hadn't gone back to live with her parents and their small village when she'd returned. No one person was to blame for her hardships, except maybe Cassie herself, and while they snubbed any insinuation of her karmic considerations, her parents had also refused to believe that her misfortune could simply be bad luck or consequences. The men in her life had been to blame, and that was that, or so Penelope had informed her.

When Leo had come back into Cassie's world, she'd been excited to tell Will, but had dreaded telling her parents. They'd reacted exactly as she'd expected—with cold indifference masked beneath a fake smile, and lies masquerading themselves as compliments. Regardless of all that, Cassie still had said nothing to call them on their behavior. There might've been a different future mapped out for her once upon a time ago, but she also had to consider how she might've never gotten to see her family again if things with Victor had gone differently.

She valued her freedom so much that she couldn't bring herself to be upset with her mother's oppressive opinions or her father's grumpy aloofness. All that mattered was that she was away from the cartel's clutches and had her family back in her life. Her parents evidently couldn't understand that, but Cassie knew it wasn't their fault. It was simply who they were. If she chose to stay away or never say the things aloud she wished she could, that was fine—as long as it was up to her.

"So, Birthday Boy," Cassie said, filling the silence by making a fuss of Will. "You have us for three whole days, what are we doing with it?" He seemed delighted, and Cassie loved the still gentle, boyish grin he awarded her.

She wrapped an arm around his waist and followed him inside, bouncing on the balls of her feet with each step she took. Nothing could bring her down, not now she was here and in the arms of the boy she'd loved since the moment their mother had brought him home from hospital. He gave her a squeeze that made her heart ache, but in a good way. "I've missed you, Snot Face," she told him with a grin.

"Missed you too, Jelly Belle," Will replied, and she giggled. He hadn't called her that in over ten years, and she guessed she'd asked for it with name-calling him first. Cassie no longer associated herself with such a silly nickname, and hadn't since they were still kids.

Now, that name reminded her of those precious sweet treats and Leo's new nickname for her. To Cassie, it also symbolized the turning point in hers and Leo's relationship. Such a silly thing, but even now a bag of the sweet candy would bring her a smile and a flutter in her chest. She looked back at Leo, having known he'd follow close behind, and she caught the stunning grin on his face. He'd obviously heard Will call her *Jelly Belle*, and was shaking his head in surprise.

In that moment, Cassie didn't care what her parents thought of Leo. She was tough enough to know the difference between love and lust this time around, and wasn't about to let her mom or dad diminish what she and Leo had. Love hurt at times. In fact, it'd come close to tearing her apart. Cassie had learned that lesson a long time ago, but knew he was well worth the risk.

# Chapter Twelve

The small group chatted long into the evening, catching up, and for Leo, getting to know one another better. Will was warm and courteous to him, as Cassie had told Leo he would be, and he appreciated the effort her brother seemed to be going to. Will had the same gentle, yet honest and sincere way about him that Cassie had, and Leo had taken a liking to him almost instantly.

Roger had made a quick introduction and then taken a spot by the door, where he'd yet to move from. His usually friendly persona which Leo had gotten so used to nowadays was gone, though. Roger was all business, and Leo was glad of it. At one point, he'd considered asking Cassie to let him go, but had come to realize how important he now was, and not just for Cassie, but for them both. Leo knew that with Roger around they could relax and be a normal couple during times away from the safety of the apartment, and he appreciated the chance to enjoy his lover's company rather than constantly worry about her safety.

After finishing his glass of Penelope's homemade lemonade, Leo was desperate for a real drink, and he politely asked Will if they had anything stronger in the house.

"Let me show you my wine cellar," Timothy replied for his son, before standing and indicating for Leo to follow him. He knew exactly what this was. It was Timothy's chance to establish dominance and pretend to be a protective father, when actually he'd been far from it. From what Cassie had told him, her dad had been absent during most of her childhood, working away from home for weeks at a time. When he had been around, by all accounts he hadn't made a fuss of his children or kept his promises to take them on days out or lavish them with attention.

Cassie had confided in Leo that it felt as if her father been there for her only when it'd suited him, and had otherwise sat back and done as Penelope instructed, just like the placid man he seemed content to be. Leo didn't like Cassie's father, he'd known before even getting here. In the interest of keeping the peace, though, he'd endeavored to be on his best behavior. Leo wouldn't give Timothy the chance to badmouth or cast judgment on him, so he stood and walked out into the hall after him with a courteous smile.

"I didn't know you were a wine connoisseur, Timothy," Leo said, and he began reeling off names of expensive bottles he too had procured over the years. Timothy's wide eyes said plenty—he was impressed. "I also have a passion for collecting beautiful things," Leo added, eyeing the art on the walls as they walked through the large house. "Back in New York, I had an assortment of vintage sports cars and million-dollar collections of fine art."

"Ah yes, your Stateside collection," Timothy replied with a scowl, and Leo noticed the change in him immediately. *Here we go,* he thought, concealing a knowing smile. "From what I understand, you paid for those things using a fortune made from exploiting the vices of others. Is that right?" His voice was calm, but his face said it all—Timothy wasn't at all comfortable confronting Leo, his domineering wife had clearly put him up to it. Leo knew that Penelope was the one he'd have to win over, or at least come to an understanding with if he were to get anywhere with Cassie's family. Timothy was merely her lapdog, and Leo pitied him.

"You and your wife are welcome to question me, my morals, values, ethics, and past misdemeanors, Mr. Taylor." Leo was cool and calm as he delivered his practiced speech. He'd known this would come at some point over their visit, and was glad that at least on this issue, Timothy hadn't disappointed him. "How I earn my money is of little consequence to how I choose to spend it, but yes—I did make a small fortune from delivering others the object of their desire for a fee. It's the same principle as your vintner really," he said as he plucked an expensive bottle of red wine from one of the shelves. "He must earn a fortune selling his wares to rich connoisseurs who can afford to indulge, and is he immoral for doing so?"

Timothy frowned. "I guess not, but when what

you're selling is women and drugs…"

"I don't sell those things, or perhaps you'd like to see my financial statements?" Leo cut him off, and Timothy shook his head. He took the bottle from Leo's hand and carefully slid it back in its place on the pristinely organized shelf. Leo knew he was stretching the truth, but he wasn't *technically* lying. Jamie had taken over that side of things, so as far as his life in the UK went, he was completely above-board and legal in his current business ventures. Plus, he wasn't about to go into any detail regarding his professional life during their visit. It wasn't any of their business, and he wasn't interested in their opinions on the state of his affairs.

"I'm sorry, Leo. It's just that Cassie's been through so much, and I would hate to see her get hurt again, that's all," Timothy replied, and he visibly softened. His mask dropped, and the weak, weary man shone through again. He'd evidently said his piece, and Leo respected the sentiment.

"I get it, but I'm not the bad guy. I worship Cassie, and did everything I could to save her back in New York. I almost lost everything getting her away from that monster, and I'd do it again in a heartbeat. I see things through to the end, Mr. Taylor, so don't ever think I'd up and leave, or hurt her knowingly." Leo was sure Timothy's eyes were glistening with tears he'd held back over all the years, and he had to take a breath to stop his voice from faltering too. "I've made it my life's work to make your daughter happy, and I would never let anyone else cause her pain ever again. Cassie means

172

everything to me, and I'd die without her," he told him, and was surprised by his own words. They were so honest it hurt, but seemed to do the trick. Timothy's face lit up, and he smiled from ear to ear.

"In that case…" He pulled the wine back from the shelf and rubbed at the label thoughtfully. "I guess we should be celebrating more than just Will's birthday."

\*\*\*

Cassie chatted away animatedly with her little brother while their mother cooked up a storm in the kitchen and Roger watched over them all from his seat beside the door. Leo and their father still hadn't emerged from the cellar, and she guessed they were having some version of "the talk" Timothy had given Jonah once upon a time ago. She cringed at the sheer thought of it, but knew Leo would stand his ground, whereas Jonah had crumbled under her parents' scrutiny.

"So, come on, be honest. There must be someone you've got your eye on? Weekend hookups are all well and good, but now you're through university and the long days and nights with your head stuck in a book…there has to be more?" Cassie demanded, grinning broadly at her brother.

She couldn't ever remember a woman he'd brought home to meet their parents, or whom he'd mentioned as more than a passing fling during their phone calls, and she hoped he might finally be ready to move on from bachelorhood and find something special now that he was finished with his studies.

"Well, there's this one girl…" Will replied, and his shy smile said it all. Cassie jumped up and down in her seat, clapping her hands with girlish delight. Her brother scowled and shook his head. "Calm down, sis. It's early days yet, but we've had a few dates, and I like her."

"Are you going to invite her out with us tomorrow?" she asked, mentally planning their night out in the nearby city to celebrate Will's birthday. He shrugged.

"I'd said about going to see a movie or something, but I can text her and ask if she's up for a night out with us instead? You coming to visit was a surprise after all, so I couldn't ask sooner." Will grabbed his cell. He stared at the screen thoughtfully, and Cassie decided to give him some privacy to come up with his message to the girl she could already tell had made her mark on him.

She stood and walked the few steps to where her bodyguard sat watching her with a smile. She rested her hip on the sofa beside his perch.

"All good?" she asked, and he nodded.

"All good," Roger repeated with a smile. "It's nice seeing you with your family, especially him." Cassie knew he was talking about Will, and she nodded.

"There'll always be a big place in my heart for that boy." She peered back over her shoulder to watch as her brother spoke quietly into his phone, evidently having opted to make a call to his new girlfriend rather than just send a text. "It feels good to be with him again. In fact it feels good being with all of my family, regardless of the past."

"Damn straight," Roger replied with a warm smile, and she patted him on the shoulder before heading back over to where her brother was sitting. She stopped en route and stared at the handful of photographs that littered the nearby mantle, and smiled. The first few were of the pair of them as young children, and each was so very happy and carefree, the epitome of innocence. She was a quirky, fun, and adventurous young girl, but had later caved to peer pressure in her teens and followed the herd. During those years, Cassie had been at a completely different end of the spectrum to her lighthearted old self, but at the time she hadn't cared enough to miss who she'd once been.

Somewhere in the house would be an album filled with pictures of a dark-haired teenager who looked like her, and yet that same girl was an entirely different young woman to the one that stood there now. Her mother had called her a diva, a "right royal pain in the bum," and even a bitch— and she had been. Cassie had wanted it all, and downright expected it. Now? She'd happily settle for peace and normalcy. Well, that and her now regular bursts of excitement only Leo could seem to awaken in her between the sheets.

Leo and Timothy appeared in the doorway after a short while longer, looking relaxed and far more at ease with one another than when they'd left. Cassie knew without asking that her hunch was correct, and they'd had their obligatory talk. However, this time it seemed Leo had passed whatever test her father had put him through at the behest of their matriarch. Even Cassie knew her father didn't have the wherewithal to give her partner too much hassle without being prompted, and she smiled to herself at how domineering her mother seemed to be. What a complete contradiction Cassie knew she was to Penelope, and yet she didn't care. She'd never wanted to end up like her mother, regardless of her affection for her, and had evidently succeeded.

"Do you fancy a glass of real wine?" Leo asked when he reached her, and he brushed her cheek with a delicate kiss. Cassie looked down at the bottle of aged red wine in his hand, and knew it must've cost hundreds of pounds to buy, but also that it'd be wasted on her palate. She shook her head no. "I thought you'd say that," Leo said before she could answer, and then pulled a second bottle from behind his back.

"That's much more like it," Cassie said with a smile, and she snatched the bottle of sauvignon blanc from his hand before following him over to the drinks cabinet to grab a glass. She poured one for Will too, and handed it to him with a wink. His eyes were bright, happy, and he returned the gesture with a soft smile. Cassie liked this new girlfriend of his already. Just talking with her on the phone made him light up, and she couldn't wait to see how they were together in person.

By the time they'd all settled back in their seats and were sipping on their chosen drinks, Will had his date arranged for the following evening, much to Cassie's elation, and their mother had begun delivering plates of appetizers. The siblings tucked straight in, while Leo waited courteously as Timothy took a few bites, and then he had a taste.

She watched him the entire time, unable to stop from admiring the man she loved with every inch of her body and soul. Cassie envied the wine glass as he brought it to his mouth and pressed his lips to the rim. She was jealous of the admiration and respect he showed to the vintage wine as it passed over those lips, and when his tongue curled around a piece of Parma ham-wrapped fig, she felt herself blush. A surge of desire blasted through her, and it was all Cassie could do not to jump on him and demand he take care of those needs the way only Leo knew how.

She'd shocked herself. Never had she experienced such a horny rage like it, and knew she had to be sending him some hormonal energy waves from across the room, because when his gaze met hers, he was like a caged animal. His intense stare seemed to penetrate her from feet away. Behind his cool exterior, Cassie knew there was a power in him that could, and would, have her floating on air the second they were alone, and she craved him. It didn't matter that she was stronger now and more independent than ever. She no longer cared about how she ought to feel or what she was meant to want from a modern relationship. She wanted the same thing she'd asked him for the first night he'd come back for her—to be owned by Leonardo Solomon.

"So, Leo. What made you head over to the States for your education rather than stay here?" Her father's voice broke the intense silence, and Cassie forced herself to push aside her needy, salacious mood. She sipped on her wine, but oddly wasn't enjoying it, so she opted to focus on a loaded bruschetta that sat in front of her instead. As Leo contemplated his answer, she realized she didn't know all that much about his life from before he'd moved to America either. When they'd talked about their childhoods, he'd been so reticent after telling her how he'd been orphaned at such a young age that she'd decided against pressing him for any more information. Like with all things deep and meaningful, Leo had to open up those vaults inside of him at his own speed, and only when he was ready.

She was glad he seemed to be in one of his more agreeable moods, and soon realized she was listening to his answer as intently as her father seemed to be.

"I was offered a scholarship with NYU after college in the UK, so moved there when I was eighteen to pursue my degree," Leo told him, and Timothy nodded in understanding. Cassie was sure she saw a renewed respect in his expression, as though he hadn't necessarily considered Leo to be so highly educated. In all honesty, she couldn't blame him. With a reputation as a notorious gangster and felon, Leo must have found it commonplace to receive that sort of reaction while meeting new people.

"Let me guess, football or boxing?" Timothy asked, refilling their glasses.

"No, civil and urban engineering," he replied with a kind smile, surprising him with his answer.

178

Cassie caught the wry grin on Will's lips beside her, and loved that her brother was enjoying this little show too. The many assumptions her parents had undoubtedly made about Leo were being proven wrong—left, right, and center. It was wonderful to watch, and when their mother returned to inform them dinner was served and to take their seats, she seemed taken aback by the change of atmosphere. All three members of the Taylor family were leaning forward, listening to Leo intently, and even Penelope took a second to compose herself.

Leo didn't say another word; he simply left his revelation hanging while the small group followed her order. Each member of the Taylor family took their seats at the huge dining table, and then Leo accepted the chair at the end of the table opposite Timothy. Roger joined them and remained quiet, but he accepted the hostess's offer of a home cooked dinner with a courteous smile. Penelope served up a delicious meal of roasted chicken with a variety of perfectly prepared and cooked side dishes.

"Cassandra, will you help me serve, dear?" she asked, and while she hated the old-fashioned way of it, Cassie agreed. She piled up a plate for Roger while her mother served both Timothy and Will, and then it was her turn to dish up some food for Leo. Care and attention to his preferences came as naturally as if she were plating up her own meal, and Cassie surprised herself by enjoying such a simple task as preparing his dinner for him. When she rounded the table and set the plate down in front of Leo, she realized he was watching her every move like a hawk, and she felt the rush of heat spread out from her core again. Their eyes met and she had to bite the inside of her cheek, afraid she might moan with the desire curling her insides and twisting her gut.

Cassie forced herself to step away, knowing they'd soon start making everybody feel uncomfortable again, and grabbed her empty plate. She'd just leaned over to start dishing up her own meal when Leo's voice was in her ear, and she jumped in surprise. She hadn't even noticed him stand.

"My turn to serve you, I believe," he whispered, and he took the plate from her hands. He indicated for her to take a seat, and began doing the same as she'd just done for him while the others watched on in shock. Penelope seemed surprised beyond words, and took her seat with her mouth pursed and her plate only half filled. Will seemed to be enjoying it tremendously, and he even offered Cassie a wink when she caught his eye.

Being traditionalist, it simply wasn't the way Penelope or women of her generation and class did things, and she'd tried to instill the same traditions in her daughter since birth. However, Cassie hadn't been the type to give control of herself to anyone in the same way. She wanted respect but also wanted her chance to submit when appropriate. She adored how Leo was so ready to show her family how much he honored Cassie in those small moments of kind gentleness. Cassie knew it must be an odd dynamic for their parents to get their heads around, but one her mother would have to respect. Hers and

Leo's mutual respect for one another shone through any layers of indifference or iciness that plagued most couples, and he neither degraded nor belittled her by serving her in return for her having attended to him.

His rebellion against the prim and proper methods Penelope seemed intent on still living by didn't seem to have been done with malice. It was more as if he simply wanted to remind her of the changing of the times. He clearly wanted to show them that while he was dominative, he wasn't intimidating, at least not with Cassie. Leo cared for her, and had showed it in so many ways she wasn't sure there'd ever be enough she could do for him in return to even the keel.

Leo delivered Cassie her meal with a kiss, and then took his seat without another word about it. The small group ate in silence at first, but soon enough the conversation began flowing again, and her now seemingly interested father picked back up where they'd left off in the sitting room.

"I must admit, I thought with your build you would've been a sportsman, Leo. But engineering you say?" he asked, taking a bite of his chicken.

"I will be honest, I was quite slim as a young man, Mr. Taylor. I only began weight-training and boxing in my late teens," Leo informed him, and Cassie had to stop herself from grinning at the stereotypical jock her parents had clearly assumed he had to have been. "Engineering was always my calling, even as a child. When I was fourteen, I invented a water purification system that was later taken on by the government to treat areas of the UK where filtration is outdated. After that, I went on to invent, patent, and sell on other devices designed to enhance and improve on the methods used previously. I honed those skills over the years that followed before eventually being offered the scholarship to NYU."

The room was suddenly eerily quiet, but Leo seemed either oblivious or indifferent to the fact that both Penelope and Timothy had stopped eating and were watching him with fascination. It was the best thing Cassie had ever seen, and she loved Leo even more for having successfully dumbfounded her folks. "Once I was immersed in the field, I completed my degree with honors, but changed course due to personal inclinations towards the business world. I still own the patents and earn royalties from my designs and their uses, which is why I was able to come back to the UK and start my company here."

"So, you didn't buy it with all your dirty money, baby?" Cassie asked, filling the silence that followed his impressive statement with a clear poke at her parents' assumptions, and Leo shook his head.

"Not at all," he agreed.

# Chapter Thirteen

Cassie awoke late the next morning with a yawn. She tried to stretch out her arms, but was halted when she caught sight of a knot that still tied one of her wrists to the headboard. Her stockings were ruined, but she didn't care, and let the nylon springiness pull her back toward the center of the bed. With her free hand, she tried to unwind the knot Leo had put in it the night before, but it was no use, so instead she fished around behind her in an attempt to locate the other end. Cassie found it after a few seconds of searching, and then giggled when she caught Leo watching her intently from his pillow beside her.

"And what do you think *you're* doing?" he asked, untying the knot from around the wooden beam. He weaved the nylon around his lithe fingers. The over and under move wrapped the thick stocking around his knuckles and palm, pulling her closer and closer with every winding motion he made. "You're not getting out of that unless I let you out," Leo teased. He grabbed Cassie and pulled her close to his chest so that their naked bodies collided. He kissed her deeply, raking his free hand over her back, ass, and then down her thighs, which he then pried open. Leo took his place between her legs while turning her onto her back and commanding her body with his. "Tell me what you want," he moaned into her open mouth, nibbling her bottom lip gently.

"You, Leo. I want you," Cassie purred, arching her back so her core met his impressive morning-glory, but he resisted. "I'm so wet for you, baby. Make me come, please."

"Like I did last night?" One dark eyebrow cocked as he peered down at her on the bed, and Cassie nodded. "I told you, didn't I? I said I was gonna tie you to this bed and make you scream, Cassie. And you wanted it so badly, didn't you?" Leo kissed her again and ran his hand over her cheek to her breast. He tweaked her nipple, caressing it with hard pinches that only left her wanting more.

"Yes, I did. I also wanted you to fuck me all over my parents' house, if only I could've got them to leave us alone…" Cassie was silenced when Leo's mouth covered hers again, and she knew she hadn't been wrong—he'd felt it too.

The tease was over. Leo's huge erection found its target and he was inside before she could take her next breath. He rode back and forth, hard and fast, and when she neared her release, Leo sat back on his heels. Her hips were soon pulled upwards to meet his deep thrusts, and he peered down at her now exposed body. Leo watched every stroke as he pressed himself inside of her, seeming so engrossed, and instead of turning shy, Cassie adored having his eyes on her. He didn't stop staring, even when she came, and she too took the chance to watch his amazing body as he continued to pleasure her.

His pecs were huge and unmoving, whereas his amazing abs rippled with every curl of his spine as he impaled her. His incredible hip muscles were more pronounced than ever thanks to the exertion, and Cassie followed the curve down to where their bodies met. She watched him make love to her and was in awe of how perfectly they fit together.

With one last, heavy thrust, Leo shuddered his release and leaned back down to kiss and hold Cassie against his still slowly thrusting hips. She welcomed the heavy weight of him against her.

"Don't ever leave me," Leo whispered into her embrace, and his voice was so quiet she almost hadn't heard it. "I'd die without you."

"Never. I promise," she replied, kissing his forehead tenderly.

When they'd finally pulled themselves away from the bedroom, and each other, Leo went for a run. Cassie took a shower then caught up with Roger, knowing he'd probably been up hours waiting for them to get out of bed. Her suspicions were proven right when she spotted numerous empty instant coffee sachets in the small bin in his room. She was surprised he wasn't jittery as hell after having had so much caffeine.

"Leo handled himself well yesterday," her protector told her over his coffee mug, and seemed to be back in friendly mode for the time being.

"Your folks are pretty intense, but he won over your dad. It's just your mum who doesn't seem completely on-board, and she was definitely shocked by his actions at the dinner table. I don't think she'd ever let your dad do something so chivalrous even if he tried."

"That woman takes feminism to the extreme," Cassie agreed, grabbing a bagel from the room-service tray. "She seems to think that being a doting housewife is fine as long as it's on her terms, and yet she's tried so hard to turn me into her protégé over the years without a care for the exploitation some modern men are capable of. In her view, if a man starts to expect being taken care of, he's a sexist pig, but at the same time the woman should take pride in serving her man, looking after him, the house, the children—blah, blah, blah. It's an impossible standard these days. I'm too busy trying to run my own business and deal with everything life's thrown at me." Cassie knew she was having a rant about her mother's impossible expectations, but was glad she was able to get a few things off her chest to someone she could trust. She took a breath and laughed off her mood. "I honestly don't think she was prepared for my and Leo's strange way of balancing out those parts of our relationship, but I have to admit I liked shocking her."

"Good, I was glad. When we first got there I was sure I saw you wilt a little under their scrutiny, and I was pleased to watch as you climbed back up again. You are who you are, Cassie. Leo or not, you're much stronger than either of them might ever give you credit for," Roger told her matter-of-factly.

Cassie launched herself at him. She threw her arms around the hulking man and hugged him tight, whether he wanted to or not.

"I bloody love you, Rog. Don't ever forget that," she told him, and when she didn't let go, he wrapped his arms around her in return.

"I guess you're okay," he teased, but held on until she released him.

Cassie's cell rang in her purse, and she jumped off the bed to grab it in time before the call went to voicemail.

"Hello?" she chimed, listening intently. "Will?"

"Hey, sis. Glad I caught you. We're all sorted for tonight, do you wanna pick us up at eight?" Her brother's deep tones echoed down the line, and Cassie grinned.

"Sure, but there's something I need to do first." Before he could ask what, she burst into song. Cassie sang "Happy Birthday" loudly, and with so much energy that all Will could do was laugh. When her rendition was over, he thanked her before saying goodbye and hanging up the line.

She turned back toward her bodyguard with a smile, and Cassie jumped when she discovered a sweaty Leo standing just inside the connecting doorway. He and Roger were both watching her with open-mouthed stares, and she felt her cheeks burn.

"I've never heard you sing like that before, Cassie," Leo told her. "Your voice is beautiful."

"Why the hell would you paint theater sets and make costumes when you have a set of lungs like that?" Roger added, shaking his head.

"Not everyone who runs away with the theater dreams of being center stage. I love what I do, and never even tried out for the leading roles back in my early days in London. Drawing is what I love, art and design," she told them, but appreciated the praise. Cassie had played many roles over the years when it'd come to her personal life, and knew she wouldn't want to do it every day in her professional life too. No matter her love of fairytales, she didn't want to play the part of the young heroine locked in an ivory tower while the beast below fought to win her affections. She'd lived it for real with Victor, and hadn't set her heart by those fairytales ever since.

Shaking off the eerie chill that'd swept down her spine with the sheer thought of her dear departed ex, she informed Leo and Roger of the plans Will had just confirmed with her. Cassie then busied herself with getting ready for an afternoon of shopping with her mother, and deliberated over her outfit for far too long. Roger insisted on accompanying them, while Timothy had arranged to play a round of golf with Leo at his local club, and he'd not been offered the choice to refuse.

"I'll miss you," he told Cassie when she was finally ready. She grabbed her things, informing Roger that she was good to go.

"Me too, but it'll be nice just you and my dad getting some time alone to bond, and hopefully you'll not come back hating each other. I'm not sure the same can be said for me and my mother," Cassie grumbled. Leo didn't answer. He simply held her close and planted a powerful kiss on her still tender lips, and she loved the bruising sting it left behind.

She spent the day following her mother around various shops in which Penelope insisted on choosing Cassie an array of new outfits. They chatted some, but not about any of the important issues, like her daughter's recovery or how she and Leo were managing being back together. Penelope insisted on gossiping about the local residents and their exploits, while only asking about her life in London to determine whether the theater was bringing in enough money for her to deem it an adequately reputable business for her daughter to be involved in. Within a couple of hours, Cassie felt tired and achy. She wanted to call it a day, but Penelope seemed intent on carrying on.

"Ms. Taylor, please excuse my intrusion, but we need to get going," Roger informed Cassie politely while checking his watch in an overly obvious manner. She could've kissed him, but simply nodded her head in agreement and made her excuses to her mother about needing to get ready for Will's birthday night. The matter sorted, Penelope gave her a small hug. They said goodbye, and Cassie was soon on her way back to the hotel. "You're welcome," Roger added, watching her through the rearview mirror with a smile in his eyes.

That evening, Cassie and Leo climbed into the four-by-four with Roger and were driven across the small village to where her brother lived. They collected Will from his apartment, along with his girlfriend, Lana. She seemed a little shy at first, but quickly shook it off when Cassie pulled her into an affectionate hug. She gave her no choice but to let her get on with it, and within seconds the young woman relaxed. Cassie then watched as a more natural, genuine smile took the place of the forced one, and she was glad Lana seemed to settle in with them so quickly. The guys greeted each other, and Leo wished Will a happy birthday before handing him the big bag of gifts they'd brought with them.

"You didn't have to!" Will exclaimed, but soon started digging in excitedly. Cassie let go of his still quiet girlfriend and watched as he began unwrapping their array of gifts. The first was a small box, and inside were a set of diamond cufflinks that sparkled brightly despite the fading sunlight. "These are too much, I can't..." he began, but Cassie stepped closer and wrapped her hands around his.

"You can and you will. We wanted to spoil you, and I've lost the receipt anyway so you'll just have to keep them," she told him, winking over at Lana, who grinned back. Will nodded, admitting silent defeat. He simply kissed his sister's cheek, and then started on the other presents. Cassie knew she'd gone a little crazy this year with the elaborate arrangement of trinkets, especially when she'd usually just send him loaded gift cards or small presents. This time she got to watch him open them and spend the day celebrating together, so she'd indulged her generous streak. Will seemed absolutely astonished by his assortment of presents, but also incredibly appreciative. Cassie had bought him designer clothes, tickets to see his favorite band in concert, a driving experience day with one of his idols of the racing world, and an IOU for a weekend trip to London for him and Lana whenever they wanted it.

Lastly, Cassie reached behind her for one more gift, which she gave to Lana. Inside was a stunning designer handbag she'd picked up that afternoon, and she watched with satisfaction as the young woman's eyes lit up in surprise. Cassie didn't even give her the chance to object or make a fuss, she simply headed back to the car, climbed into the front seat, and shouted for them all to join her.

After carefully putting the presents away inside Will's apartment, they all piled in and Roger drove them the short distance to the restaurant, where he dropped them at the door before parking around the back.

Leo took Cassie's hand in his as he led the way, and before long they were sat enjoying plate after plate of incredible tapas while the wine flowed freely. Roger joined them, but once again stayed quiet as he ate. Cassie had hoped he might relax a little, but could see him watching the doors and other customers constantly, rather than keeping track of the conversation. She could understand it, though, and welcomed his careful attitude and attentiveness toward her. He truly was an incredible asset, and Cassie knew she couldn't have found a better bodyguard even if she'd searched high and low. She thanked whichever forces of fate had sent him to her that day she'd contacted the elite security agency he'd been registered with, and was sure she'd never need another protector as long as he was around.

The others chatted effortlessly, and Cassie

enjoyed getting to know Lana, as well as having the chance to see her and Will together. They were clearly into one another, and she was sure that in time they'd both realize it and take the next step.

Once their bellies were full and they'd had enough of the rustic restaurant, Leo paid the check and they climbed back in the car. Roger soon delivered them to another doorway, but this time to a huge warehouse-style building they'd not discussed visiting when plans had been made earlier that day. Cassie was about to ask where they were when Roger opened the door and she heard the thumping music coming from within. After climbing out, she could see the sign over the doorman's head that said **'*Casanova,*'** and was immediately confused. Leo noticed, but held his finger to his lips to shush her. He then led the way toward the burly guy manning the door at the front of a queue that lined the street as far as she could see.

"Hey, I don't feel like waiting, and my friend here's celebrating his birthday, so what do you reckon we can cut in?" he asked the man, who scowled in response. Leo tapped his chin thoughtfully for a second as though deliberating. He shrugged and turned back to the others. "Looks like we'll have to wait. There's another option, but you'll have to promise not to tell anyone I used my powers, okay?" he asked a confused Will, then leaned in closer to the bouncer. Leo waved his hands around in front of his face using circular motions, and snapped his fingers as though he'd just hypnotized the glowering doorman. "You're going to let us in now, no questions asked," he said, his voice low and rumbling, and Cassie had to force herself not to giggle.

"Come right on in," the man replied, lifting up the rope so their group could step over the threshold and into the doorway. Will opened his mouth as if he were just about to ask Cassie what on earth he'd just witnessed, when the doorman called after them, "Enjoy your evening, Mr. Solomon."

"Dammit, Paul! I had them fooled for a minute there," Leo called back with a loud laugh, and the now grinning man shrugged before turning back to the entrance, dropping his broad smile, and adopting his scowl again.

The group continued inside, and Leo grinned down at Cassie. He pulled her close, laying a soft kiss on her lips, before turning back to the others so he could explain himself. "This is one of my clubs. I stopped by earlier to check in on things and gave Paul a heads up that we'd be stopping by tonight," he informed them, and both Will and Lana laughed when they caught on.

Leo led them into the VIP area, where they were offered every drink imaginable and treated like royalty. Roger accepted a glass of lemonade, and Cassie joined him. She felt too full from dinner to drink much yet, and even a little nauseous.

"I did wonder when I saw the name outside," Cassie told Leo after they were settled in one of the private booths.

"It wasn't just the one in London, I bought the entire chain. There are ten in total all over the UK. What do you think?" he asked, and Cassie loved how excited he was to show her his most recent business venture.

"It's great. I love the vibe, and the music. And, judging by the line outside, I'd say it's doing well."

"Seems so," he replied with a wink. His coyness when it came to money was endearing. He seemed to like being loaded, and she could never imagine him struggling for cash, but he never appeared to want to flaunt his wealth either. She'd been the one who'd gone out buying the gifts for Will, while Leo had been uneasy. He liked expensive things, but she'd noticed he didn't show them off all that often. Leonardo Solomon was unlike any millionaire she'd ever met before, but then again, she guessed she must be as well because she didn't flash her own cash all that often either.

Cassie thought back to the strange inheritance Victor had left for her, and how she'd put it to good use creating a new life for herself in London. Her accountant had been honest and told her he wondered if Victor had put the money in her name not as a safeguard for her future, but as a way to launder money into offshore accounts. He certainly didn't seem the sort to care enough to leave money in trust, and she too believed it was only coincidental that she'd received that fund after killing him in cold blood.

Strangely, no guilt tore at her gut at thinking of how she'd ended up with millions while he lay six feet under. He'd had to die. Regardless of those rare good moments he'd given her when they were together, he was still an unrepentant monster right until the end and had deserved what he'd got.

Instead of dwelling on the past, Cassie immersed herself in the energy of the night, and she watched the crowd for a moment, mesmerized by the sea of clubbers and their vigor. She also basked in the happiness it gave her having those she loved so close by. Will and Lana were already dancing amidst the throb of people a few feet away, and Roger was liaising with the security staff over by the bar. She slid further into the booth with her man, and Leo immediately put his hand between her knees. He kissed her neck as he squeezed the soft flesh of her thigh gently, kneading her in circular motions while moving up towards the apex. Cassie's heart pounded and her core reacted instantly to his touch. She was soaking and ready, panting in response to just the simple touch of his palm and fingers to her thighs.

"Take off your knickers, I want them," he whispered in her ear, and Cassie froze. She tensed up in shock so fast that Leo quickly pulled his hand away. He stared at her in surprise at her sudden recoil, and then cupped her cheek with his other palm. "What's the matter, love?" he asked, and pulled her still tense body closer in an attempt to soothe her. Cassie tried to shake off the memory that'd forced itself back into her thoughts, seeming intent on disrupting their fun, but it took her a moment before she could even meet Leo's gaze, let alone explain her reaction to him.

"Did you ever meet Eduardo?" she eventually asked, staring at the collar on his shirt in an attempt to avoid his gaze. Leo nodded his head.

"Yeah. He's a massive douchebag. He was one

of the guys that beat me up that night at my house. He also raped Tina…" His voice faltered, and Cassie gasped. She'd never liked Eduardo before learning those two horrific facts, but hated him even more now. She'd always had a strong feeling that he was one of the worst guys in Victor's team of top henchmen, and it seemed her instincts had been right. "Did he hurt you?" Leo asked as he pulled back and stared down at her. Cassie shook her head.

"No, but when Victor took us all out to make him his second in command, he dressed me up and showed me off like some fucking prize. He asked me to give Eduardo my knickers in the nightclub to say congratulations for being promoted. The sleaze didn't take his eyes off me after that, and I was always scared he'd try something," she told Leo honestly, and shuddered at the thought of what he was capable of. She had no doubt now what Eduardo would've done if he'd ever found her alone in that compound.

Leo pulled her into him roughly, and the move made the breath catch in her lungs.

"I had no idea, or else I would've never asked for you to give them to me. I was just messing around. I'm so sorry, love," he said, kissing her forehead lightly as he held her.

"Hey, are you okay?" Will's voice chimed, and Cassie looked up in time to catch the concerned look on his face as he took his seat beside her. She nodded a little too enthusiastically and he frowned. "Liar. What is it, Cassie?"

"Honestly, it's nothing." She tried to be convincing, but his face said it all—she was failing miserably. Under his scrutinizing gaze Cassie suddenly felt lost. She'd never gone into the deeper, darker details about her ordeal with him. Will knew she'd had it bad and had nursed her through the aftermath, but he'd never pried, and she'd never wanted him to know the extent of her trauma. She still saw him as her innocent baby brother, someone to protect and care for, rather than the other way around.

"Sometimes things trigger a memory from her past, and I inadvertently reminded Cassie of something. She'll be fine. Come on, let's go grab another drink," Leo stepped in and took control, as always, and Cassie was grateful. She gave him a nod, silently telling him she was ready to reveal more of her tale.

"You guys go to the bar will you. While I take a minute, Leo can fill you in on some of the things I haven't been able to."

"Are you sure?" Will asked, and she nodded.

"Come on, let's give her a breather," Leo said. He motioned for Roger to come and take his place, while he ushered Will and Lana to the bar with him. She knew he would tell her brother the quick version of what'd truly happened. The lawyer in Will was a pain in the ass at times, and she knew he'd want to know the whole truth. Cassie could tell by their body language they were discussing her past in some detail. Will went stiff as a board and peered over his shoulder at her, but Leo directed his attention back to him.

"You look like you might puke, are you okay?" Roger asked, pulling her attention away from the bar. She'd almost forgotten he'd joined her. Cassie nodded, and then shook her head.

"I keep thinking I'm okay, but then stupid things set me off." A wave of nausea hit her again, and she slouched back into her seat. Roger ordered a ginger ale, and while they waited for the waitress to deliver it, he said nothing more. She was grateful for the lack of questions. She really didn't need another set of eyes on her. Regardless of the fact her brother and lover were watching her like hawks out of consideration for her wellbeing, she still hated it, and wished for normalcy in her life she guessed might never happen.

Roger wrapped an arm around Cassie and pulled her close, and she let him. She could see Leo watching them, but welcomed the silent, sexless affection and support only Roger could seem to give. Leo was too close sometimes, and she was grateful to have someone other than him that could bring her down whenever she wound herself up.

"Do you want me to schedule an appointment with Dr. Gill on Monday?" Roger asked after the ginger ale was in front of her and Cassie was sipping on it slowly. The thought of having to go back to her shrink was enough of a kick up the ass, and she instantly shook off her unease. Psychoanalysis was the last thing she wanted, not after all her progress.

"No, absolutely not," she replied, sitting up in her seat and looking him in the eye. She knew he'd probably mentioned her psychiatrist for this very result, rather than actually meaning to book her in, and Cassie was glad he had. It'd worked. She pushed all thoughts of Eduardo aside, finished her drink, and peered over to where Leo and Will were still talking intently. "I'm gonna go to the bathroom. Do you need to accompany me, or are we good?" she asked with a small laugh.

"We're good," Roger replied, rolling his eyes, but he still watched her walk away, and she knew he'd hover outside the door in wait.

*** 

"Trust me, she's gone through a lot and she's better, but there's still some healing left to do," Leo said, finishing up his quick tale of Cassie's past. Will had seemed shocked to learn some of the truths Leo had told him, and he hadn't even delved properly into her ordeal with Jonah or the depths of her forced submission with Victor.

"She never told me any of this, just that she'd gotten mixed up with the wrong guy in Mexico and he'd killed Jonah. I knew you were involved, but had no idea how much she'd really gone through..." Will tailed off, and Leo placed a hand on his shoulder.

"Cassie didn't want you to know, and she hid it from you because the last thing she wanted was to burden you with her woes. She doesn't want to be pitied or get asked to talk about the things she's buried away, so how about we ditch the seriousness and get back to having fun? That's the whole reason we're here, and I know she'll hate thinking she's ruined the night by causing a fuss." Will nodded in agreement and grabbed a shot from the bar. He seemed truly grateful for the drink Leo had lined up awaiting him, and took another.

"You're a good man, Leo. Thank you for taking such great care of her," he said in toast to the man beside him before knocking another back. Leo smiled, but felt uneasy. He still couldn't deal with it when people said things like that to him. Part of him wanted to tell Will all the ways in which he wasn't a good man, but instead he bit his tongue and downed a shot of his own.

When Cassie returned from the bathroom, Leo took her hand and led her to the dance floor, where he pulled her close and cradled her protectively. She seemed to melt into him, as though thankful for the support, and the turmoil within him silenced instantly. She wanted him, needed him. There could be one hundred friendly faces in the room, and she would still seek him out. He knew it without her ever saying so, and knowing how much she loved and trusted him gave Leo hope.

Despite his own progress, he'd still convinced himself he wasn't good enough for her. That he was a sociopath who cared about no one but himself. But when their bodies were against each other's and she calmed the chaos within, Leo trusted her judgment. If Cassie said he was good, he couldn't believe it. But when her body wordlessly told him through her willing submission and love, Leo couldn't deny she made him feel like a good man. Maybe one day he might finally believe it to be true.

They moved together slowly despite the upbeat song blasting through the speakers, and before long she climbed up onto her tiptoes to reach his lips with hers. Leo gave himself to her, not caring who might see. He needed the connection just as much as she evidently did, and neither one broke it until they absolutely had to.

# Chapter Fourteen

On their way back to their booth, a loud squealing screech pierced the air, and all of them turned to check out where and from whom the calls had come from.

"Cassie? Cassie Taylor!" She froze. Roger stepped in immediately to assess the situation before whoever it was reached her, but Cassie already recognized the voice's owner. Part of her wanted to keep walking, but the other part was actually kind of interested to see one of her high school friends again after such a long time.

"It's okay, Rog," she said, stepping around him, and lo and behold, there she was—Holly Madison. The school's Queen Bee. Cassie plastered a huge smile on her face and took in the sight of Holly and her small group of friends-slash-minions. They were the same bunch she'd hung around with at school, just ten years older. "How have you been, Holly?"

"Great, obviously," she replied, but then elaborated when Cassie's face must've said it all.

Clearly everybody around their small village knew how amazing her life had apparently turned out, well, apart from Cassie, much to Holly's distaste. "I'm a teacher now. I've just been promoted to Deputy Head." Her lips curled into a smile that reeked of self-obsession, and Cassie could tell Holly was still used to being adored and followed everywhere by her gang of cronies.

"Congratulations," she managed, and found herself disinterested in catching up with the old crowd already. She looked around and saw faces she'd known years before, but who weren't her friends, and whose lives were very different to her own. She didn't care who they were or who they thought they were, and she didn't give a damn what they thought of her. In fact, Cassie didn't even feel the need to outdo Holly by informing her of her own achievements. She simply smiled sweetly and made to walk away. "Well, it was nice seeing you, but we'd best be going back to our table. Enjoy the rest of your night."

"Whoa, are you going to the VIP area?" Holly asked, her eyes alight. Cassie nodded. "How'd you manage that?" she spat, and her words had a bitter edge Cassie couldn't help but revel in. After that reaction, she kind of did want to flaunt her status and relationship with Leo, but then again, what did it matter if someone like Holly was jealous of her? There was nothing in it for Cassie, so she simply shrugged.

"It's Will's birthday so we came for a visit," she replied, and Holly followed her gaze over to where Cassie's brother was chatting to one of the guys he seemed to know from their group. She nodded and fumbled with her hands, not seeming to know what to say next, and Cassie got the impression she was hoping for an invitation to join them in the VIP section—an invitation she most certainly wasn't going to get. The conversation seemed to have come to a quick and natural halt, and Cassie was eager to get on her way. She knew Roger and Leo were standing motionless behind her, watching and waiting patiently for her to wrap it up, and she was glad to have their support so close by. "Well, bye," she told Holly, and turned to go.

"What do we have here?" A voice Cassie knew very well boomed from her right, and she turned toward the man who'd just joined them. Her first ever boyfriend and childhood sweetheart, Tate Reynolds, headed through the group and stood staring at her from Holly's side. He eyed Cassie up and down with a satisfied smile, and then rolled his eyes when Holly caught him and gave him a nudge. "Long time no see, Cass. You're looking good."

"Thanks, Tate. You too," Cassie replied with a forced smile. She didn't mean it. In actual fact, he looked scruffy and old.

"Word was you ran off and joined the theater." He laughed as if he'd just told the funniest joke in the world and Cassie scowled.

"Yeah, something like that," she told him, and stepped back into Leo's towering shadow in readiness to leave. She didn't feel like explaining herself or her lifestyle choices to the likes of Tate.

"Got yourself in all sorts of trouble from what I heard. Drug dealers and murderers…"

"If you want to stay in my club one more minute, I suggest you shut the fuck up right now," Leo's voice rumbled from just above her ear, and Cassie realized he'd stepped in even closer behind her. He wrapped his arm protectively around her waist, and she watched as Tate's face dropped in shock.

The pair of them had dated all their way through high school, and at the time she'd been absolutely besotted with him. Now, however, there was absolutely no comparing him to Leo. Yes, she had run away when it'd come to going off to college. In fact, she'd chosen to attend a university in London not only for their arts program, but for the distance from their small life in that village. Even away from it, the same people and their same judgments had found her life's ups and downs a worthy point for discussion, and Cassie was suddenly ready to go home.

She watched as Holly also did a double take, then scowled. She clearly hadn't expected such a turn of events, and Cassie couldn't deny it felt good having the upper hand after all the years she and the other girls had spent living in Holly's shadow.

"Sorry, I was just messing around. I didn't think..." Tate replied with a stutter. He peered up at Leo and cringed, but her powerful man gave no further threats. He didn't need to. "I was only messing, you know that, right?"

"It wasn't funny, *Tate*. And no, you obviously didn't think before you opened your stupid mouth." Leo's voice was full of venom, and even Roger seemed to notice the impending outburst if Tate didn't shut the hell up and stop digging himself into more of a hole. Roger closed the gap, stepping right in front of Cassie so she was sandwiched between him and Leo, and laid a hand on Tate's shoulder.

"No, mate. That's the problem, you didn't think. And now we have a problem, 'cos you've not only upset Ms. Taylor, but pissed off the club's owner too. I suggest you keep your thoughtless opinions to yourself, and get back to hanging with your buddies here. Enjoy your night." Tate had been dismissed, and when he opened his mouth to say something, presumably an apology but Cassie couldn't be sure, Roger shook his head.

Cassie took the opportunity to escape, turning on her heel without so much as a goodbye to Tate, Holly, or the others. They weren't important to her or her life now, so she left them behind just like she had years before. She took Leo's hand in hers and led him away. He bristled, and even hesitated as though hankering after a fight, but she kept pulling and eventually won their silent battle of wills. Their night had hit a rough patch already, and she certainly didn't want another one happening simply because her ex had no filter.

After depositing Leo back in their booth along with her brother, Cassie headed to the bathroom again. Lana joined her, but evidently decided against bringing up her turmoil or her past, and Cassie was glad. Instead, after they'd finished their business she simply smiled sweetly and thanked Cassie for their lovely evening.

"You're very welcome. I guess you might have this figured out already, but I tend to have some drama or another following me," Cassie told her with a sad smile. "But I'm not here that often, so things should go back to being pretty quiet when we go home tomorrow."

"Don't say that." Lana seemed shocked at her apology. "I've never seen Will so happy. He's loved having you guys here, and he wouldn't care even if you threw the biggest strop and caused a huge scene. All that matters is he's sharing his birthday with you. The explanation is absolutely unnecessary."

A sob caught in Cassie's throat, and she forced away the tears pricking at her eyes. She grabbed Lana and hugged her tightly.

"I knew I'd like you," she told her with a smile, and Lana returned the compliment before hugging Cassie back to show her she meant it.

\*\*\*

When the girls returned, the air was much clearer, and Leo felt far more relaxed after chatting with Will and Roger for a few minutes. He watched Cassie intently, mesmerized by his strong and beautiful girlfriend. There was nothing he wouldn't do for her, and while he still had to recognize when to pick a fight or walk away, he was learning.

Every step she took towards him was a feast for his eyes. Cassie had no idea how stunning she was, and that just added to her beauty. Her long legs stretched out beneath her short dress, but there was just enough hidden to still look classy. His eyes scrolled upward and lingered on those ample breasts of hers. They were bulging out the top of her neckline, and he could see the mounds wobbling slightly with each step she took. He'd adored those two mountainous peaks from the first moment he'd seen them on the camera at his New York mansion, and still did. Most of the women he'd known had huge fake breasts, and he'd enjoyed fondling them back in the day. But with Cassie, they were natural, and he couldn't get enough of them.

Cassie was smiling coyly, clearly having caught his lingering looks, but she didn't shy away from him. She was finally letting herself enjoy his attention, and he was pleased to see her confidence shining brightly despite the night's couple of setbacks. She looked good enough to eat, and Leo knew he would be doing exactly that before too long whenever he got her good and naked.

By the time she slid into the booth next to him, Leo's hard-on was already straining in his pants. He'd need a minute before he could stand. He felt her hand go to the pocket of his jacket, and peered down just in time to see an edge of black satin disappear inside with her fingers.

"You did ask nicely, and it's my pleasure to do everything you want of me," Cassie whispered in his ear. She slid her tongue out to trace the edge of his earlobe. "No one owns our pleasure but us, and my pain is yours to command as well, Leo Solomon. We're making our own memories, with no more looking back."

"No looking back," he repeated, and turned his head, capturing her mouth with his. The world around them fell away. All that mattered was Cassie and her lips, her body as she pressed it against his, and the way her hand held on to his bicep tightly. She was pulling him closer, deeper, and further into their kiss than he ever thought she would in front of others. When they finally broke away, Leo laid two more soft kisses against her cheek as he found her ear. "That mouth of yours is going to get you in trouble," he told her, and felt rather than heard her sharp intake of breath. "I'm going to fuck it tonight, and then I'm gonna come on your tits. But first, I want to taste how wet you are, and not stop until you're screaming my name. Will you do those things for me, love?"

"Yes," she groaned, and Leo was sure he caught her crossing her legs tightly, as though clenching her core in anticipation.

"If you dare have a single orgasm in this club I'll take you in one of the rooms out the back and spank you so hard you'll see stars." His tone was powerful, and despite his growing need for her, his threat was a sincere promise. Cassie's eyes widened and Leo was sure he heard her gasp again. *Game on*, he thought.

He checked the room around them, pleased to discover Will and Lana had taken themselves off to the dance floor again, and that Roger was over by the bar. They had some stolen alone time, and despite his direct order for her not to climax while at the club, Leo intended to make it as hard for her as possible to follow it.

She'd accepted his challenge without a word, and he watched as she continued to clench. Leo pulled her back into the small seclusion that the booth provided, and he thrust his hand between those delectable thighs she still held tense. His thumb caressed her clit with gentle strokes while his fingers delved inside her soaking pussy, and Leo was shocked at how wet she was. "Don't you dare come, Cassie. Your ass will be so sore on that drive home tomorrow you won't be able to sit still," he teased while doing everything he could to ensure she did just that.

She soon began clenching and throbbing against his hand, and her bosom heaved with her panting breaths. Leo watched Cassie reach her glorious climax and then come down from her high. She peered up at him cunningly.

"Oops," she whispered with a sexy smile. Leo felt a low growl make its way up his throat. He was in awe of her, but also filled with an urgent need to punish her. In one quick move, Leo had straightened them both up and stood. He took her hand and pulled her toward one corner of the club, heading straight through the door marked **'Staff Only.'**

He found the small office he'd visited earlier and locked the door closed behind them. Leo stood and stared at his incredible lover, taking in the flushed color to her cheeks and the cheeky grin on her red lips. Cassie walked over to the small desk, pulling up her dress as she went, and leaned across it, exposing her naked ass to him. "I've been a bad girl, Mr. Solomon." Her voice quivered as she spoke, and damn if it didn't make him harder.

"Yes, you have." Leo stepped closer and cupped her mound with his palm, hissing with delight when she leaned back into him and groaned. "I'm going to punish you, and if you come again I'm going to fuck you here." Leo slipped two fingers inside her soaking core. "And then here." He slid the same fingers up to her tight back opening and massaged it.

Cassie gasped, but she didn't stop him, and he had to wonder. Leo decided it was time he pushed her even further. He slid one finger inside and caressed her gently, guiding the digit deeper and deeper with each thrust. He was so hard he could barely contain himself, and seeing how willing she was to accept his explorative advances had him ready to take her there and then.

First, though, he had a punishment to administer. Leo forced himself to retreat, and as soon as she let out an unsatisfied moan that he'd left her empty, he knew he'd be fucking that amazing ass before they left this tiny room.

He didn't let her say or do anything before his first slap made contact with her cheek. Cassie held on to the desk tightly and said nothing to stop him, so Leo struck her again. This time he smoothed the skin and kissed it afterwards, knowing he'd hit her hard, but her panting breath told him she wasn't hurt—in fact it seemed she'd loved him using a firmer hand. After two more slaps he moved on to the other cheek, where he delivered another four to her increasingly reddened ass.

Deep down, there was a part of him that sadistically delighted in hurting Cassie, but only as much as she wanted. He truly enjoyed giving her what she needed from him. Leo was doing everything he could to pleasure her, like a good

Dom should. She wanted the pain, for whatever reason, and he was strong enough to deliver it to her safely. Panting, glistening, and groaning with pleasure, Cassie arched her back and opened her legs wider. Leo knew exactly what she needed, and slapped her right on the clit.

Leo thanked God for the thumping music that drowned out the sound of Cassie's scream. At first he thought he'd hurt her, but when she peered back over her shoulder at him with a desire he felt in his soul, he knew she'd just exploded in pleasure rather than pain. He pushed down his pants and was inside her soaked opening in seconds, and she was still clenching as the last remnants of her orgasm echoed through her. "Fuck, Cassie. You feel so good," he groaned, and then hissed when she wriggled against him, burrowing him deeper inside.

Leo pounded hard, pressing into her while driving his own climax ever closer. When he could wait no longer, he pulled out and teased her tight ass with the head of his cock, coaxing his way inside without asking permission or having to tell her what to do. Cassie relaxed immediately and welcomed him, and Leo groaned at the tightness she held him with. He came after just a few strokes, but didn't stop his movements. He was too hard to be satisfied yet, so carried on just a little bit longer, and watched in awe as she came for him one more time.

Leo pulled himself out slowly. He then helped Cassie to the small bathroom, where he got cleaned up while she composed herself. She looked utterly fucked, and he supposed she was. She seemed surprised when he soaked the handkerchief from his jacket pocket in warm water and cleaned her up as well, as though she thought he would be too disgusted to clean up his own mess, but it was quite the opposite. Leo loved how she'd taken him so willingly, but he also took great pleasure in knowing she was comfortable and cared for even after their epic lovemaking session was over. "Have you done it properly before? Not just what we've done?" he asked, and didn't look into her eyes when she replied with an almost silent affirmation.

Leo didn't ask for any details. He didn't need or want to know who had taught her how to do it, nor did he want to embarrass her by making Cassie tell him. It needed to stay in the past where it belonged. They were moving on together. Cassie had shown him that by pushing her panties into his pocket even after she'd told him about the disgusting memory of Eduardo and the present she'd been forced to give him. He knew he'd never make her feel bad for her sexual past. He'd had hundreds of women over the years, in many different ways too, so he could never judge Cassie or her preferences in the bedroom. In fact, he downright loved that she was opening up more and more about what she craved, and knew he was more than willing to give her everything she wanted.

***

The next day, they bid farewell to the Taylor's and headed back to London. Cassie was more emotional than she would've thought she'd be, but wouldn't let herself cry. Her parents had been their

213

usual selves, but she really thought Leo had made a good impression on them both, and hoped he'd be a welcome addition to her life now that they'd gotten to know him better. Will had firmly embraced him as his brother-in-law, regardless of the constant reminders from his big sister that they weren't planning to get married. Her parents had brought up the subject as well, but Cassie had shot their comments down right away.

A part of her considered herself to have some kind of curse when it came to having a husband, and the thought of getting married a third time was depressing. Cassie was widowed twice over, and that was more than enough for one lifetime. She and Leo would be together for the rest of their lives, she had absolutely no doubt about it, and she didn't need a piece of paper or a ring on her finger to know that.

Not caring about the travel sickness, she climbed in the back to sit with Leo for the ride home. She had to be with him, so she popped a tablet with some kind of herbal remedy to help ease her nausea and then settled in beside her man. Leo wrapped an arm around her and pulled Cassie closer, and with a cocky smile he rested one hand over her ass. She was still a little bruised, but not as sore as she would've thought, and her memory of the night before only made her want more. She had to admit, she'd thoroughly enjoyed all three elements of what'd gone on in that office, and was more than willing to do them again whenever Leo asked her to.

Everything was perfect, and while the pessimist

inside wanted to warn her that trouble might just be around the corner, she pushed it away. Only the positive thoughts were allowed into her mind right now, and she intended to keep it that way.

# *Chapter Fifteen*

Happy days together turned into blissful weeks, and before long Cassie fell into a wonderful routine of work and home life that she never dreamed she could have before. Leo had remained his ever-forceful self, at times still closed-off, but he was working on it, and she didn't push him. They explored her interest in the darker, more violent sides of his sexual prowess, and as promised, tried their hands at a little roleplay of their own.

She woke late one morning to find him gone, but a note was left behind in his place. Cassie grabbed it and read his fine handwriting with a smile.

*My love,*
*I've gone to the office, but I won't be long. The game is on, and today's the day I teach you how to be ravaged, Cassie. Watch your back, as you won't know when or where I might pounce. Fight back all you want, but don't*

*forget I'll only stop for the safe word--*
*Jellybeans.*
  *Yours anticipatively,*
  *Leo x*

Cassie bit her lip with excitement. It seemed he was finally willing to show her the last of those things he'd told her about months before, and she was more than ready to try it out. She climbed up out of bed and got herself ready for a day of cleaning and running errands, figuring she'd best go about her ordinary tasks while waiting with bated breath for him to strike.

By mid-morning, the wait was already torture, and she showered with one eye on the door, all the while failing in her bid to ignore the sweet, burning desire building in her gut. She was a twisted knot at first, watching every movement from the corner of her eye like a paranoid lunatic, and had to force herself to calm down. Cassie did some breathing exercises and stretched out with a bit of yoga.

With one ear on the door, figuring she'd hear Leo when he came home anyway, Cassie then set about completing her chores. As she stood at the kitchen sink washing dishes, she was so deep in thought she finally forgot all about their game. She daydreamed of a future life with Leo. Yes, she still had her damaged past and the baggage that came with it, but so did he, and together they were mending those broken parts of one another. Their future could be as bright as they wanted it to be, and she was sure ready for less of the chaos and drama.

A gloved hand suddenly covered her mouth, and

a wall of heavy muscle pinned her to the counter from behind. Cassie jumped and tried to scream, but the sound was drowned out by the epic force holding her still and silent. Her heart was beating out of her chest and her breath was ragged, and when her attacker's breath tickled her ear, she shuddered.

"I'm going to remove my hand, and if you dare scream you'll be sorry. Understand?" the rumbling baritone voice murmured against her cheek, and Cassie nodded. She knew it was Leo right from the start, and wasn't scared, but was also well aware of the game he was playing. He was the cat and she was the mouse. And, like a cat, he was an unrelenting force hell-bent on catching his prey. But she was a crafty mouse who was already enjoying their game, so much so that she wasn't quite ready to give up just yet.

As soon as he dropped his hand, she shoved an elbow back into his ribs. A deep grunt was all she got from him, but Leo stepped away just enough for Cassie to slide free from his hold and make a run for it, and she knew he'd let her go on purpose. She charged for the door, but only made it as far as the hall before being swept off her feet and into the air. She cried out, kicking and squirming in an attempt to get free, but it was no use. His hand was back over her mouth again, and no amount of struggling could get her free.

Leo flung her over one end of the couch on her stomach, and Cassie knew she had no options left. He was holding her by her wrists at the small of her back, and was pressing her face into the sofa cushions, while her ass was sticking up over the raised arm of the sofa completely at his mercy. His free hand grabbed at the waistband of her pants, ripping the clothing from her in a rush, and Leo buried himself inside of her from behind.

After just a few hard thrusts she was putty in his hands, and any fight she'd tried to keep hold of was quickly lost. But she did it all willingly, wanting this and so much more from her intensely sexy lover. The excitement drove her wild, as did his body as he forced himself into her over and over. He roared as he came, and Cassie was right there with him. Her body clenched around his pulsing length, taking everything he had to give her, and when he finally stilled they both fell into a crumpled heap of bodies entwined.

"Whoa," she breathed, and nestled deeper into his hold.

"Yeah," Leo replied, and despite his earlier savage treatment, he kissed and caressed Cassie with gentle touches. When she'd come down from her extreme high, she peered up at him through her lashes and marveled at the man who loved her so much she felt breathless in his arms. He was a brute, through and through, yet Leo was also tender, caring, and gentle when he let himself be. He loved her with everything he had, and she adored how he wasn't afraid to show it. "Did you like it?"

"Well, obviously," Cassie teased, and she laughed when he tickled her rib playfully. "You didn't keep me waiting too long either, but I enjoyed the anticipation."

"I've been hiding in the apartment all day,

waiting for the opportune moment," he told her, and Cassie laughed even harder. "I never went to the office, it was all part of my master plan to have you fooled."

"Wow, you're a good stalker. I didn't even know you were here!" she cried in response, and Leo took a half bow. He sat them both up, checked Cassie over, as though to make sure he hadn't been too rough, and then led her away to get cleaned up.

\*\*\*

No amount of sickness remedy was working this time, and Cassie's stomach lurched at the very idea that there might be something more behind her symptoms than she'd first thought. One possibility kept coming back to her, though, the idea quickly becoming less and less impossible to imagine. Siobhan had gone on a few times about how her pregnant sister hadn't had morning sickness, but a general queasiness that'd lasted until around halfway through her term, and it seemed almost feasible that it could be the reason behind her now constant nausea. With the implant in her arm, Cassie's periods had stopped anyway, so she hadn't skipped any, but she definitely felt strange. There was an "off" feeling she couldn't shake.

"I'm taking my lunch break," she told Siobhan, who immediately offered to go with her. Cassie refused. She didn't let on, but she needed some time alone, albeit with her bodyguard in tow. Thankfully, Roger knew when it was in his best interests to stay quiet, and that this was one of those times.

It was a quick walk down the street to a chemist, and less than thirty minutes later, Cassie was staring at the two small blue lines that read as a positive result on the pregnancy test in her hands. "Oh, God," she groaned, and then stashed the test in her purse. Cassie wasn't sure how to feel, somehow both elated and terrified at the same time. She made her excuses to Siobhan, asking her to close up for her, and let Roger drive her to the casino so she could talk to Leo about her incredible discovery. There was no waiting or hiding it from him, and she needed him to be delighted with their impending parenthood before she could even begin to contemplate celebrating the news.

Cassie bypassed the lobby and its horde of young women waiting to greet the guests. With Roger at her side she rode up to Leo's office in silence. Usually, he'd leave her to it when she got to the casino, but this time he'd stayed, and Cassie was glad.

"It'll be okay," he mumbled. Cassie felt a lump form in her throat. She wasn't ready to talk, not yet, but she appreciated having her trusty companion and his always so ready encouragement. "Don't be scared."

"But, what if…" she began, but Roger cut her off.

"What if the woman he loves comes and tells him she's going to give him the one thing he's been missing his entire adult life? What if the woman he adores tells him she's going to give him a child? I'd say he'll be pretty bloody happy about the news, and if he isn't quite jumping for joy, it's just 'cos he's scared—like you."

Cassie took a deep breath and steadied herself. Roger really did need a raise, and she made a mental note to make some fuss of him very soon. He'd been a silent support no end of times, and at other times a source of fun to help take her mind off the seriousness shrouding her daily life. Then there were the moments like this, when he offered her heartfelt advice and a shoulder to cry on exactly when she needed it most.

"Thanks," she told him when they reached Leo's office door.

"Any time, boss lady," he replied with a wink, before taking residence in a chair across the hall.

She knocked and went inside, and found Leo and his cousin Brian browsing through some paperwork at the huge desk. They both looked up in surprise, but each grinned in welcome. Brian made his excuses and left them to it, while Cassie hovered across the desk from her gorgeous lover. She didn't know how to say it. Her mind went blank.

"What's wrong, love?" Leo asked, and stood so he could walk around the desk and gather her up in his powerful arms.

"Leo, I'm…you're…" she stammered. "You're going to be a daddy," she finally managed, feeling as though she might be sick. Leo grabbed her chin and tilted her face to meet his, dazzling Cassie with the most radiant smile she'd ever seen. Tears poured from her eyes uncontrollably as she took him in. Leo wiped them away with his pocket-handkerchief without a word. He sniffed, as though fighting back the tears himself, and continued to peer down at her adoringly.

"And you're going to be a mommy," he purred, his accent lilting with the American sound he'd somehow become accustomed to mixing with his British inflection. She laughed.

"Yeah, I guess that too," she mumbled, and then sobbed when he planted a deep and loving kiss against her lips. She wasn't afraid, not anymore, but she was damn well shocked to imagine that this could actually be happening for real. It wasn't a pipedream and it certainly wasn't planned, but Cassie thanked God for sending them this baby, and knew they'd both love it more than either could ever have imagined.

When she'd finally calmed back down, Leo took her to sit with him behind his desk. She climbed into his lap without a care and then watched as he finished his work and cleared the table.

She dozed in his hold, and came to when she felt herself being lifted up into his strong arms. "Leo?" she asked, rubbing her bleary eyes.

"It's okay, love. I've got you," he told her, placing her down on the sofa across the room from his desk with gentle hands. "I've called for a gynecologist, she'll be here within the hour." Panic flared within again, but this time it wasn't to do with her nerves, but her excitement.

When the doctor arrived, they made quick work of discussing Cassie's contraceptive uses before agreeing that her implant had somehow failed. The kind and warm young woman was methodical as she then ran through Cassie's medical history with her. Cassie paled when the question, "how many surgeries have you had and where?" came up.

Leo held her hand tightly in his, and his strength helped Cassie be honest about her reconstructive labial surgery after Jonah's attack.

"Okay. Well if you've still managed to continue with normal sexual health since then, I assume the surgery was a success?" Dr. Singh asked, and Cassie nodded. The doctor's dark brown eyes were suddenly warmer, her gaze less business-like, and her features had noticeably changed. Cassie couldn't be sure if she was like this with all her patients, but she certainly felt put at ease by the approach Dr. Singh continued on with. "And, is this your first pregnancy? Including miscarriages, etcetera?"

"Yes," Cassie answered honestly, and was glad she didn't have anything else to discuss with the doctor about her torrid past.

After analyzing a urine sample, the doctor was able to confirm the pregnancy. Cassie caught Leo's broad smile. His happiness spurred her on, and while she hated needles, she stared over at him to keep her mind off of it when the doctor then took some blood.

"How about we try listening to the heartbeat?" Dr. Singh then asked, and both parents-to-be sat a little higher in their seats. Cassie wanted to hear that sound more than anything else in the world, and hadn't even considered they might be able to listen in so soon. She immediately followed the doctor's instructions to lay down and lift her shirt. Dr. Singh felt around for a while, seeming pleased with what she found there, and she took out a small device she then lubricated and ran across the base of Cassie's stomach. Within seconds, a fast thumping noise came through the handset, and the doctor grinned. "Perfect. I'd say you're around nine weeks along. Congratulations," she told them, and passed Cassie a tissue when she began crying again.

\*\*\*

Leo had never been happier. Things were falling into place for him and Cassie, and he truly felt as if their luck might've changed for the better. They were so in love, regardless of the ups and downs, and he knew they'd make great parents to the tiny new life miraculously growing inside of his amazing girlfriend's womb. He watched her sleep for hours that night, his hand resting gently on her stomach, and finally drifted off in the early hours when his exhaustion overtook his excitement.

Cassie woke him later that morning by grinding against him, her hips stretching back to find the morning hard-on he always had for her, and he was surprised to discover her still asleep when he pried open his eyes and peered down at his hot and horny girlfriend.

Lying on her side with her back to him, Cassie was panting, trembling, and mumbling something he couldn't hear. Leo stroked her face in an attempt to rouse her, but Cassie remained in the deep throes of her dream.

"I want you, Leo. I want you to own me," she whimpered, sending his mind back to their rekindled night together. The memories of her request for him to own her came crashing to the forefront of his thoughts. She was dreaming of him, she had to be, and she groaned as if she was enjoying the vision playing out inside her subconscious mind. Cassie arched back against him again, and this time the tip of his cock ended up nestled directly at the apex of her thighs.

She needed him, Leo knew it, and he curled his hips up to meet hers while spooning around her from behind. His hardness found her heat and slid inside with ease. She was soaking already, and moaned when he drove himself home and started rocking. Cassie gasped and grabbed his hand, bringing it to her mouth so she could kiss his palm. He could tell she was now awake, and was glad she hadn't minded him taking what her unconscious body had offered.

"I've got you, Cassie," Leo groaned and he let out a hiss when she slid two of his fingertips into her mouth. She sucked them, swirling her tongue in the same way she'd caressed his cock countless times, and the motion sent his hips thrusting in a frenzy. He stilled, pressing himself deep inside. "I love you so damn much," he whispered, and then slid his fingers from her mouth. Cassie groaned, but let him go, watching as he moved those same, glistening fingertips down to her clit. She whimpered as he teased it, bucking against him in her pleasure, and Leo started moving inside of her again.

When she came, he was right there with her, and he adored watching as she unwound whatever tension had been coiling in her belly while dreaming. They then fell back into a satiated sleep, and this time Leo had no problem drifting off.

# *Chapter Sixteen*

After another busy night on the casino floor, Leo swung past his office on his way home, feeling more than ready to head off and wrap his arms around his stunning girlfriend. All he could think about was Cassie, and the baby growing inside of her—his baby. Could this really be happening? Was he, the big, bad gangster, finally going to be a father? All evidence pointed to yes, and Leo couldn't be happier with where their lives were headed.

He took a seat at his desk and checked the casino's security feed. All good. He then tapped into the feed for his office, finding the image of himself sat at the desk in real time, and hit rewind. There'd been a whole lot of nothing going on in his empty office, which was just how he liked it, and Leo reactivated the camera recording before shutting down and grabbing his jacket.

"Hey, boss," a sweet, sassy voice welcomed him in the hallway, and Leo forced himself to smile even though the last thing he needed was to be dragged back into work.

"Evening, Suzie," he replied, locking the door behind him and stashing his keys. Leo walked away, but she was hot on his heels, so he turned back to her, hoping to get whatever it was she wanted out of the way so he could get home. "What's up?"

"Oh, nothing much, I just wanted to see if you fancied having a drink with me?" she asked. Leo had to stop himself from rolling his eyes. He looked Suzie up and down, and pitied her. She'd kept her dark hair and now seemed to be dressed in the exact same outfit Cassie had been wearing a few days previously. He figured perhaps Stuart had been right to warn him about her after all, and maybe she was actually a little unhinged. Suzie was clearly emulating Cassie in a bid to catch his eye, but Leo couldn't be less interested in playing games or indulging her foolish crush.

"I'm in a relationship, Suzie. And even if I weren't, I'm afraid it'd still be a no," he told her coolly, trying not to hurt her feelings, but at the same time wanting to make it perfectly clear where he stood.

She didn't listen to his attempt at letting her down gently. Suzie burst into tears, screaming and wailing into her hands. When she pulled them away, her panda eyes were out of control, and Leo handed her a tissue from his pocket. He wasn't a complete bastard, but didn't much feel like taking care of a clearly insane woman, so rather than comfort Suzie, he did nothing but stand there while she dabbed at her eyes.

"What more can I do to get you to notice me?" she cried, sobbing harder. She was a mess, anyone could see it, but Leo didn't really give a shit. He guessed he really was a sociopath after all, because he couldn't care less how she felt or if he'd hurt her. All he was bothered about was getting home to his girl.

He stepped closer and put a hand on her shoulder, and Suzie peered up at him with a smile, clearly hoping he was going to say something gentle and romantic.

"You're a fucking state and I'd never look at you no matter what. I'm not interested in being your sugar daddy, and I'm certainly not fooled by this 'poor me' routine you've got going on. I know psycho bitches when I see them, and you're right up there with the best of them, sweetheart. Go home, sort yourself out, and stop copying my girlfriend in an attempt to catch my eye, otherwise you can kiss your job goodbye," he told her, and then walked away without another word.

In the elevator, Leo grabbed his cell and dialed his cousin. "Bri, looks like Suzie's going to be a problem. Full-blown-crazy-bitch-mode," he said.

"Damn, I thought she seemed a little bit too interested in you," Brian answered, and Leo heard him wince. He knew that tone. His dear cousin had clearly gotten too close to Suzie and it was going to be a problem Leo didn't want to have to deal with.

"You got something to tell me?"

Brian cursed. "Yeah, I've been fucking her. She was asking me questions about you and Cassie, what she likes and dislikes. I thought she wanted to be her friend, but then things started seeming a bit less like she was merely interested and a bit more like she was obsessed. I told her to back off and haven't seen her since." Now it was Leo's turn to curse.

"You sort her the fuck out, man, otherwise you'll both become problems I'll have to deal with myself, and you don't wanna push me. Got it?"

"Got it, and I'm sorry," Brian answered. Obviously he knew Leo's threat wasn't half-hearted. If he had to, he was more than willing to teach his cousin a lesson using his fists. They were incredibly adept at doing the talking for him whenever Leo was truly pissed, and he was more than willing to let off a little steam if necessary. It didn't matter that Brian was family; if his men fucked up, they had to learn their lessons. "I'll call her, tell her to back off," Brian added down the line.

"You'd better. I don't want Cassie getting upset over this," Leo replied, and he abruptly ended the call. He cursed. Nothing ever stayed simple.

The drive home didn't do anything to calm him down. By the time he got back to the apartment, Leo was still a tangled mess of anger and rage, so he grabbed his sneakers and gym kit from the trunk and went for a run. It didn't matter that it was the dead of night; he ran like he wanted to stomp holes in the sidewalk itself. Suzie and her infatuation with him was nothing but a pain in the ass. He didn't want anything to do with her, and yet she had somehow wormed her way into his thoughts rather than letting him carry on about his business as normal. He didn't care about her, only the trouble she might cause him. It was a problem he really didn't need, or want.

Leo ran harder, faster. By the time he rounded the corner back to where his car was parked, he'd already decided that she was Brian's problem, not his. He'd have to get her in line or show her the door. Simple. Leo wasn't getting any more involved with her, and Cassie never had to know a thing about his new stalker and her foolish crush. He'd known women like her in the past, and had done the same with them. After a period of stone-cold iciness from him, they always got the hint—even the really fucked-up ones.

Cassie was asleep already when he finally headed inside, curled into a ball beneath their huge duvet with a book lying beside her head as if she'd drifted off reading it. Just the sight of her calmed him some more, but she also stirred his other senses, and Leo knew he was still far too wired to sleep.

He took a shower, hoping the cool jets would help. They didn't, and when he'd dried off, he turned out the light and climbed in behind her, kissing Cassie's shoulder and neck in an attempt to wake her.

\*\*\*

Cassie stirred when she felt lips caressing her skin and hot hands that turned her over onto her back. A rush of cool air hit her skin as the duvet was lifted, but was quickly replaced with a hot body, damp from a recent shower. She groaned, but

232

didn't stop him when Leo wrenched her thighs apart. In fact, in her half-awake daze, she lifted her hips up, attempting to meet him halfway. However, it appeared he had other ideas. Leo pushed her back down and she felt him dip beneath the covers. Hot breath met her even hotter core, and he pounced on her like a man possessed. His hands dug into her hips, keeping her in place, while his tongue and lips preyed on her, staking his claim. He was somehow inside, on top, and all over her body, while also inside her head and heart. He knew exactly what she needed before she even knew herself, and delivered her pleasure without a single word or command. Leo didn't need to. Her body reacted to his touch on some primal level, and Cassie cried out as a wave of sheer ecstasy rolled over her from the inside out.

She was suddenly full, stretching and throbbing around the hard rod that'd plunged inside her soaked opening. Leo went hard and fast, as though he was on some mission to leave her nothing but mush when he was done. When he came, he collapsed on top of her, kissing and caressing every inch of her his hands could reach.

"Whoa," she breathed against his temple.

"Yeah," Leo whispered, rolling off her. "I didn't hurt you, did I?" he checked, and she quickly reassured him that she was far from hurt.

"No, baby. I'm wonderful." She turned so she could snuggle against him.

"Yeah. Yeah, you are," he agreed, holding her back tightly.

# *Chapter Seventeen*

After finishing up early at the theater, Cassie decided to head straight over to the casino to surprise Leo. The new play was going really well, as were his ventures, and business was booming for them both. The past few months together had been the best of her life, and as far as she was concerned, they could keep on going strong in the coming months and years stretched out ahead of them. A few weeks had passed since they found out about the baby, and the pregnancy was still a shock, but she was dealing with the surprise well, as was Leo. The world of diapers and sleepless nights seemed far less scary than the world she'd found herself in a few years before, and she honestly felt ready to take the next step. Cassie had already told him she didn't want to get married again, but now their child was growing inside of her, and she had to admit, she was starting to rethink things.

Roger walked her to the doorway of the casino and waved goodbye as she stepped into the elevator, clocking off for the evening only after seeing her to

Leo's premises safely. As always, she appreciated his continued hard work. She rode up in silence, aware she had a cheesy grin on her face, but didn't care. Life was good, and Cassie felt like nothing could get in her way.

That was until she rounded the corner and heard giggling coming from Leo's office. It wasn't the friendly sort, or the polite. It was lust-filled and teasing, the sort a girl threw at the man of her dreams over candlelight and wine. Her stomach dropped, but Cassie had to see for herself what was going on inside before she could react. *You're such a fool. Of course you wouldn't be enough for him. You were never enough before, why did you think things would change now?* Her brain teased and tormented her relentlessly, and Cassie had to fight the urge to scream or puke, or both. She reached out to grab the handle and noticed the door was open just an inch, so she peered inside.

"Come on, Leo. She'll never have to know. I've told you before, I'm very discreet..." Suzie was inside, perching against Leo's desk, while he sat in his huge leather chair across from her. Cassie couldn't tell whether she thought he was enjoying her advances or not. His face was icy but his eyes seemed to be burning into her with a regard that made Cassie's blood boil.

"Suzanne, I have told you repeatedly not to harass me. Your behavior is trashy, to say the least." Cassie felt relief tinge the edges of her anger, and hoped with all her heart he was being sincere. "I told Brian to get you in check, and he's clearly failed. You're fired with immediate effect. Get your things and go."

"I'll tell everyone you fucked me anyway. Your precious girlfriend will leave you in a heartbeat, and then I'll sue for sexual harassment. I'll say I was too intimidated to say no," Suzie bit back, clearly disgruntled that he'd refused her offer.

"You can say what you want. I have all our conversations on tape to prove exactly the opposite. We're done here, you can leave." Leo's tone was vicious and stern. He'd never spoken to Cassie that way, and she hoped he'd never need to. She'd always known how scary he could be, but the man sitting behind that desk was something else entirely. His features and tone were calculated and malicious enough to send shivers down her spine, and she wasn't the one he'd said it to. Mr. Solomon was clearly in the room, not her Leo, and part of her actually felt bad for Suzie. But then again, maybe not.

Cassie opened the door fully and walked in with a scowl. "Are you gonna get out, or am I gonna have to throw you out?" Suzie seemed startled by her entrance, whereas Leo didn't appear fazed, and she had to wonder if he'd noticed her there already. She wasn't completely sure of his innocence, but for now all she cared about was taking out the trash.

Leo pressed a button on the intercom, calling to his cousin, and Brian came rushing in. He took Suzie by the elbow, and didn't say a word as he frog-marched her out the office. Cassie was glad to watch her leave. She just hoped Brian wasn't planning on coming back until she'd completely left the premises, and for good this time.

Cassie was furious, and didn't delay in making it known to her beau. Leo sat and took every vicious word she spat without retaliating, and when she finally started to calm down, he stood, walked around the desk, and wrapped her in his arms.

"I'm so sorry, love," he whispered, running his hands up and down her back. "I promise you I didn't do anything with her. She's been stalking me and trying to get close, but I only learned the full extent of it recently. It seems she's become a little too obsessed, and I'm sorry you had to hear her saying those vile things, but you know they aren't true. You're my one and only, Cassie. Us against the world, remember?"

"Yeah, I remember. It's just hard to believe it sometimes. I'm sorry," she replied, leaning into him. "What's she been doing, then?"

"It started with flirting and harmless eyelash fluttering, but then I noticed she'd dyed her hair and styled it to look like yours." Cassie looked up at him in surprise. She hadn't even noticed, but now she thought about it, Suzie had gone from being a dye-job blonde to a brunette seemingly overnight. "She started to dress like you and listen to the same music. Even when she started trying to talk to me about plays and the theater it didn't click. I'm not sure she was even aware of what she was doing, but it appears she thought that if she could look and act like you, I might fall for her."

"Whoa, crazy bitch," Cassie murmured. It all fell into place. There had been a handful of conversations during her visits when Suzie had asked her about herself and her hobbies, and Cassie had been polite and chatted back with her. She'd seemed perfectly harmless to her at the time, but she guessed that was exactly the point. Suzie had *seemed* harmless, when in fact she was an overdramatic lunatic who could've potentially driven a wedge between her and Leo forever.

Leo groaned when she pulled away, but Cassie needed some space. Just a minute so she could fully calm her fraught mind. She used the bathroom and reapplied her makeup to hide her panda eyes, all the while deep in thought. When her cell chimed to tell her she had a text, she jumped in surprise, but her anger soon returned when she saw what was written there.

**Suzie: So, did he tell you a bunch of lies to hide the fact he's been fucking me every day for the past few weeks? Don't trust a word your player of a boyfriend says. He told me he loved me. He made me promises he didn't keep. How long until he breaks your heart too? Luckily, I'm not upset, I'm angry. I just keyed his precious car, what do think he's gonna say about that?**

Cassie flung her cell back in her bag. She was ready to go out there guns blazing, but knew Leo wouldn't let her if she told him about the text. She decided against letting him know that she'd even gotten the message. She wanted to deal with that stupid girl herself.

"I'm going down to get a drink," she told him when she came out of his private bathroom a few minutes later. "You don't need to come with me. In fact, I could do with a few minutes to myself."

Leo looked hurt, but he nodded in understanding. She'd believed him when he said nothing had happened with Suzie, but still felt like the whole thing had put some distance between them. Cassie wanted to go back to how she'd felt while travelling up in the elevator, and forced herself to push her anger aside. Rather than hash it out yet, she just gave Leo a chaste kiss and left him to it while she headed down to take care of their little stalker issue once and for all.

She pushed open the back entrance door and stepped out into the cool night air. Cassie looked around but couldn't see any sign of Suzie, so she grabbed the cell from her purse and called up the contacts list. Then, a soft whimpering caught her attention, and she followed the sound around one of the trucks, where she found Suzie lying face-down on the ground. Cassie leaned over to check her, but could already see blood trickling down her face from a wound on her head, as though she'd been knocked out.

She stood and turned to run back inside when she collided with a wall of a man who had seemingly been hiding in the shadows beside Suzie's unconscious body. "Please, take my bag, you can keep all the money inside. Just don't hurt me," she pleaded. Rather than convince him to snatch her purse and go, her appeal earned her a deep laugh in response.

"I don't want your money, Cassie." Her blood turned cold, and she peered up at the man standing before her in the darkness. She couldn't see his face, but she knew right away who he was. Her blood turned to ice as the hoarse voice sparked fearful memories that quickly came rushing back. She wanted to run, but was halted by the sound of the man's voice and the overwhelming presence he had over her.

"GG? Is it really you?" she asked, stepping over Suzie's outstretched legs as she stumbled further into the loading bay. "What are you doing here?" Cassie was shaking. This was far from the reunion she'd always hoped they might have.

"Don't call me that anymore. I'm certainly no Gentle Giant. In fact, I'm far from the man you once thought you knew. And all of that's thanks to you, though, isn't it? In your bid for freedom you threw me to the wolves, Cassie, and now you're gonna pay for what you've done." His voice was bitter and cruel, Grayson's words callously tormenting her in a way he'd never done in all their time together in Mexico. His icy demeanor made her crumble, and she shook her head. As much as she hadn't wanted to turn him over to the police along with the rest of Victor's crew, his arrest had been unavoidable, and she'd done her fair share of beating herself up about it since that day.

Realizing her cell was still in her hand, Cassie looked down at it, hoping she might have enough time to press the alarm that'd alert Roger she was in danger. "Don't even think about it," Grayson said, stepping closer to her.

Cassie didn't listen. She unlocked the screen with a tap of her finger and hit the app that would send her protector an alert and their location. Cassie managed it just in time before Grayson reached her and threw the phone from her hand. She knew it had to have smashed on the hard ground, but hoped with all her heart that the cavalry would arrive regardless.

Grayson stepped closer still, pinning her to the truck behind, and a flicker of light illuminated his face. He'd aged a lot more since she'd last seen him. He had even lost the soft, caring look he'd always had about him where she was concerned, and all that was left was an empty, heartless shell. He'd once treated her like a sister and made her feel safe and protected with him, but the man standing before her seemed adrift. Grayson was nothing but a thug, and he was right, she was to blame.

He grinned maliciously and reached behind him, pulling a ringing cell phone from his back pocket, which he seemed to take great delight in showing to her. When the screen lit up, she blinked and focused. It took her a second to figure out what she was reading, and she sobbed when she realized what it must mean.

### Alarm triggered. Location stored and ready for GPS navigation.

Grayson had Roger's phone, which meant he'd also paid her bodyguard a visit, and she let out a cry for her dear friend's safety.

"What've you done, GG?" she asked. "Where's Roger?"

"I knew you'd have a way to contact him, so I went to his apartment and made sure he wouldn't be able to respond to your alarm when you triggered it. In fact, he won't be doing much of anything anymore," he told her with a sneer. "You've become so predictable, Cassie. You played right into my hands."

Cassie felt like she might be sick. Grayson hadn't said it specifically, but he'd hinted that Roger was either in a bad way or dead. Her Gentle Giant was truly gone, and she tried to fight his hold over her, but it was no use. Grayson was twice the size he used to be, and overpowered her easily. He pinned her to the truck by her shoulders and stared her down.

"Okay, okay," she conceded. In a moment of clarity, Cassie decided against fighting him. She knew she had to keep him talking in the hope someone would either stumble onto them or Leo would come looking. It was her only choice. "And what about her?" she eventually asked, nodding over to where Suzie still lay unconscious.

"I befriended her a while back, showed her a good time. She was incredibly forthcoming with information about the new boss and his girlfriend. I'd barely even got my dick wet before she was spilling the beans about you and your new life here in London," he scoffed. "Oh how she went on and on about the gorgeous Mr. Solomon and how she wanted to be just like you. Deranged skank thought she could take your place, so I spurred her on. I knew I couldn't get near you with Roger and Leo around, so I watched and waited. Bided my time. You made sure they kept you close, made sure you were safe."

"Like you used to," she tried, but Grayson's scowl told her he wasn't ready to reminisce about the past yet.

"I told Suzie before her shift tonight that she should try one last time to proposition Leo, that he'd kept her waiting long enough. I wanted to really rile him up, hopefully enough so that he'd forget all about taking proper precautions for your safety. I intercepted your precious Roger on his way home and took care of business the only way us thug types know how, and then I waited." He grinned, and the sight of his hateful smile made Cassie's blood run cold. "After that, it was a case of me sitting and waiting for the opportunity to get you down here. I figured you'd be furious that she'd dared try it on with him, and when she came storming out saying you'd thrown her out of his office, I knew exactly what to do."

"So you knocked her out and texted me on her phone so I'd come after her?" Grayson nodded. "And what now?"

"Now?" His cruel tone was back. "Now you pay for everything you've done, *Mrs. Sanchez.*" She shuddered at the name, and shook her head. This couldn't be happening, not after all this time. Cassie had been assured that the cartel couldn't travel into the UK, nor would they be able to find her if they did. She'd legally changed her name, and her business was registered to holding companies, so she was as untraceable as she could be. Leo hadn't hidden his identity like she had, but he had people working for him both here and in the States that took care of his protection and would know if anyone was snooping around in his business. Grayson had clearly been lurking in the shadows for weeks, if not months, and she knew for sure now that he meant everything he'd said. He was the polar opposite to the man she'd left behind almost two years previously and was clearly there to make her pay.

Her adrenaline kicked in, and Cassie used every ounce of strength she had to punch Grayson in the jaw. He groaned in shock, rather than pain, but she used his moment of disbelief to send a knee into his groin and then ran as fast as she could back toward the doorway.

Just a few feet from the entrance, she was tackled to the ground with such force she was winded instantly. All she could think about was the baby. Cassie knew that if she kept fighting him, she'd lose it, so she went limp in his hold in defeat.

It didn't stop Grayson mocking her. "We're doing this the hard way, huh?" he asked rhetorically, ignoring when she shook her head pleadingly. He then pulled a syringe from his jacket pocket and stuck it straight into her neck. Within seconds, Cassie was floating away. The last thing she felt was her body being lifted into Grayson's huge hold as he carried her off into the darkness, but she had no way of fighting him.

\*\*\*

"Where the hell is she?" Leo barked at Brian, staring him down angrily. "I told you to keep an eye on her!"

"You said she was going to the bar, so I went there first. She wasn't there and nobody had seen her either. After searching for a while I came straight to you, Leo. No one knows where Cassie is."

"Keep looking," Leo growled. He slumped in his chair and held his head in his hands. Her cell phone was off, Roger wasn't answering, and Siobhan hadn't heard from her. Leo was going out of his mind with worry. She never took off like this. Cassie's own fear of something bad catching up with her always made sure he could contact her or get eyes on her whenever he needed to. He'd even been known to have her followed on many an occasion thanks to his paranoia for her safety, but had never once lost her. He failed to comprehend how she'd gone missing from his casino without anyone knowing. She had to be somewhere.

Leo knew invading her privacy wasn't right, but he hadn't been able to relinquish all his bad habits the past year, and for his own sanity he had been keeping tabs on Cassie wherever she went. He'd known when she'd gone out to buy the pregnancy test, and he'd guessed the news when she'd come to see him looking pale and terrified an hour later. His surveillance made it almost impossible for her to surprise him, but he was happy to forgo the excitement if it meant he felt secure. Having lost her to Victor was soul destroying, and he'd done everything in his power since getting her back to make sure it didn't happen again. Short of implanting a microchip into her body, Leo would do whatever it took to make sure Cassie was safe. He'd never rest unless he knew where she was at all times, even if that made him much more of a crazy stalker than Suzie had ever been.

He lost all track of time as he sat there and wallowed in his worry, but came around quickly when the door to his office flung open and Brian came inside. He was carrying a dark-haired woman in his arms. She was limp and barely moving, but Leo knew right away it wasn't Cassie.

"I found her out by one of the trucks. She used her phone to text Cassie not long after we kicked her out. That much I could see. There's no sign of her out there, but I did find this." Brian put Suzie down on the couch and reached into his pocket. He pulled out Cassie's broken cell and handed it to his cousin with a sour look on his face.

Deadly rage boiled inside of Leo. He flew over to where Suzie was still lying unconscious on the couch and shook her awake, not caring about any injuries. When her eyes opened, he bombarded her with questions and demands. He couldn't stop until he knew what'd happened, and the only person with any answers was sitting before him in stunned silence. Suzie seemed terrified of him, but Leo was glad. Maybe she'd think twice before messing with him or Cassie again; but before he could address any of that, he had to get his answers.

"Get what you can out of her, I'm trying Roger again," Leo told his cousin, who nodded and kneeled before Suzie with a kind smile. While Leo paced the room, he could hear Brian talking to her softly, apparently taking the gentler approach, and it seemed to be working. After getting nothing but endless ringing from Roger's number, Leo stopped his prowling and listened to his former employee as she began opening up about her foolish actions at long last.

"This guy. Him and me were fooling around and he made me feel good—special. He told me I was more than good enough for Leo and that I should make my move tonight, so I did. After everything kicked off here, I called him and begged him to pick me up. When I went outside to meet him and told him what'd happened, I expected him to hug me and tell me it was okay. Instead, he punched me straight in the temple," Suzie told Brian between sobs. "I fell down and he punched me again. I've never seen someone be so violent for no reason before," she explained. Tears fell from her eyes, and while Brian was still being attentive, Leo's heart was sinking.

"What was his name?" he asked, his voice grim.

"He said his name was Joaquin," she replied, sniffing and wiping her eyes on a tissue. "Joaquin Grayson."

Leo fell to the ground. His knees hit the floor hard and he doubled over, grabbing his hair roughly in his hands while tears forced their way out of him. He howled as he rocked and curled into as tight a ball as he could, desperately trying to forget the words that had just been said.

After what felt like forever, Leo unfurled his weak body and stumbled back over to his chair. He retrieved his cell and sent a text to Roger's phone. He knew Grayson must have it. There was no way he could have Cassie and not have taken out her bodyguard first.

*Leo: I know you have her. Bring her back and I'll let you walk away, name your price and I'll pay it. Please, Grayson. Don't let them ruin her all over again.*

# *Chapter Eighteen*

"Aww, how sweet. Your boyfriend thinks he can bribe me into taking you back." Grayson's voice filtered through what'd been deafening silence until then, and Cassie started to wake from whatever sedative he'd injected into her. As her eyes fluttered open, she took in the room around her. Grayson was sat in an armchair at one end of the small space, while she was lying on a bed on the opposite side. Cassie guessed it must be some kind of old motel or perhaps a disused hospital, and she contemplated screaming for help, but knew he wouldn't be foolish enough to take her somewhere full of other patrons. Her hands were bound above her head tightly, and even though she and Leo had toyed with the roleplay, it made her feel like a prisoner again, and she hated it.

"Please, GG. Please let me go. What do you even want with me?" she pleaded, needing to know why he'd come all the way from Mexico to track her down.

"It's not me who wants you," he said, standing

and going over to the window to peek out the edge of the curtain. "Did you really think you could murder Victor, put us all away, and then run off with his money? Are you that foolish you believed no one would come after you?" He was the same icy, hard-faced, Grayson she'd spoken with in the alley. Cassie had to wonder if what he'd said was true, and her Gentle Giant really had gone. "I'm taking you back to Mexico, where you're going to settle your debt to the cartel. They're ready to watch you pay for everything you did in blood, sweat, tears, and with that precious cunt Victor held so dear."

"No! Grayson, please," she cried. Going back to that hellhole was a fate worse than death, and Cassie felt as if she was going to throw up. She fought against her restraints, thinking she'd rather fight and risk it all than go back there. She'd barely made it out in one piece the last time she'd been dragged there to be Victor's whore. "I'll give you back every penny. The court gave it to me, I didn't steal it. I'll give it all back and run off properly this time. I'll stay hidden."

"Regardless of the details, that money was never yours, and you do not just get off with killing Victor. Everything crumbled after you murdered him, and you landed the rest of us in prison. Luckily, Eduardo had some sway even from across the border, but we've all had to sacrifice our humanity in order to survive. Now that he's got all his crew back, and he's got the cartel running at full power, he's finally ready to make you pay."

Cassie broke down in tears. She tugged at the

bindings on her wrists and writhed on the bed, desperate to try and escape, but it was no use. Grayson watched her struggle without even a hint of compassion on his face. It didn't matter to him how she was hurting, or that she was terrified. He didn't even care that she was going back there to die or be swallowed up by Eduardo and his disgusting pimps. He simply didn't care. She could see in his blank stare that his soul was lost. The part of him she'd once loved and had missed so terribly was long gone.

When she'd calmed down a little, Cassie stopped struggling against the ropes and stared back up at him.

"All that time you were caring for me, teaching me how to handle Victor's moods, and how to survive in that god-awful place. And now you're just gonna take me back there to be raped and whored out to Eduardo and his customers? I won't go without a fight, and you can guess again if you think I'll just let you walk me through airport security and onto a plane. I'll scream and shout until my dying breath if it means I don't have to go back there," she said, spitting as much venom his way as she could muster.

Quick as a flash, Grayson was on top of her on the bed. He pinned her down and effortlessly forced open her legs, which he slid between. Cassie groaned in disgust at both how easily he could overpower her, and that he would even contemplate doing so. With a look of sick satisfaction, Grayson stared into her eyes from mere inches away. She squirmed against him, but he just pressed into her harder and she shuddered.

"It's all in the detail, Cassie. We've been planning this for a long time, believe me," he said, his voice almost a whisper. "I've got a private jet in a small airfield just a few miles away. Inside that jet is a compartment, completely invisible from the outside. It's tight, smaller than a coffin—and completely soundproofed. You could scream and shout to your heart's content, but you'd do nothing more than use up precious oxygen."

"Who the hell are you?" Cassie whimpered. Her body and mind were in so much pain that she could feel herself growing desperate. The Grayson she'd once known had been kind and gentle. He'd been loyal to Victor, but he'd also loved her like a brother. That man had taken such good care of her that Cassie's isolation atop Victor's ivory tower had almost been bearable.

"I'm a heartless, ruthless gangster now. I fuck and beat whores who step out of line, and I don't care about anyone other than myself. Isn't that who you thought I should've been all along? You were always so surprised to find such a nice guy like me in Victor's employment. Well now you can see what two years of fighting for your life every day does to a man. Prison ruined me. You wanna talk about rape? You don't even know what I went through because of you and Leo."

Cassie's heart broke for him, and she went limp in his hold. Grayson truly had been beaten in many ways, and she knew she had to take some blame for where his life had taken him.

"I'm so sorry. I had no control over your trial. I

barely had any say when it came to my own. I have no excuse, and I know you want to punish me for it, but please remember how we grew close and how you once cared so deeply for my safety. All of that can't mean nothing now that you've been to hell and back?"

Grayson started laughing. It was an evil, cruel laugh, and it gave her chills.

"That's exactly what you mean—nothing! You women, all the fucking same. I tell you a sob story and you go all soft, feel sorry for me, and even apologize for what happened. I've tied you up and am dragging you halfway across the world against your will, and you're saying sorry to me?" he roared, laughing again. "Are you forgetting what's gonna happen to you when we get to Mexico? Eduardo is finally getting his hands on the prize Victor kept hidden away. He'll break every bit of free will you think you have, and before you know it he'll own you in a way you never even thought possible. Eduardo will have his fun, and then when he's had enough, he'll throw you to the wolves. After we've all had a piece of you, it'll be straight to work under one of his pimps, and believe me when I say you're gonna be a bestseller. The one who got away. The pale-skinned prized possession of our former overlord…"

Grayson pressed his hips against her thigh, giving her a nudge with the hard-on she couldn't quite believe he could have given the situation. She cried out in panic. "I've seen what's under here, don't forget," he groaned as he ran his hands over Cassie's breasts, cupping each one roughly. He seemed to revel in her disgust of his heavy-handed touch.

Cassie saw red, and figured it was her turn to say her piece.

"All that time you were being a good little minion in the hope that Victor might shove his cock in you, or at least let you have a taste of it. And now, because you never got to be his bitch, you think by having me it'll make you feel better?" Cassie let her anger rule her for a moment in a bid to hurt him too. "Let's go then, GG. If you think you've got the balls, I'll show you how a real woman fucks." She arched her back, grinding against him, and grinned when she saw him recoil.

Cassie took the slap Grayson swung against her cheek without any complaints, and then it was her turn to laugh, even though things were far from funny. Grayson climbed off her in a heartbeat, stalking the length of the small room. He was trembling with rage, and as much as it scared her, Cassie was glad she'd gotten him good and riled up. Sick satisfaction bloomed within, and she realized he wasn't the only one who'd changed.

"Do you have any idea the shit I had to do to keep you safe back then?" he bellowed after a few minutes of pacing. "Who was the one guarding your bedroom door when Eduardo decided he'd done waiting for his turn with you? Me! I had to take a beating off him and shove my gun in his face before he'd finally leave, and all because you'd given him such a good fucking show the night before."

Cassie knew exactly what night he was talking about—the time Victor had gotten drunk and paraded her around like his prized pony at the club. She knew she'd caught Eduardo's eye, but had no idea he'd been so determined to have a piece of her, regardless of Victor's order that she was off-limits. "And how about this little nugget? Why do you think I had to prepare all your meals?" Cassie shook her head, too shocked to even fathom an answer. "After Lolita's little tantrum the day of Luis's funeral, she tried to poison your food. She wasn't the only one either, and so I got the job of hand preparing your food for you," he spat, and began pacing again. "I even had to save you from Victor on occasion. There were nights when he was in destructive, vicious moods, and I kept him away on purpose. I knew you'd be the one paying for his fury, so I did whatever I had to do to protect you from his wrath. How can you still be so naïve to what was happening all around you back there?" Grayson huffed as he slumped down into the chair at the other side of the room again.

A few dreadful minutes of silence passed between them, and Cassie heaved a deep sigh.

"I'm pregnant, GG," she told him. "We've finally moved on and are making something of our lives. Please don't take this away from me."

Grayson said nothing. He simply stared at the ground for a long time, and Cassie let her last couple of sentences hang in the air between them.

Deep down, she knew some remnant of her old friend had to still be in there, even if it was just a tiny bit. He wouldn't have told her all of that if he didn't want her to know how much he'd cared back in Mexico, and she hoped the cold version she'd witnessed was all just a front he'd been forced to put up since they'd last seen each other.

Cassie had hated being locked away in that bedroom of Victor's mansion day after day, but now, the alternative petrified her. If Eduardo had gotten inside and forced himself on her, Victor would've then seen her as tainted, and he would've discarded her. Also, if Victor had ever hurt her badly in a moment of rage, his guilt would've consumed him, and she'd have been tossed aside just the same. Her safety had been an intricate game played out on a knife's edge, and she'd never realized just how close she'd been to falling. Grayson had saved her all of those times, and probably more, and she had to believe he'd do the same for her now.

After a long wait, he stood and stalked into the bathroom without so much as a backward glance at her. Cassie watched as he splashed his face with water and washed his hands methodically, as though still lost in thought. "Grayson?" she called out softly, hoping he might be ready to talk.

"Don't, Cassie." His voice was barely even a whisper.

"Fuck you. I'm not gonna make this any easier on you. I want you to look me in the eyes when you seal my fate, and the fate of my child. Joaquin Grayson, are you listening to me?" she bellowed, using every bit of strength and nerve she had left to scream as loud as she could for the world to hear. Cassie knew she had to get through to him, before it was too late.

He stormed out of the bathroom toward her, then

turned and punched three holes into the chipped and faded door. His mighty fists flew and Cassie flinched on every impact. Only when he was bloody and panting did he stop. Grayson turned back and peered down at her, his gaze softer but still incredibly distant. He didn't say a word. After a few seconds, he stalked back into the bathroom and grabbed at the roll of toilet paper to dab at his cuts.

"Yeah, I fucking hear you," he said, clenching and unclenching his fists while clearing up the blood. "Either you're telling me lies, or else you've got Leonardo Solomon's baby in there." He pointed at her stomach. "Maybe Eduardo won't be so hard on you after all, because once he gets his hands on that little bastard, it'll be the ultimate vengeance for what the pair of you did to Victor. He'll probably raise the child as his own, and you'll never get near it again. Either that, or he'll cut his losses and drag you down the clinic to get rid of it," he told Cassie with a sneer, and she felt her heart breaking at his awful words.

She couldn't believe he was saying such vile things to her, and she turned her face away. Cassie could no longer bring herself to even look at him. Her Gentle Giant was so lost there had to be nothing of him left, and she despised the monster standing a few feet away. "I don't even know you anymore…"

He didn't so much as groan in response.

"I need some air. Stay put, Mrs. Sanchez. Our ride will be here in a few hours." Grayson grabbed his jacket and pulled a cigarette from one of the pockets before heading outside, where she could hear him lighting up.

Cassie waited until she heard his footsteps in the distance before she began pulling and twisting her hands again in an attempt to pry them loose from the ropes he'd bound her with, but it was no use. Eventually, she decided to try breaking the wood of the old bed instead, and used her entire body weight to push against the headboard. It creaked and eventually broke apart after a few exhausting pulls, and she fell back onto the sheet, panting. Cassie jumped up and looked around, and she found Roger's phone lying on the small table beside the armchair Grayson had been sitting in when she'd woken up.

Even with her hands still tied, she grabbed it and dialed Leo's cell, hoping to God he'd answer...

"Listen to me, you asshole. You lay one finger on her and—"

"Leo, you have to find me," she cut in, desperate to say what she needed to in time. "Can you track Roger's phone?"

"No, I already tried, love. Please tell me you're okay? I'm going out of my mind here," he begged, and Cassie had to admit he sounded terrible. It was good to hear his voice, but she knew they had to hurry.

"I'm as okay as I can be, but I only have a minute before Grayson comes back. He's not the same guy he was, Leo, not by a long shot. He says he's gonna take me to Mexico where Eduardo will turn me into a whore so I can pay my debt to the cartel. God, Leo. I couldn't bear it." She knew she was rambling so forced herself to focus. "I don't know where I am. He drugged me and I woke up here. It looks like an old motel or hospital, and I can't hear any other people here so I think it must be abandoned. He said there's a plane waiting to take us away, but in a private airfield."

"Okay, Jellybean. I'm going to find you. I will not let that plane take off with you inside, do you hear me?" Leo's voice was powerful and determined, and she believed him. "I'm coming for you, Cassie. Please stay strong."

Grayson stepped inside and glowered at her from the doorway. Cassie let out a shriek of surprise and threw the handset right at his head. When he reached up to rub the swollen bump she'd left there, Cassie tried to make a run for it, but Grayson was too fast.

"You think you can run from me? You think I'd just let you walk outta here? Not a fucking chance," he growled, slapping her across the cheek before throwing her back down on the bed. Cassie sobbed and screamed, calling out Leo's name while Grayson retied her bonds. "It's about time you shut the hell up." When he was done, Grayson stuffed her mouth with a rag from his pocket.

Cassie could hear Leo's anxious, angry cries from the still-connected call, and once she was secure, Grayson retrieved the cell from the hard floor. He held it to his ear and grinned down at her. "I hope you just said your goodbyes, 'cause that's the last time you'll ever hear her voice."

He hung up before Leo could answer, and then smashed the phone to pieces beneath his boot.

# *Chapter Nineteen*

Leo screamed insults and murderous promises into his handset, knowing full well that Grayson had hung up already so wasn't hearing them, but he couldn't stop it. His brain had turned to mush, and he slumped back in his chair, rubbing his tired eyes. He wanted to tear that guy apart, rip him to shreds, and then piss on his corpse before torching it. Nothing would be left to identify him once he was done. Having been forced to listen in as Grayson hurt Cassie caused all kinds of old wounds to open up in him again, and he was quickly dragged under by the demons of his wretched past. He'd brought all of this upon her, and now once again Cassie was in the clutches of a monster.

His cousin came into the office, took one look at Leo, and headed straight for the coffee machine. Brian handed him a double espresso, and Leo took it with a grateful half-smile. He couldn't focus on anything, but knew they needed to make a plan, and fast. He had to get her away from that vile man as soon as possible, no matter what it took.

Leo then told his cousin about the call he'd just taken.

"She's terrified, Bri. I could hear him slapping her around." His voice faltered, and Leo shook away the tears. He focused on the coffee cup, and took a long sip while he steadied his nerves. "She said they're in a motel or hospital, but it seems either empty or abandoned. And she said there's a plane on a private airfield waiting to take them to Mexico. We cannot let him drag her back to that godforsaken place."

"No way." Brian grabbed one of the laptops from Leo's desk. "I'll find it. One way or another, I'll track him down, Leo."

He believed him, but still grabbed the mouse on his desk and started searching for clues alongside his trusty sidekick. Two hands were definitely better than one in this scenario, and it felt good to finally have a lead to go off.

\*\*\*

Cassie stirred, forcing herself to wake up. She knew she hadn't been asleep long, and had drifted off out of exhaustion rather than comfort, but she didn't want to waste any time sleeping that she could be using to try and get away.

It took her a minute to realize her hands were no longer tied, and that the rag had been removed from her mouth. However, it was the sound and feeling of soft breath brushing against at her ear and a thunderous heart beating beneath her that pulled her from her slumber. They weren't Leo's breaths, and she started, staring at the man who had his thickly muscled arms wrapped around her tiny body. Grayson peered back at her, and for a reason she couldn't fathom, his expression was warm and soft. Her Gentle Giant had seemingly returned, but for how long, she couldn't be sure. Cassie looked into his eyes, and sobbed when she saw the pain in them.

"I'm sorry I hurt you," he whispered, pulling her back into him, and Cassie let him. She laid her head down to rest back on Grayson's chest, staring across at the battered bathroom door. She wanted to relax, to trust and hope that the old him would come through for her in the end, but she couldn't be sure. She'd seen a side to him that terrified her, and could tell one more wrong word might bring that side of him out in a heartbeat.

"Please, GG. I can't go back there. I barely survived last time." She could feel herself trembling. Grayson turned onto his side and held her closer, wrapping both arms around Cassie's back while pressing her head against his chest.

"Ssshh. I just want to enjoy this without you ruining it," he said, and she nodded. Cassie finally understood how broken and damaged her old friend had become after everything he'd been through as well. She'd underestimated how badly Leo had been affected when Victor had taken her, and knew now that she'd done the same with Grayson. She waited a long while, but it eventually became too hard to stay quiet. Cassie needed answers.

"Tell me about it, GG. Make me understand," she said against him, and he flinched. Grayson took a few deep breaths, as though steadying himself, and when he finally spoke, his voice was hardly more than a quiet rumble against her ear.

"Our crew didn't even get a proper trial, we were just processed and thrown in prison. Even with Eduardo's sway with some of the gangs, we were still picked off by the strongest or most dangerous inmates in the place. There were some with allegiances to the cartel, and they were offered incentives to keep us safe. I was given to a predator called Neo—a fucking gift-wrapped bribe from my gracious new leader." Grayson tensed up, and Cassie instinctively raised a hand to comfort him, deciding on giving him just a gentle stroke on his arm. "After I was broken in, it was simply a case of enduring it until I got out. I was Neo's bitch for almost two years, but in some ways I got off easy. A couple of the guys were beaten and gang raped repeatedly, and another was murdered in his bed."

Cassie shuddered. She tried to force the imagery away, but her imagination kept conjuring up all kinds of awful visions, and she wanted to cry for him—for all of them. "The entire experience left me hating everything and everyone. I lashed out, the desire in me to make people pay for my pain was too strong to deny. The voices inside my head screamed for blood, and I spilled it from whomever Eduardo told me to." His voice had turned wistful, as if he were no longer there with her but lost in his memories, and Cassie knew he had to be fighting no end of demons within if that was the life he'd been forced to live after she'd left him behind.

"I don't know what to say, GG. I'm sorry you ended up there, and that you were treated so badly.

Leo won't talk about his time in prison, but I know it had to have been awful too," she replied, and her heart was aching just thinking about him and of how broken her man must be right now.

"Oh, don't worry about Leo," Grayson replied with a snide edge to his tone. "He set himself up pretty good."

"Yeah, he said he used his money to buy himself an easy time," she agreed, but Grayson laughed gruffly, and Cassie tensed. The story had seemed hard to believe, but his reaction said it all. Leo had clearly lied to stop her from worrying.

"No, Cassie. He used his fists—or anything else he had to hand—to beat or murder the other guys so he could reach the top. The guards were in his pocket out of fear, and probably the odd bribe, but he most certainly wasn't anyone's bitch during his time inside. Your precious Leonardo Solomon undoubtedly has his demons after the things he did in there, but not because he was the victim. He was the predator."

She didn't reply. She couldn't. As much as she hated the idea of him acting out like that, she'd seen Leo crumble under the weight of his burdens, and knew he'd never chosen to become that guy. He'd been as forced as Grayson had, so she refused to let him portray Leo as a monster. "A couple of my guys got transferred to his prison, and they didn't even last a day. You're man had them strung up and butchered like cattle." She wanted to reply with a vicious comment about how they'd probably deserved it, but bit her tongue. Cassie needed to keep the softer and gentler Grayson around for as long as possible, so stayed quiet.

"Can I please use the bathroom?" she asked, pulling away slightly, and was glad when he let go. He didn't say a word, but she saw him sit up and watch her as she pushed open the splintered door. Cassie knew without him having to say so that she had to leave it open, and so she did her business without commenting or even bothering about how Grayson was watching. It was their old routine all over again, and she found it strange how quickly she could settle into those ways.

If she made it back to Mexico, she knew things would be vastly different with Eduardo as her captor, though. He wouldn't bother to keep her protected the way Victor had. He wouldn't care for or love her the way her former husband had, and he certainly wouldn't stop the others from having a piece of his predecessor's pie.

"Do you still draw?" Grayson asked when she climbed back onto the bed and into his arms. She should hate him, but their embrace brought her comfort, and Cassie had to admit, she could use all of the affection she could get.

"Yeah. I make most of my sets and costumes now. I employed an apprentice to help as well, but it's what I love. Well…loved." Grayson ignored her comment, and she jumped when she felt his hand press down gently on her stomach.

"How far gone are you?"

"Eleven weeks, or there about. I have my first scan booked for next week—had," she told him, correcting herself again, and she pushed his hand away in a huff. He didn't get to touch her there and pretend as if he cared, not when he was the one dragging her away to endure certain misery and agony at Eduardo's vile hands.

Cassie pulled out of his hold and sat up, crossing her legs beneath her and resting her elbows on her knees. She stared at the door, knowing she was closer to it than Grayson was, but that it'd still be foolish to try and run. She wasn't strong enough to beat him, or take another heavy-handed tackle, so she just sat there and stared, thinking how near and yet so far her freedom was. "How long do we have?"

"I haven't made the call yet, but when I do, it'll be three hours, give or take."

"Why haven't you called them?" Hope fluttered in her chest. "Why can't you just say you never found me? Leo and I can take off and we'll disappear properly this time. Can't you do one last thing to keep me safe, GG? Can you be the friend I know you are?" She looked over her shoulder at him, pleading with him to show her some mercy. "You were like a brother to me. You didn't let them rape or hurt me before, why can't you be that man now? Be my Gentle Giant..."

Grayson said nothing, but he didn't get angry either, and Cassie hoped her heartfelt words had sunk in. He climbed up off the bed, grabbed his duffel bag, and then threw her a cereal bar to eat, which Cassie devoured in three bites. Her heart was pounding in her chest, but all she could do was stare as he rifled through the huge bag with a thoughtful look. Part of her wondered if he was even searching for an item in particular or if he simply needed to do something to keep his hands busy, but she didn't want to ask and bring him out of his thoughts.

When he stilled and pulled his hand free, Cassie watched in horror as he took out a small firearm and checked that it was fully loaded. She paled as Grayson then screwed a suppressor onto the end of the weapon, and pulled out a cell phone.

She cried out and lunged forward, desperate to stop him from making the call. Cassie fell off the end of the bed onto her knees, and when she looked up, Grayson had the gun pointed right at her head. She crumbled before him, trembling and sobbing, while the lethal end of the weapon pressed harder into her temple.

"Package ready for extraction," he said to whomever was on the other end of the line. "What's your ETA? Very well," he added before ending the call and crushing the cell beneath his boot like he had Roger's handset.

Cassie howled in her misery, clutching at her ribs to try and ease the ache in her chest as the realization dawned on her that this was really happening. No matter how hard she'd tried to get through to him, Grayson was taking her back to Mexico. There, she knew she'd pay dearly for what she'd done to Victor and to the cartel. Her life was over, and there seemed nothing she could do about it. "Look at me, Cassie," she heard him demand, but she shook her head.

"How could you?" she sobbed into her hands. "How could you do this to me, to my baby?"

"LOOK AT ME!" Grayson bellowed, and the sound reverberated around her so hard Cassie was sure she felt the floorboards shake beneath her knees. She finally did as he'd ordered, and looked up into the face of the most broken man she'd ever seen in her life. He lifted the gun away from her temple and spun it in his hand, offering her the handle without a word. She took it, but didn't understand what on earth he was doing.

Grayson then fell to his knees and took her face in his hands. He stroked her cheeks gently and kissed her in such a tender way tears sprung from her eyes again. "I love you, Cassie, and I'm sorry. Go and live your life, but you promise me you'll run away and never look back. Promise me now," he said, and the conviction in his tone made her believe he was telling the truth.

"Come with us, GG. We'll all go together, keep each other safe?" she tried, and her offer made him smile broadly at her. Grayson shook his head and kissed her again.

"It means the world to me that you'd even suggest it after everything I've done, but it has to be this way. They'll think you managed to somehow get the gun from me and ran, and this'll be a clear message to let them know you won't let yourself be found again. Eduardo will have to give up looking for you, and you and Leo will be safe with that precious little baby of yours." Grayson grabbed her hand with the weapon in and yanked it toward him, pressing the gun to his own head. "Do it," he told her.

"No, I can't!" she cried, shaking her head.

"You have to, there's no other choice. They'll be here in two hours, but the trail to you ends with me, so do this now. Let me go from this terrible place. Let me be free, and then you go and do the same." She couldn't believe what he was saying, but the desperation in his eyes let her know he was being deadly serious. He was willing to die to keep her safe, but she had to be the one to do it.

"I love you, Joaquin Grayson. You'll always be my Gentle Giant," she told him with tears streaming down her face.

"I love you too. My sweet, sweet, Cassie. You're strong and beautiful, and far kinder than I deserve after how I've treated you. Now, do it, be free…"

When she pulled the trigger and watched as his lifeless body fell to the ground, Cassie screamed in pain. Every inch of her body yelled for her to run, but she couldn't take her eyes off him. She shouted curses at his lifeless body, yelling at him for daring to make her choose her life over his, but knew it was pointless. Grayson was gone, and she only had a couple hours before his cartel buddies would arrive. Cassie had to be long gone by then.

After calling on the numbness she once had been forced to maintain every day to return, Cassie stood, stashed the gun in the back of her jeans, and grabbed Grayson's car keys from his jacket. All the while, she couldn't look at the corpse she was leaving behind.

She closed the door behind her and calmly walked down the corridor to the nearest stairwell. It turned out the place was a derelict old house. Cassie had no idea where, but all she knew was that she had to get away. She felt like a zombie as she forced her feet forward, something living and breathing, but not alive. Her body was numb, along with her heart. On auto-pilot, she checked as she rounded every corner using methods she'd watched the cops do on television. Cassie pointed the gun around in search of any moving target, and breathed a huge sigh of relief when she spotted the solitary black sedan parked outside by the base of the stairs.

She slowed a couple steps short of the bottom when she saw someone leaning casually against it, clearly expecting her. Cassie crept forward, unsure how to proceed, when a soft, yet terrifying sound reached her ears. It was only a small, satisfied snigger, but it halted her descent in a heartbeat. It was a sound that turned her blood to ice, and her steely resolve to mush. Eduardo had evidently come along for the ride, and was openly amused to have discovered her fleeing Grayson's captivity.

"I knew he wouldn't be able to do it," he said, and laughed again. "That's why the mission took so long, isn't it? Not that he couldn't find you, but that he couldn't quite bring himself to decide your fate, *Señora Sanchez*," Eduardo added, stepping into the doorway so she could see him fully. He too had aged incredibly since she'd last seen him, but that intense dark stare of his still gave her the creeps. Eduardo was a true monster; she'd seen it right from the start. This time, though, she had no one there to protect her from him. Cassie took a step back. She didn't know where she might go, but hiding or running in the opposite direction seemed like a good place to start.

"Don't even think about it," muttered another voice from the shadows by the base of the stairs.

She heard a gun cock. Figuring it had to be trained on her, Cassie turned to find the voice's owner, but couldn't see through the darkness.

"Drop the gun, *puta*. If you do as you're told, I won't hurt you. I promise," Eduardo told her, and she realized she was still holding the gun in her hand. She lifted it higher, her hand shaking as she trained it on her oppressor. She didn't believe his lies for even a second.

With a sneer, Eduardo reached to his hip where he pulled a knife from its sheathe on his belt. Cassie recognized the blade instantly, and saliva flooded her mouth when a wave of nausea struck. It was Victor's knife. The same one his brother Luis had given him as a teenager, and the one she'd later used to stab him and take his life.

"You've three seconds to drop it, otherwise I'll shoot you in the stomach," the voice in the shadows warned her, and Cassie gasped. Whoever was there somehow knew she was pregnant, and she had to wonder how.

"No, José. I'll use this to cut the *bastardo* out." Eduardo stepped closer, calling her bluff with the gun. "It's the justice you deserve, but I won't make it fatal to you, no. I need you alive so I can get my money's worth," he told her, and Cassie retched.

In her moment of disgust, he lunged and grabbed the gun. She fired, but Eduardo had already pushed her hand skyward and the bullet hit the wall behind him. He flung the weapon away, and then tackled her.

As he pushed Cassie down onto the stairs beneath them, Eduardo slid the blade between two of her ribs in a calm and calculated move. He didn't go deep, but it was enough to leave her writhing beneath him, gasping for agonizing breath.

He watched her with a smile, and brushed her hair away from her face in a move she might've considered gentle if he hadn't just stabbed her.

"José? Please, is it really you?" she whimpered, closing her eyes so she didn't have to stare up into Eduardo's piercing gaze any longer. He was mere inches away, his body crushing hers against the hard stairs beneath them.

"*Sí, Inglés aumentó,* it's me." She heard him take a step toward them. "I lied when I told you I meant no harm. You were right not to trust me."

Cassie nodded. Being proven correct wasn't remotely as sweet as it ought to have been. She finally opened her eyes. Eduardo had her exactly where he wanted her, and there was nothing she could do to fight it. Cassie gave in to the pain radiating from her side, letting the calm numbness trickle out from her heart to the rest of her tense, aching body. It was better to be an emotionless shell for what she knew was coming, and the pain actually helped her focus her energy on retreating into herself.

Eduardo watched Cassie give up, and he smiled. Clearly delighted by her lack of fight, he ran his thumb over her lip before sliding it down to her breasts and then waist.

"Go do a perimeter sweep, will you?" he ordered without looking away, and José stalked off without another word. "I'm going to fuck you now," he murmured when they were alone, unbuttoning

Cassie's jeans. "And if you scream or fight me, the knife will go here next." He rested his hand over the small round of her belly. Cassie said nothing. She simply screwed her eyes shut, waiting for him to proceed. Waiting for the pain and the anguish to hit her along with his disgusting violation. But nothing happened.

She opened her eyes again just in time to watch as Eduardo's brains splattered against the wall beside them. A misty cloud of blood settled on her face and chest, and Cassie could do nothing but stare up at the gory mess in shock and disbelief. She turned to where the shot had come from, and saw the blood-covered face of a man she knew all too well on the other side of a shattered windowpane. Roger was standing there, albeit with a significant sway. He had a pistol in one hand and a cell phone in the other.

He grinned as though pleased with what he'd just done, but Cassie couldn't believe her eyes or feel gladness for what had just happened. She guessed she had to be hallucinating, and did nothing but scream until she eventually passed out.

# *Chapter Twenty*

They were bumping along when Cassie started to come around. Something stung at her side, the pain eventually forcing her awake. She groaned and coughed.

"Try not to move." Roger's voice was in her ear, and the sound shocked her back to full awareness. She blinked awake and turned her face toward it. He was really there, not dead like Grayson had let her believe. Roger had clearly been injured, but he was okay. Her protector was back by her side, and he was pressing down on her stab wound with a wad of bloody cloth. The bumping she'd felt was because they were in the back of a car, and Cassie quickly realized they were driving off, away from both Grayson and Eduardo's corpses.

"How did you find me? Where's José? Who's driving? You're alive?" She mumbled question after question, and eventually fell silent. Cassie lifted her hand to touch Roger's cheek and sighed. "Tell Leo I love him, and I'm sorry," she said, fretting that she might not make it after she saw just how much blood was soaking through the gauze in Roger's hands.

"You'll be telling him yourself in a matter of minutes, Cassie. Trust me," Roger replied with a scowl. He was trying not to show how worried he was, but his expression said it all. She was in a bad way.

"You always were a bad liar," Cassie groaned as the world started to spin. Roger sighed, and rather than respond, he turned his head to glance over his shoulder at their driver.

"I hope you've got your foot to the floor, José?" he asked. Cassie's breath hitched. Her eyes widened in fear, but Roger shushed her. "It's okay. He's with us, Cassie. He's on our side."

"Well in that case, I want a fucking word with you, José," she managed.

*"Sí, Inglés aumentó,* you may have as many as you desire." His voice filtered over to the backseat, and Cassie smiled. Whoever he was, trusted ally or cartel scumbag, Roger seemed at ease with him there, and so would she be.

Pain spurred from her chest again and Cassie sucked in a hissed breath. The car was spinning, so she closed her eyes and prayed that she'd at least get to see Leo one more time. While she hoped the baby was okay, all she could think about was him, and when the darkness dragged her under again, it was his face she saw in her mind's eye.

\*\*\*

Leo paced, pounding the floor hard with his size

elevens in an attempt to leave holes in the linoleum. Being powerless and without any information at all wasn't his idea of fun, and he glowered at the man sitting behind a steel table opposite him.

"Tell me again why I'm here?" he demanded, coming to a stop before him.

"For your protection," the man answered, crossing thickly muscled arms across his chest. Leo sized the guy up, trying to determine if he could take him, but then figured it wasn't the best idea, seeing as he'd declared himself as a Secret Service agent and all.

He thought back to a few hours earlier when a couple of mean looking behemoths had stormed into his office unannounced and asked him and Brian to go with them. They'd barely said a word, and yet the underlying message had been abundantly clear—there hadn't really been any choice in the matter. The men had told him how they knew that Cassie had been taken and who by, and how they'd put measures in place that'd ensure she was extracted and safe by the end of that day. However, Leo had been offered no proof of their claims, and had spent the past few hours demanding answers from the men whose lips were annoyingly sealed.

"Where is she? What's going on? Who the ever-loving fuck are you guys?" he tried again, but his stoic companion said nothing—again.

Leo slumped against the wall, holding his head in his hands. He felt broken, and so desperate for the answers his tight-lipped companion seemed either unwilling or unable to give him, and it was making him angry. "I need something, man," he murmured, but his heartfelt plea was met with nothing but silence.

After an age, the door opened and in walked another man Leo had never seen before. Unlike his gargantuan comrades and their all-black getup, he was dressed in a suit and tie. He seemed different to the others, and Leo tensed. This guy was clearly *someone*, and his otherwise indifferent guard jumped to attention and then took his leave without being given a word of order.

Leo mirrored the new man's movements, and quickly took the seat opposite him at the table, while silence descended that was so thick he was sure he could taste it.

"Mr. Solomon, my name's Colton, but people call me 'The Boss.' I'm the director of this particular branch of the Secret Service."

"Funny, that's what people call me too," Leo replied with a smirk. "Looks like we're either gonna get on like a house on fire—or not."

"I'm hoping the former," Colton answered, and Leo fixed him with a serious look.

"Well, that depends on how long you're planning on keeping me locked up…"

"Only as long as necessary. I trust you've been well taken care of?" he asked, and Leo shrugged. He fixed Colton with a hard stare, trying to read him, but it was no use. The man opposite was more than a closed book, he was a bound and sealed bag of cold and calculated nothingness. Leo shuddered. In many ways, it was like looking in a mirror.

"I was told to go with your boys out there, taken

halfway across the city to where I'd hoped to find my girlfriend safe and well, only to be shoved in here without so much as an idea of her whereabouts or condition. I've been given nothing. I've been told nothing…I need answers, Colton, and I hope to bloody God that you're here to give me some."

Colton awarded Leo a flicker of a smile, but otherwise didn't react to his ramblings, as though having expected every single word of Leo's anxious response. He crossed his knees and linked his hands over the top, evidently going with the more casual approach.

"She's in our custody, and you can see her shortly." He paused while Leo let out a sigh of relief. "While she's being taken care of, I thought we might have a little chat. Do you know who we are and what we do here, Mr. Solomon?"

"With all due respect, Colton, I don't give a shit," Leo snapped, thinking how this was not the time for a game of "guess the special branch while having a pissing contest with the Big Boss."

"Don't you want to know why we found and rescued Ms. Philips, or how? Aren't you at least the slightest bit intrigued as to how we knew where to find you, or why we chose to intervene?" Colton pressed. Leo guessed he wasn't leaving their small room until he at least showed his willingness to play along, so he shrugged.

"I was warned I'd be being watched, so can't say it's a huge surprise old Big Brother has been keeping tabs on me," he answered. "Let me guess, MI6?"

Colton gripped the hem of each sleeve in turn,

straightening himself while sitting taller in his seat.

"We don't work for the government, but we are affiliated with the Secret Intelligence Service, yes," he agreed. "Organized Crime Unit, specifically drug related."

"Specifically, cartels and highly organized drug rings?"

"Specifically, yes."

"Then what, pray tell, do you want from me? I won't go back inside." Leo had transformed. He was no longer the man trembling with anxiety, fearing the worst. He was Mr. Big, Bad Solomon, and when he felt backed into a corner, his alter ego certainly wasn't one to back down. Colton seemed hesitant to answer, so Leo leaned over the table towards him, and added, "You might want to get to the goddamn point, and quick."

***

Cassie stirred, feeling ready to throw up. She turned her body and retched, and was surprised when the rim of a cold metal bowl touched just below her lips.

"We've got you, Cassie." Roger's voice filled her ears, and the wondrous sound immediately eased her nausea. She turned her face toward him and let her eyes flutter open. It was so bright it took her a few blinks to come around, but when she did, she saw the loveliest sight.

"You look like an idiot with that bandage on your head," she teased, and smiled. He'd been patched up, as had she, going by the gurney she was laid out on and the thick gauze now wrapped around her ribs. It was tight, but she felt no pain, and guessed she'd been doped up pretty good. "The baby?" she mumbled in question, and her heart fluttered wildly when Roger grinned.

"Fine," he answered quickly. "Everything's fine." He lifted up a sheet of black and white images, and Cassie took them from him with a gasp. It was a set of sonogram pictures. She stared at the little blob in shock while Roger helped sit her up against the thick cushions.

"What's going on, Rog? And where the hell are we?" He pulled up his chair so he could sit beside her and hold her hand.

"I hope you're ready for this?" he asked with a smile, and she nodded.

# *Chapter Twenty-One*

"So, José's a Secret Service agent and not a cartel goon?" Cassie double-checked, trying to piece it all together in her mind again. Roger nodded.

"He was working undercover in Mexico while you were there with Victor. His branch of the Secret Service knew you'd been held there against your will and his team was assessing their potential extraction options when Leo lured you both back into the States with the help of the FBI. The case then went cold until recently."

"When Leo returned to the UK?"

"Yeah, because two known members of the Sanchez cartel were identified as having followed him into the country. José came to speak with me not long after he came back into Siobhan's life—and their backstory is true, by the way. She really did grow up with him and knew him years ago before he was recruited. Their relationship is real, and he's recently told her the truth about his job, but she couldn't tell you. I know it ate her up to have to hold something back, and I was the same."

"She was mad as hell, but understood my reasons." José carried on Roger's story, joining them at Cassie's bedside. "I'm sorry I lied to you and made you distrustful, but I had to have Eduardo and the others fooled. I needed to be the one ordered to meet him at that derelict house, so I made sure I was given the task of being Grayson's liaison in London. I passed information back and forth between him and the Cartel, and was the person he called before you managed to get away," he told her, and Cassie had to look away from his questioning gaze. Even thinking of how that'd panned out made her want to either cry or retch again, probably both.

"Grayson had no idea José was working both sides, so when I caught him tailing me back home, I warned José that your old foe was making his move at last. Grayson caught up with me, knocked me out, and put me in the trunk of his car, and I was just coming around when José popped the lock and sprung me loose. I was ready to go covert ops right by his side, but he shushed me and handed me a weapon. As soon as I saw what was going on between you and Eduardo in that stairwell, I knew what had to be done, and took his life before he could take anything else from you." Roger seemed to choke on those last words, and Cassie knew it must've been awful finding her there under Eduardo's command.

Not that she'd ever even doubted it, but she knew now just how much Roger truly cared for her. He'd taken the life of the man who'd threatened her future. He'd rid her of a demon she'd been forced to cower before, and Cassie knew she'd be eternally grateful for both his and José's actions earlier that day.

"I love you too, Rog. Thank you," she mumbled, taking his hand in hers. He smiled and kissed the back of her palm.

"The mission was to do the handover and then take Grayson and Eduardo into custody, but a monster like him had to be put down, so I let Roger be the one to do it rather than get in trouble for not completing the assignment. He was well within his rights as your bodyguard to act accordingly," José carried on, and Cassie nodded in understanding. She guessed the official statement might say something along the lines of Roger having acted alone while José's back was turned, and didn't care that things had needed to go that way.

Another cartel boss was dead, and Cassie was glad, even if the memory of his brains splattering against the wall of that stairwell would haunt her for a while. It was just another one to add to her collection, and one she'd gladly live with if it meant she was free from another of her tormentors.

"Grayson wanted me to be free in the end. He handed me the weapon and forced me to take his life," Cassie told them, and neither seemed surprised to hear it.

"Some people simply can't come back from the edge, no matter how hard they try," Roger muttered. "But at least he showed you one final kindness by letting you go. He'd struggled with his order to kidnap you for months, and we wondered if he'd even manage it at all."

"GG and I had a special friendship while I was in Mexico, and I hate how different he became after I left him behind to rot in prison so I could be free. He was himself at the very end, though, so I can't hate him. He did the right thing by me and the baby when it counted." Cassie groaned as she repositioned herself in a bid to get more comfortable.

"He loved you, no matter what. I saw that myself during his darker days. I want you to know, I had no idea Eduardo was planning on using the knife, otherwise I'd have gotten it off him. I'm sorry you were injured," José told her, seeming earnest, and Cassie nodded.

"I know. The main thing is the baby's not hurt," she replied, staring at the sonogram pictures again. "When did they take these?" she asked, watching as Roger pointed to the small blur, showing Cassie which parts were which.

"While you were out cold. That's one strong little bugger you've got there, by the way. I refused to leave your side while they were working on you, so got to see when they gave you the scan. It was wriggling around like mad."

"I'm glad it's safe. Any baby Solomon was always going to be a stubborn little thing, like its father," she replied with a grin. "Speaking of, where's Leo?"

"He's…um," Roger began, and Cassie scowled, feeling instantly fretful. He noticed her panic and shook his head. "Nothing bad, it's just he's currently under lock and key. Talking with The

Boss," he added.

"About what?" she demanded.

"Goddam Secret Service tried offering me a job, but I told them to go fuck themselves," Leo answered from the doorway with a huge grin, and he bounded over to join the others at Cassie's side. He touched her with care, remaining delicate and careful, but she grabbed him and yanked him down to meet her embrace. She needed to feel him against her. When her tears returned, she didn't fight them, nor did he make a fuss. The pair simply held one another while Roger and José chatted quietly between themselves for a minute.

"Leo, I'm so sorry. I shouldn't have stormed off after Suzie without a chaperone. I should've been honest about her message," she told him, but he shushed her.

"The bad guys had us surrounded regardless. No matter how, no matter when—they were on their way to get you. All that matters is that when it came to it, we had these guys on our side," he replied. Leo climbed up and offered José his outstretched hand. "I'm forever in your debt."

"Don't mention it, I'm just glad she got away in one piece," he answered with a smile, but then frowned. "You know that if I could've helped it, she wouldn't have been injured at all."

"She's back here with me, José. And, that's all any of us could've prayed for." He patted José on the shoulder and grinned again. "So, Secret Service, hey? Didn't feel like sharing that little truth with me at any point?"

"Sorry, man. It was classified," José answered.

285

"Nah, I get it. I just can't figure out why they'd try and get me to join. As if I'd ever say yes…"

"I did," Roger interjected, and they all stared at him in shock.

Cassie reached out and took his hand again.

"When?" she asked.

"This afternoon while you were still asleep. Leo wasn't the only one who was offered a new job."

"You know you can't leave me, right?" Cassie demanded, and she wanted him to know she was deadly serious. Roger laughed and lifted her hand so he could kiss the back of it.

"Oh, you sweet thing. You're the widow of one of Mexico's most high profile cartel bosses, and you just took down his successor. I don't think you realize just how much you'll be seeing of me during your time in witness protection," he told her.

"Witness protection? Are you serious?" she groaned, and Roger simply shrugged. She looked up at Leo, hoping he might be able to offer a different option, but he gave her the same look as Roger.

"Looks like we need to disappear again, baby. For good this time," Leo said, perching beside her on the gurney. "They'll keep us safe, all three of us."

"You, me, and the baby against the world?"

"Yep, but this time we're going to be ghosts. No messing around. You and the baby are everything to me, and I'll never let anyone harm you again as long as I live," Leo answered, pulling her close for a kiss, and Cassie knew he meant every word.

# *Epilogue*

### *Ten Years Later...*

"Where is your father when I need him?" Cassie bellowed, grabbing the jackets and boots from the cupboard under the stairs. She was hot and bothered, flustered, and in a mad rush. It didn't help that her husband had gone missing in the vast expanse of English country manor house that'd been their family home for the past eight years.

"He's gone to work," nine-year-old Leo Junior told her, scrunching his nose when she glared at him crossly. He knew she wasn't angry with him, and shrugged with a cheeky grin that matched his father's perfectly. "Dad told me when he came to wake me up."

"What? He didn't tell me he had to be in today!" she grumbled, forcing Junior's feet into his wellington boots.

"Calm down, sis." Will's cheerful voice boomed from the entryway of the huge house. He had his namesake, six-year-old William, by his side and ready to go. How he'd managed to persuade the boisterous boy to get both his boots and coat on was beyond her, and the usually so mischievous scamp simply smirked at her from beside his favorite uncle. "What are you up to today anyway, seeing as I'm taking this lot out?" Will asked, and Cassie smiled coyly.

"Well, we *had* discussed spending the day together, but seeing as my darling husband has disappeared on me in favor of spending some time with his newest prototype, I might as well head to the studio."

Cassie peered across the courtyard at her purpose-built annex. It'd been made into her private art studio, her place of solace, and she truly adored the refuge she found there. In the years since Eduardo's attack, they'd not only moved to an isolated, secure mansion nestled in the heart of the countryside, but she'd also found her art again. The dark and dismal within her had come up for air, as had the beautiful and light work she'd drawn throughout the years.

After leaving the city behind, their collective assets had been liquidated, and Cassie had finally caved on the issue of marriage. Leo had popped the question the day their eldest son was born, and she had been so in love with the two Leos in her life she couldn't say no. It'd been a small wedding—she couldn't have faced another big, white ordeal even if he'd wanted it—but Leo hadn't pressed her for anything more than a registrar and a ring on her finger.

Ever since the day they'd first met at that party

in New York, she'd belonged to him, and Cassie knew she'd never fight his hold on her ever again. In fact, she still craved the satisfaction she felt in giving every part of herself to him. Leo was her everything, and he'd not only changed his life for her over and over again, he'd changed hers too.

"Mum, will this do?" A soft voice interrupted her reverie, and Cassie looked down the hall at the little girl who was her absolute double. At only four years old, Gee-Gee Solomon knew exactly what she wanted, and how to get it. The little angel was smiling sweetly, and had pulled on her boots like her mother had instructed, yet she'd teamed it with a tutu and a tiara. Her jacket was on, so she'd also followed Cassie's other order, yet she'd topped the ensemble off with a set of fairy wings that matched the bright pink netting bunched at her waist.

"I don't know...Uncle Will, what do you think?" She turned back to smirk at her baby brother.

"You'll do perfectly, sweetie. Who cares if all we're doing is going to the zoo and then a sleepover at my house? A fairy princess always needs to look her best," Will replied, curtseying to his niece when she joined him.

Cassie bid her three children goodbye, kissing each and fussing over them far more than necessary, but she could never help herself. Despite having Roger and the other Secret Service agents still watching over them, she still worried. With a fake smile, she waved them off, not moving from the doorstep until the car turned out of the gated driveway and headed off toward Will's new home just a few miles away. She breathed a sigh of relief when their private security team followed his car, but couldn't fight a shudder as it swept down her spine. Cassie was suddenly aware of being watched. Yes, there were cameras and security guards around the property, but this was different. She felt eyes on her specifically, and not the house or the perimeter.

She knew she needed to let go of her fears rather than fight them, and without Leo around to help her, Cassie guessed she'd use her art to offload that dread instead. Her work was a hit, and somehow sold to collectors all around the world. While no one knew her real identity, it was a thrill knowing that her work spoke to people, calling out their fears and fancies, and she adored her new job as a stay-at-home-mom and artist.

Leo, on the other hand, had gone back into engineering after refusing the job with the Secret Service. He'd invented, engineered, and patented hundreds of different innovations since then, and while she had no idea what half of them even were, Cassie loved how he too had found his calling. Together they were whole, and their three children had brought them happiness beyond anything they could've hoped for. Life was good. In fact, it was amazing.

Cassie stepped back into the now deafeningly silent house and shut the door. She turned to walk inside, thinking that a cup of tea seemed like a great idea, when she saw a folded note taped to the bottom rung of the banister by the huge front door. It was too high up for any of the kids to reach, so she grabbed it and read the handwritten words with a smile.

*I'm watching you. Don't run, don't scream, and don't even think of calling for help. I want you, but I'll have you only when I'm done watching. Then, I will take you hard and fast, and I won't take no for an answer...*

*The game is on, Jellybean. I'm coming for you.*

Cassie knew she was blushing. She was hot all of a sudden, and could feel her heart racing as she panted with desire and a desperate need only Leo could fulfill. So, the game was on, and her darling husband was in luck, because it sure was her favorite one in all the world. They'd perfected their ravishment roleplay over the years, and she knew exactly how to get what they both wanted from the hot and dangerous game of cat and mouse.

"Come and get me, baby," she called out. It'd been Leo's eyes she'd felt on her, she realized, and she smiled. Cassie was more than ready to give him a show, and grew hotter in anticipation of when he might strike. Last time, she'd stood painting in her studio wearing nothing but an apron to tease him. However, this time she decided she'd make him work harder for it.

Cassie reckoned it was time she washed and waxed her new sleek and sexy sports car, and figured she might as well wear as little as possible while doing so, just in case of splashes. She'd wanted to christen it for weeks, and hoped her predatory lover might take the opportunity to have her over the bonnet.

But first, it was time to enjoy a nice cup of tea while she read the morning paper in peace.

## *The End*

# Acknowledgements

Once again, I'd like to thank my close friends and family for the wonderful support throughout my writing journey. Without you, I couldn't have done it. Please don't ever think it goes unnoticed.

And a huge shout-out to my wonderful PA, Jodie and my amazing team of faithful ladies—Morgan's Minions! I seriously couldn't do this without you all, so thank you from the bottom of my heart. xxx

# About the Author

Laura Morgan is a hopeless romantic with a dark side. A self-confessed computer geek, Laura spends her days looking after her two young children and their cocker spaniel Milo, as well as making the most of her free time by indulging in another of her passions, music. Laura loves going to concerts with her friends, or else listening to rock music at home while writing.

Laura loves edgy, gritty books that strip your heart and soul bare, and that leaves you with an epic book hangover at the end. That's what she aims to do with her own work, and thinks her readers agree. At times they're dark and controversial, but that's also what makes them unique.

**Facebook:**
www.facebook.com/lauramorganauthor

**Twitter:**
www.twitter.com/lauram241

**Goodreads:**
http://www.goodreads.com/laura_morgan

58052157R10181

Made in the USA
Charleston, SC
02 July 2016